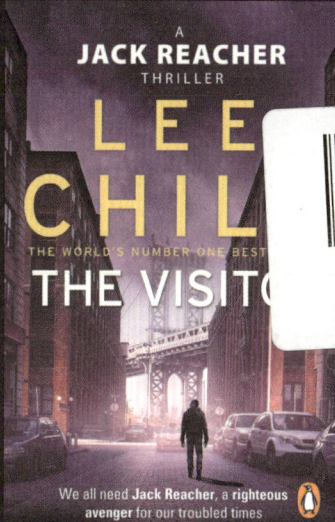

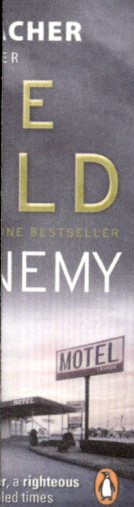
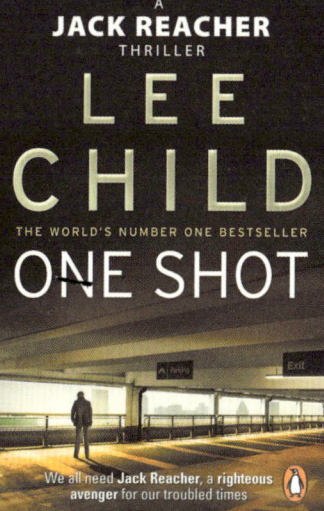
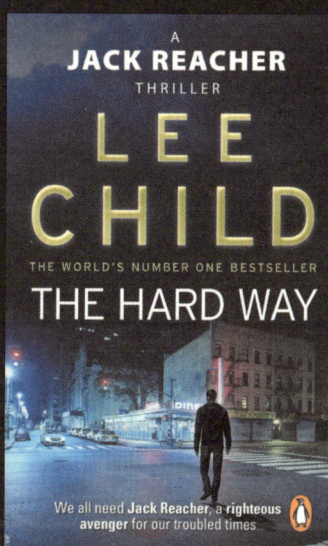

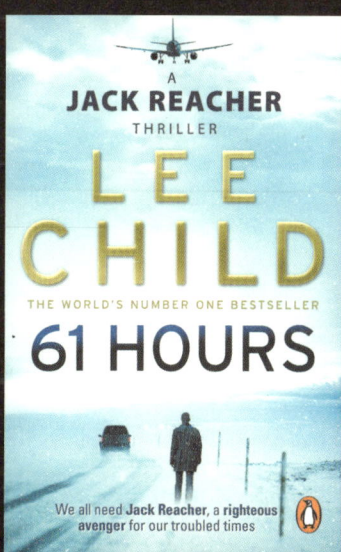
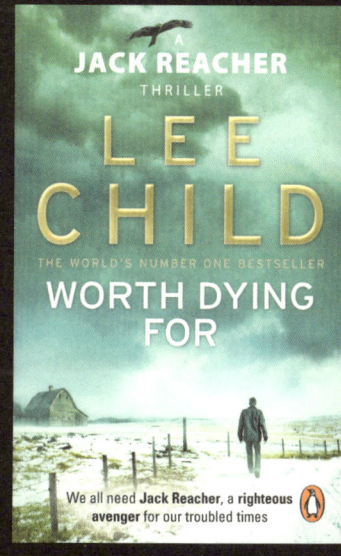

The Jack Reacher series

KILLING FLOOR
DIE TRYING
TRIPWIRE
THE VISITOR
ECHO BURNING
WITHOUT FAIL
PERSUADER
THE ENEMY
ONE SHOT
THE HARD WAY
BAD LUCK AND TROUBLE
NOTHING TO LOSE
GONE TOMORROW
61 HOURS
WORTH DYING FOR
THE AFFAIR
A WANTED MAN
NEVER GO BACK
PERSONAL
MAKE ME
NIGHT SCHOOL
NO MIDDLE NAME (REACHER STORIES)
THE MIDNIGHT LINE
PAST TENSE
BLUE MOON
THE SENTINEL
BETTER OFF DEAD
NO PLAN B
THE SECRET
IN TOO DEEP
EXIT STRATEGY

Also by Lee Child

SAFE ENOUGH (STORIES)
REACHER: THE STORIES BEHIND
THE STORIES (NON-FICTION)

For more information see www.jackreacher.com

EXIT STRATEGY

Lee Child
and
Andrew Child

bantam

TRANSWORLD PUBLISHERS

UK | USA | Canada | Ireland | Australia
India | New Zealand | South Africa

Transworld is part of the Penguin Random House group of companies
whose addresses can be found at global.penguinrandomhouse.com.

Penguin Random House UK, One Embassy Gardens,
8 Viaduct Gardens, London SW11 7BW

penguin.co.uk

First published in Great Britain in 2025 by Bantam
an imprint of Transworld Publishers

009

Copyright © Lee Child and Andrew Child 2025

The moral right of the authors has been asserted.

This book is a work of fiction and, except in the case of historical fact, any resemblance to actual persons, living or dead, is purely coincidental.

Every effort has been made to obtain the necessary permissions with reference to copyright material, both illustrative and quoted. We apologize for any omissions in this respect and will be pleased to make the appropriate acknowledgements in any future edition.

Penguin Random House values and supports copyright. Copyright fuels creativity, encourages diverse voices, promotes freedom of expression and supports a vibrant culture. Thank you for purchasing an authorized edition of this book and for respecting intellectual property laws by not reproducing, scanning or distributing any part of it by any means without permission. You are supporting authors and enabling Penguin Random House to continue to publish books for everyone. No part of this book may be used or reproduced in any manner for the purpose of training artificial intelligence technologies or systems. In accordance with Article 4(3) of the DSM Directive 2019/790, Penguin Random House expressly reserves this work from the text and data mining exception.

Typeset 11.75/16.25pt Century Old Style Std by
Six Red Marbles UK, Thetford, Norfolk
Printed and bound by CPI (UK) Ltd, Croydon CR0 4YY

The authorized representative in the EEA is Penguin Random House Ireland,
Morrison Chambers, 32 Nassau Street, Dublin D02 YH68.

A CIP catalogue record for this book is available from the British Library.

ISBNs:
9780857505613 (cased)
9780857505620 (tpb)

Penguin Random House is committed to a sustainable future
for our business, our readers and our planet. This book is
made from Forest Stewardship Council® certified paper.

For everyone who has stood with
Reacher through his first thirty adventures . . .

ONE

Nathan Gilmour knew things that other people did not.

People, like his coworkers at the Port Administration in Baltimore.

Things, like the fact that the recent death of one of those coworkers was not an accident, despite what the police report said. It was not an accident, and the man who had died was not the intended victim. Gilmour himself was.

Gilmour knew that he was the one who should have paid with his life. There was no doubt about it. And if he stayed where he was and kept on following his orders, the killers would realize they'd screwed up, too. They would correct their mistake. There was no doubt about that, either. So Gilmour was left with no choice. He had to pull the plug.

Gilmour was sitting alone in the cramped office. The

only other desk was lost under a heap of bouquets of flowers. Most of them were beginning to wilt. The air was heavy with their scent. *Their stench*, Gilmour thought. The stench of death. He began to breathe through his mouth and twisted his chair sideways to avoid the view out the window. He didn't need to see the roof of the sagging white tent. It had been put up over the center of the spot where the shipping container had hit the ground after it fell from its crane. Or was dropped. The investigators were gone but the stain on the concrete was going to be there for months. Office gossip said the guy who had been crushed by the container wound up as flat as a piece of paper. Gilmour had known the guy for five months. He had shared his workspace with him. Had come to like him. And ultimately had gotten him killed. He shivered and pulled a phone out of his pocket. A very basic one. He flipped it open and keyed in a message.

 911. Need to meet.

Gilmour entered a number. He hit Send. Noted the time – a minute after eleven in the morning – and settled in to wait for a reply. There was no way he was going to get any work done that day. Or any other day, in that place. Or in any other place, if his gambit failed.

The same time Nathan Gilmour was sending his text, Jack Reacher was stepping into a coffee shop. It was a large place, bright and busy, just a stone's throw from Gilmour's dockside office. Inside, it had exposed-brick walls, oak floors, and three parallel rows of ornate iron pillars holding up the ceiling. An old warehouse, Reacher guessed. Solid. Built to endure. The kind of place that had outlasted the industry it had been designed to serve and was now onto its second lease on life. Reacher imagined that the upper floors would be converted into chic apartments as the neighborhood got gentrified, if they hadn't been already.

Reacher stood in line at the counter, ordered his coffee – black, no sugar – paid, and carried the mug to a small round table in the corner. Someone had left a newspaper, but that wasn't why Reacher chose it. He settled there because it gave him a view of the whole room. He squeezed in behind the table and lowered himself onto the wooden chair. It wasn't built for someone his size – six foot five, two hundred fifty pounds – and it wasn't comfortable, but Reacher didn't mind. He wasn't planning to stay long. He had arrived in the city that morning on a Greyhound bus and would be leaving the same way either late that night or early the next day. He was there to catch a band he liked that was playing at a benefit for veterans. It was going to be an evening show, in the open air, it was late October, and Reacher didn't have a coat. Buying one was next on his to-do list. He figured he would take a refill of coffee or two – maybe three – then when the quantity of caffeine in his system was restored to a satisfactory level he would move on.

The coffee shop was three-quarters full. A handful of the other customers were also on their own. Two of them were reading books. The others were tapping away on laptops. Six people were crowded around a table for four in the center of the space. The rest of the tables were taken by couples. Most of the couples were focused on each other, or on their phones, but Reacher saw that two pairs had a different dynamic. One duo couldn't keep their eyes off the entrance. The man had a beard, neatly trimmed. The woman had black hair pulled back in a French braid. They were both smartly dressed, like they were there for some kind of special occasion, and the expressions on their faces flip-flopped between anxiety and excitement. The final couple was watching them. They were older. Maybe in their late seventies. They looked pale and gray and hunched. Their clothes were worn and shabby and there was just a single mug between them on the table.

Reacher finished his coffee, wriggled free of his table, and strolled to the counter. He got his first refill and as he turned back another person walked into the shop. A man, maybe in his mid-forties, dressed in a suit and carrying a briefcase. The smart couple that had been watching the entrance got halfway to their feet, the beginning of a smile taking hold on their faces. Then something about the newcomer's expression hit them. Their smiles died a sudden death. They sunk back down onto their chairs. The man's shoulders slumped. The newcomer joined them at their table and for a moment no one spoke. Then the man with the beard straightened up. He stuck out his chin and said, 'If it's bad news, tell us. Don't leave us hanging.'

Reacher stayed back by the cluster of flasks at the end of the counter and made like he was considering adding cream to his coffee. He wanted to hear how the conversation unfolded.

The new guy said, 'You have to remember what I told you. The futures market is like a violent storm over the ocean. An investment is like a ship trying to sail across that ocean. You've got high winds to take into account. Treacherous currents. Unpredictable tides. You can run aground. Get holed on the rocks. Hit delays. Maybe even sink.'

Reacher saw the old shabby guy shake his head and push his chair back like he was ready to stand up. The woman who was with him put her hand on his arm, stopping him.

The man with the beard said, 'You told us you knew how to navigate all that storm stuff. You told us you were the best. That you could turn a profit inside twenty-four hours. Maybe even double our money.'

The new guy said, 'True. I did say that.'

'So what are you telling us now? You lost our money?'

'I didn't *lose* it.'

'What, then?'

'I didn't double it.'

'So there's some left?'

'Some?' The guy grinned. 'You could say that. Because I didn't double it. I tripled it.'

The man with the beard was silent for a long moment, then said, 'Tripled? That would make . . .'

The new guy picked up his briefcase, set it on his lap, worked the locks, then upended it over the table. Bundles of banknotes cascaded out. Fifteen of them. One knocked over a cup. Two tumbled onto the floor. He said, 'Fifteen thousand dollars in less than a day. And that's after my commission. Like I told you, I am the best.'

Reacher saw the shabby couple lock eyes for a second. Some kind of silent understanding passed between them.

They each nodded, very gently. They straightened up a little. Leaned slightly forward.

The man with the beard stared at the money. His jaw sagged open. The woman who was with him shrieked and threw her arms around him so hard they almost fell off their chairs. They yelled. They whooped. They high-fived. Everyone in the place was staring at them but they showed no sign of caring. The new guy smiled. He turned his briefcase the right way up and closed it. He got to his feet and was halfway to the door before the man with the beard noticed he was moving.

The man said, 'Wait. You're leaving?'

'Why not? My work is done. Enjoy your profit.'

'No. Your work's not done.' He started to gather up the bundles of cash. 'Take this back. Invest it for us. All of it. Just like last night.'

'Are you sure?'

'I'm certain.'

'I can't promise to triple it again.'

'But you could double it?'

The new guy returned to the table. 'It's possible.'

Reacher went back to his table and watched the man with the beard gather up the bundles of money. The man retrieved the two that had fallen, righted the tipped-over cup, shook the new guy's hand, then put his arm around the woman's shoulder and went with her toward the door. They were almost skipping. The new guy set his briefcase down, opened it, and stacked the money inside. He closed it again, locked it, and turned to leave.

The shabby man heaved himself to his feet. He held up his hand, then gestured like he wanted the new guy to join him and the woman at their table. The guy looked around for a moment as if he thought the man must be beckoning to someone else, shrugged, then approached. The men spoke for a moment, then both sat down. Reacher couldn't hear their conversation. He didn't need to. He could see what was going on. And he knew what was going to happen next. Two minutes later the shabby man slid a skinny hand into his jacket pocket and pulled out some money of his own. Two bundles of banknotes. Thicker than the ones that had poured out of the briefcase a few minutes before. Maybe five thousand dollars in each one. Ten thousand total. Probably all the old couple could scrape together.

For ten minutes after he sent his text, Nathan Gilmour sat with the phone clutched in his hand. It didn't beep. It didn't buzz. Gilmour tossed it onto his desk. It slid across the shiny surface and came to rest next to his keyboard. It looked like the computer mouse's baby brother. Gilmour stared at it. That beat the view out the window or the sight of the dying flowers, but it wasn't satisfying. The phone still didn't beep. It still didn't buzz. After twenty minutes Gilmour picked it back up. He flipped it open and checked the screen, as if a reply could have sneaked in without him noticing. The display was blank. Gilmour felt a flash of anger, like the phone was conspiring against him. Like it was deliberately blocking any incoming response. He was filled with the urge to hurl it against the wall, wait for the remains to fall, then stomp whatever survived into tiny pieces. He was still fighting the rage when the phone lit up. The message he was waiting for had arrived. It said, *Noon today.* It gave an address, which Gilmour knew was not far away. Probably a restaurant or a café, he figured, because the message finished with, *Look for a man sitting alone. He'll be the biggest guy in the place.*

TWO

The guy in the coffee shop took out a large manila envelope, slid the two new bundles of cash inside, loaded it into his briefcase, shook hands with the old man and his wife, and made for the door. Reacher drained his coffee and followed. The guy crossed the street, continued past another repurposed warehouse – this one with a couple of clothing stores on the first floor – then dodged into an alleyway. Reacher stopped short and listened. He heard a car door slam and an engine cough into life. He stepped forward and saw a Toyota Camry twenty feet away. It was silver. Not the latest version, Reacher thought, although he couldn't be sure. He wasn't much of a car guy.

Nathan Gilmour closed the phone, slipped it into his pocket, and took a moment to run the logistics in his head.

He would need maybe fifteen minutes to get to the rendezvous. Walking would be best. And when he got there he would need time to find a vantage point and figure out how and where to deliver his message. It would be tight but he could do it. He took a pad of paper out of his desk drawer and reached for a pen.

Reacher moved toward the car in the alley. The guy who'd had the briefcase was behind the wheel. The couple with the smart clothes who had supposedly made a killing in the futures market were in the back. The man still had his beard but the woman's hair was no longer black and it was no longer long. It was cut in a tight blond bob. The car began to roll forward. Reacher moved to block its path. The driver hit the brakes. He honked the horn. Reacher stepped closer. The car began to move again. The driver's foot hovered over the gas pedal. He thought about flooring it but running over some nosy stranger wasn't part of the plan. It would attract attention. Unless the guy was about to attack, in which case there would be some kind of justification. But no guarantee of success. The stranger was enormous. He looked like a walking bank vault. His hands were like hams. His arms were bigger than some people's legs. The driver wasn't sure if the car would be drivable after colliding with a guy his size. There could be major damage and the airbags were bound to be triggered. So he played it safe and went with another blast of the horn.

Reacher was thinking along the same lines, only without doing anything that would cause much damage to himself. He took another step and drove the ball of his right foot into the center of the car's radiator grille. He wasn't certain about the mechanism – he wasn't much of a car guy after all – but he knew that airbags were designed to deploy in the event of an accident, and he figured that a head-on collision must be a pretty common kind. There had to be a sensor to detect a crash like that. He didn't know exactly where it would be so he went for power over precision. It worked. The interior of the car was instantly filled with a bunch of billowing white balloons. Reacher spun away toward the driver's side. The car slowed and stopped and the airbags deflated almost as quickly as they'd appeared. Reacher grabbed the handle and hauled open the driver's door. He leaned in and took the key out of the ignition. The remnants of some kind of explosive hung in the air. Presumably what had caused the airbags to inflate so rapidly. It bit into Reacher's nose and mouth but he ignored the sensation, grabbed the driver by the front of his shirt, and pulled him out, too. The guy's clothes were coated with fine, silvery, slippery dust. He looked a little dazed from the experience. Reacher kicked the door closed, spun the guy around, and told him to step back and lean with his hands against the roof. The guy paused, too stunned to move, then did as he was instructed.

Reacher opened the rear door and hauled out the man with the beard. His body was limp and floppy at first but when Reacher let him go he didn't fall to the ground. He turned and as he moved he retrieved a blade from his sock with his right hand, then straightened, legs braced, anger contorting his face.

Reacher gestured toward the knife and said, 'Drop it.'

The man flicked his wrist to the left, then the right,

holding the blade vertically, trying to reflect light into Reacher's eyes.

Reacher said, 'I have a rule. Pull a knife on me, I break your arm. Drop it now, I'll make an exception.'

The man lunged at Reacher's face but stopped short and pulled back. He said, 'That was a warning. Turn around, run, or I'm going to cut your heart out.'

The driver straightened up and started to turn away from the car. Reacher stretched out his left arm, cupped the back of the guy's head with his hand, and launched it forward like a basketball. The bridge of the guy's nose slammed into the top of the doorframe. His head bounced off the metal and he fell straight back onto the asphalt, eyes rolled up, blood pouring from both nostrils.

Reacher turned back to the man with the beard. He said, 'You're assuming I have a heart.'

The man shuffled closer and lunged again, this time going for Reacher's body. Reacher crossed his arms just above the wrists, his left under his right, and drove forward, catching the man's forearm between the edge of his hands, pushing the blade down and out of harm's way. The man tried to pull away but he was too slow. Reacher slid his left hand out and down and grabbed the man's wrist. He twisted it back, locking the man's elbow. Then he twisted a little farther.

The man yelped with pain. 'Stop!' He let go of the knife. 'I've dropped it. I've dropped it.'

Reacher said, 'Too late.' He kept the tension on the man's arm with his left hand and brought his right fist down like a hammer just below the elbow. Both bones shattered and the man passed out from the pain before a scream could cross his lips. Reacher dumped his unconscious body on top of the first guy's and crouched to look into the back of the car. The woman was still in there, but she wasn't sitting. She was standing in the rear footwell and leaning over the passenger seat, scrabbling to get hold of the briefcase.

Reacher said, 'Leave it. Get out. This side.'

The woman hooked a finger through the briefcase handle, hauled it up, and slumped back in her seat. Then she shifted her grip and swung the case around between her and Reacher like a shield.

Reacher said, 'Out.'

The woman didn't move.

'You don't try to hurt me, I won't hurt you. But if I have to drag you out of there, all bets are off.'

The woman stretched toward the door handle on the far side of the car.

'Make me chase you and you'll regret it.'

The woman's hand kept moving.

'Think you can outrun me? Maybe you're right. But can you outrun a car?' Reacher held up the key he'd taken from the ignition a minute earlier.

The woman pulled her hand away and scooted slowly to Reacher's side of the back seat. She didn't lower the briefcase. She said, 'What do you want?'

Reacher said, 'The old couple you took money from in the coffee shop. Who are they?'

The woman shrugged. 'Don't know. Just some dumbass losers.'

'How much did they give you?'

'Ten grand.'

'When did you promise to hand over their profit?'

'Tomorrow. Same time. Same place.'

'Only you won't be there. There won't be a profit. And the old folks will lose their life savings.'

'No shit, Sherlock.'

'Give me the briefcase.'

The woman pulled the case tight to her chest. 'No.'

Reacher gestured to the two men lying immobile on the ground. 'Want to join them?'

The woman didn't answer.

'Does conning seniors come with health insurance? I hear that a long stay in the hospital is expensive.'

'Fine.' The woman tossed the briefcase onto the ground. 'But if anyone's looking at a hospital stay, it's you. The guy we work for, you can't just rip him off. There'll be consequences.'

'The guy you work for? Who is that?'

The woman was silent for a moment. 'I'm not saying his name.'

'No matter. Because I'm not ripping him off. The money's not his. It belongs to those old folks. I'm going to return it to them.'

'You're not serious.'

'Watch me.'

'Why would you do that when you could keep it?'

'If you need to ask, you won't understand. Now go. Tell your boss what happened here. Then make sure I never see any of you again.'

The same time Reacher was leaving the alley, Harvey Jones was climbing out of a cab. He was moving slowly, and that was not just because of his size. Jones was six feet seven and weighed three hundred pounds. He was feeling demoralized by the phone call he'd received a half hour earlier. The call offering him the job he was on his way to now. Jones was an actor. At least he wanted to be an actor. But whether it was his height or his weight – actors are mostly tiny, for some reason he could never understand – or a lack of good scripts, he could never land a decent role. The only work he could get was playing an enforcer and putting the fear of God into assorted lowlifes for a local *businessman*. A guy he'd met through another resting actor after his latest agent dumped him. He told himself he was doing a good deed. The threat of a beating is better than the real thing, morally speaking. Making the performance believable took skill. And at least it paid well. He did have to eat after all.

The old couple was still at the same table when Reacher got back to the coffee shop, but they were looking a lot less gray. They were sitting straighter in their seats, laughing and giggling and holding hands, and there were two drinks in front of them. Tall conical glasses full of foamy milk with horizontal stripes of espresso shot through them.

Reacher walked up to their table, settled into one of the empty chairs, and balanced the briefcase on his lap. No one spoke for a moment, then the older guy said, 'This table's taken. Find your own.'

Reacher said, 'I'm here to deliver a message. I'm not staying.'

'What message? Who are you?'

The woman nudged her husband and gestured to the

briefcase on Reacher's lap. Confusion had replaced all the happiness on her face.

Reacher said, 'You dodged a bullet.' He wrenched both locks, took the manilla envelope out of the briefcase, and set it on the table.

'Is that . . . ?' Deep lines ate into the older guy's forehead.

'It's your money. Take it.'

'I don't understand. Why so soon?' The guy picked up the envelope and looked inside. His hands started to shake. 'Wait. Where's our profit? We were promised—'

'You were conned. There is no profit.'

'There is. There will be. Those other people – they tripled their money. We need . . . What have you done? How . . . ? Who are you? You've ruined everything!'

Reacher slid his hand into the briefcase and pulled out a random bundle. He dropped it on the table.

'What's this?'

'The other couple's *profit*. There are fourteen more, exactly the same. Go ahead. Count it.'

The old guy looked at the bundle for a long moment, like he was expecting it to grow legs and move on its own, then cautiously picked it up. There were three elastic bands holding it together. One in the center and one at either end. The guy hooked a fingernail around the band on the left and tugged it free. He fanned the bundle out. There was a twenty-dollar bill at the top. A twenty at the bottom. And between them, nothing but pieces of cut-up newspaper.

Harvey Jones caught his breath, pulled out his phone, and started to walk the final block toward the venue. He couldn't risk being seen getting out of a taxi – a black town car with a chauffeur would be a different story – and it gave him a final chance to run through the brief from his employer. Reading in a moving vehicle always made him sick. The instructions said that he was to find a guy named Gilmour, who had asked for an urgent meeting. Why he wanted to meet was unknown. Two possibilities had been surmised. Gilmour was losing his nerve and wanted to bail on whatever job he was supposed to be doing. Or Gilmour was losing his mind and wanted to renegotiate terms. Either way, the answer was the same. Not a snowball's chance in hell. Gilmour was to stay the course. He was to stick to the terms of their deal, or bad things would happen. What those bad things would supposedly be was left up to Jones. He would get to improvise. To showcase his talent, albeit to an audience of one.

Jones put his phone away and allowed himself a moment to daydream. He was heading to the Lyric Theatre in Manhattan, not some yuppified coffee place in downtown Baltimore. He was Sir Ian McKellen's understudy about to step in and save the day with the most inspired performance of the decade, not . . . Wait. There was something wrong with his left arm. A jolt of pain surged from his shoulder to his wrist. His fingers tingled. He felt like a steel belt had been thrown around his chest. Someone was tightening it. Clamping it down. His legs gave way. He fell face down on the sidewalk. Managed to wriggle and roll onto his back. Then wished he hadn't, because a safe fell onto his chest. Followed by a truck. And that was the last thing he ever felt.

THREE

The older couple stumbled out of the coffee shop shell-shocked, despondent, but with their money tucked safely back in the husband's jacket pocket. Reacher was left at their table with their barely touched foamy drinks. He pushed them away, set the briefcase on the floor, waited a minute to give the couple the chance to get clear, then stood up to leave. But instead of heading to the exit, he joined the line at the counter. He'd only had two cups when he was there earlier. He'd cut his consumption short in order to follow the guy who'd first had the briefcase. It was not quite noon. He had plenty of time. So he ordered another coffee and took it to his original table, which was still free, complete with its abandoned newspaper.

Two single customers and the group of six left while he was drinking his coffee, but no one new came in. No one paid any undue attention to anyone at another table. No other scams were unfolding, as far as he could see. The only slightly weird thing was that a couple of times he spotted a guy peering in through one of the windows without ever coming inside.

Reacher finished his cup then picked up the paper and glanced at the story on the front page. It was a rabble-rousing piece about a crisis that was brewing on the border between Turkey and Armenia. The gist was that a separatist faction from a small region in Armenia was helping Iran to refine weapons-grade uranium in return for support with their territorial claims. A whistleblower had defected from the group and had smuggled out video footage of the nuclear centrifuges in action. Clips had been posted online. Experts had chimed in. Condemnation was growing throughout the West. Diplomats were pressuring the separatists to quit, forthwith. The separatists were denying any involvement. Negotiations had hit a brick wall so talk was turning to the likelihood of a US-led invasion. No troops had yet been committed, but there were reports of a private contractor stationing its operators on the Turkish side of the Armenian border, primed for a rapid response if an intervention became necessary.

Reacher turned the page. He didn't like private military contractors. The idea of war for profit didn't sit well with him. The next story his eye fell on was about the evils of social media. Reacher had no experience in the field, and even less interest, so he put the paper down and fetched a refill of coffee.

Reacher drained his second cup, took another refill,

then made his way to the door. As he went out the guy who'd been at the window finally decided to come in. He made it over the threshold right as Reacher got there. The other guy raised both hands, palms out, and leaned back like he was trying to get out of the way. One hand grazed Reacher's shoulder just as their torsos brushed together. A classic pickpocket maneuver. An innocent contact to distract from a sinister one. Reacher kept an eye on the guy in case he bolted for some hidden rear exit and at the same time took a rapid inventory of the contents of his pockets. He felt his toothbrush. His expired passport. His ATM card. And a modest bundle of cash. Nothing was missing. It was a false alarm. Reacher continued on his way.

Reacher had one task to accomplish – buying a coat – and all afternoon to do it, so he took his time. He saw that a gaggle of pedestrians had gathered on the sidewalk a half block to the west. No one had been there when he returned from the alleyway, not long before, so he paused to see what had caught their interest. An ambulance had stopped in the middle of the street. A cop car was angled on either side, keeping the traffic at bay. A pair of paramedics were wrestling with a loaded gurney. Trying to heave it into the back of their vehicle. They were struggling, but not hurrying. A figure was strapped to it, covered with a blanket. Mostly covered. A giant pair of shoes protruded from one end and Reacher could see a shock of carefully styled brown hair at the other. A man's arm in a wide black sleeve dangled down from the side. The fingertips almost grazed the pavement. Reacher watched until the gurney was finally secured and the ambulance's doors were closed. Then the paramedics made their way to the cab, climbed on board, and pulled away. Gently. There were no lights. And no siren. Which meant there was no chance for the guy in the back, Reacher thought. He wondered what had happened. He hadn't heard any gunshots while he was in the coffee shop. No screeching of tires to suggest the guy had been run down. Nothing that pointed to a car wreck. And the cops on the scene looked pretty relaxed, so he figured it must have been some kind of innocuous accident. The random hand of fate, striking when it was least expected.

Reacher melted away with the rest of the crowd and began to wander the streets, heading generally toward the center of the city but zigzagging here and there to pass an interesting building or avoid waiting at a busy intersection. He didn't want to spend too much on the coat, partly because he had no interest in fashion, but mainly because he never kept clothes of any kind for very long. Shirts, pants, and underwear he bought, wore for two or three days, junked, and replaced. A coat could theoretically last longer, but he didn't know how long he would need it. He could be on a beach the next day. Or in a desert. So he avoided streets with any hint of high-end boutiques and eventually wound up at a mom-and-pop hardware store. Inside, he saw a selection of work jackets. Beige or brown. Faux-fur linings or plaid. He found one with sleeves that were just about long enough and took it to the register. He figured the tax and pulled out his cash so he'd be ready when he got to the front of the line, then stopped and stepped aside. He saw that he'd been correct about one thing back at the coffee shop: Nothing was missing from his pocket. But now a whole other kind of issue had come to light. Something extra was in there. Something that shouldn't have been. That hadn't been when he paid for his second round of coffee. A quarter of a sheet of letter paper, roughly torn on two sides and folded into a compact square. Reacher opened it. A message had been written in the center in bold capitals. It said:

MUST DISAPPEAR
LIFE IN DANGER
NEED HELP!
VACANT WAREHOUSE, ARGYLE & HORSEFERRY,
MIDNIGHT TONIGHT
COME ALONE
BRING WHAT I'M OWED

And at the bottom of the sheet, in paler, shakier letters, like it was added as an afterthought:

PLEASE.

FOUR

Nathan Gilmour stayed in the coffee shop for half an hour after Reacher left. He stood in line, constantly glancing over his shoulder, bought a cappuccino, and took it to the table that Reacher had been using. Not because he was stalking Reacher. He still had no idea who Reacher was. But because that was the table with the best view of the entrance. Gilmour was pretty sure he hadn't been followed, but the circumstances called for caution. He needed to be certain. He kept an eye on the door as he sipped his drink. He took his time. He emptied a quarter of the cup. Half. Then when he was confident that no one was paying him any attention he took out his phone – the one he'd used for texting – and switched it off. He held it under the table, out of sight, slipped off its back cover, and removed the battery. He had made contact with the person he'd been told to find.

The biggest guy in the place. He had no doubt about that. So he wouldn't need to send any further messages. Or to receive any. And even though Gilmour had no reason to believe that the man he'd been communicating with had the means to track his phone, he saw no reason to take the risk.

The note Reacher had found in his pocket wasn't intended for him. That was clear. The guy at the coffee shop had planted it on the wrong man. *Bring what I'm owed* implied a degree of familiarity with the guy's situation that Reacher did not have. Reacher had no idea how the guy could have mistaken him for someone who did, but he figured he had a more urgent question to answer: what to do about the note. He didn't know the guy who had planted it. He didn't owe him anything. He hadn't asked to get involved. So there was nothing to stop him from dumping the note in the trash and getting on with his day.

Except . . .

The note did make it sound like the guy was in serious trouble. If he were crying out for help and this message was the key to him getting it, Reacher felt it was only right to let him know it had gone astray. He would want someone to do that for him if the shoe were on the other foot. Plus returning the note shouldn't be difficult. It shouldn't take long. It wouldn't stop him from catching the band he'd come to town to see. And most important it shouldn't stand in the way of his plan to leave town without delay.

Except . . .

An abandoned warehouse at night could be a smart

place for a rendezvous. Especially for someone who was in danger. Who was wanting to fly under the radar. But it could also be the perfect venue for an ambush. Which made it the kind of location that Reacher usually made a point of avoiding, even when he wasn't the intended victim.

Reacher inspected the torn edges of the piece of paper the note was written on. He checked both sides. He was looking for traces of a letterhead or a logo or an address that could tell him where the paper – and therefore the guy – had come from. He found nothing. He held the note up to one of the ceiling lights in the hardware store, searching for a watermark. He found nothing there, either. He laid the note flat on his palm and gazed along its length, hoping to see the imprint of whatever had been written on the previous sheet, but the paper was smooth. It held no clues. Nothing to tell Reacher where he could intercept the guy ahead of the rendezvous at the warehouse. So he was left with the same two options he had started with. Trash the note, or try to return it and risk walking into a trap.

The smart thing to do would be to walk away. Reacher knew that. He had no skin in the game. No obligation to help a total stranger. But he did have a curious nature. He couldn't help wondering what this guy must have done to be in fear for his life. Where he had honed the sleight of hand needed to slip the note into Reacher's pocket without getting caught. And on top of that his eyes kept getting drawn back to the final scrawled word at the bottom of the page. *Please*. Something about the way it was written resonated with him. It tipped the scale away from *trap*, making it feel more like a genuine plea. Not the kind of thing Reacher found it easy to walk away from.

Reacher folded the note and tucked it back into his pocket. He figured that an abandoned warehouse was likely to be dark so he looked for a display of flashlights. He selected one that would fit in his pocket then returned to the register, paid for his items, and asked the clerk for directions to Argyle and Horseferry. Then he left the store and started walking, more purposefully than before. He had time before the concert was due to start so he figured it wouldn't hurt to head to the address stated in the note. Take a look at the place. Get a sense of what level of risk was involved, then make a final decision.

Nathan Gilmour's next destination was a cramped third-floor walk-up apartment in a plain, unrestored building. It was a quarter of a mile away from the coffee shop but it took him two hours to reach it. He started out walking. He meandered along for half a dozen blocks, crossing the street at random intervals and using the reflections in storefront windows to see if anyone was following him. No one seemed to be. He dodged into an alleyway, pressed his back against the rough brick wall, and waited to see if anyone turned in after him. No one did. No one even glanced in his direction. He came back out and hailed a passing cab. He gave the driver the name of a bar. It was a ten-minute drive. Gilmour paid the fare in cash, entered the bar, and made his way straight to an exit at the rear that he knew led to another alley. He hurried to the next street. Walked another ten blocks. Hailed another cab, and this time he asked the driver to take him to a car rental office. He used a Delaware license with a fake name and a bundle of cash to pay for a Chevy Malibu for a week. The car was midsize. Its contours were bland. It was an insipid silver color. It was totally boring in Gilmour's eyes. But that was the whole point. On the road it was as close to invisible as he could get.

Gilmour parked a block away from the apartment building and sat behind the wheel for ten minutes pretending to look at his phone. When he was happy that no one had followed him he walked to the building's main entrance, let himself in, and took the stairs to the third floor. There were two apartments leading off the landing and neither had a name or a number on its door. There were no identifying marks whatsoever. Gilmour liked it that way. He had no idea how his neighbor felt about it. He had never met them. He liked that, too.

Gilmour worked the lock, which was stiff with age and a lack of maintenance, pushed the door open, and stepped into a narrow hallway. The space was dark and the air was stale and heavy with dust. Gilmour nodded to himself. That meant he could be reasonably sure no one had been inside snooping around. Not recently, anyway. He checked that his go bag was in its usual spot on the floor and continued to the apartment's main room. It had one window with no kind of a view – just the crumbling bricks on the side of the next building – but that didn't matter to Gilmour because he kept the drapes permanently closed. He flipped the light switch. There was a small kitchen area in one corner, which was adequate for anyone whose interest in food extended no further than brewing coffee and reheating frozen dinners in an ancient microwave.

There was a dining table with two chairs. And a black leather couch with splits in two of its three cushions. Gilmour lowered himself onto the one cushion that wasn't ripped, reached for the TV remote, then paused. He felt safe for the first time since leaving the coffee shop. He couldn't go back to his office. He knew that. He couldn't go home. But this place – threadbare and unkempt as it may have been – was secure. He had started renting it a year ago when it became clear that access to a bolt-hole was turning into more than a luxury. He paid cash, as far in advance as he could afford. He used a false name. And he made sure that no one else knew about it. He'd only ever let its existence slip once, to one person. A woman. It was in a very special circumstance so he wasn't worried that she would mention it. Even if she remembered or realized the significance, there was no way she could ever breathe a word.

Zack Weaver checked his phone for the fiftieth time that afternoon. Was there signal? Still yes. Was there a text from Harvey Jones? Still no.

Weaver forced himself to stop pacing in front of the desk in the room he used as an office in his home in Fells Point, which felt like a different world from Gilmour's apartment. He crossed the room and flopped down in the beat-up leather lounge chair in the corner by the door and balanced the phone on its arm so he could see the screen. Another minute ticked over on the display. Then another.

The anger that had been boiling Weaver's blood ever since Jones failed to check in on time was starting to cool.

It was giving way to fear. The job Weaver had sent Jones to do was simple: Scare some sense into Gilmour. Make sure he knocked it off with his *911 emergency* BS and held up his side of the bargain. And Gilmour was so paranoid and flaky that a Boy Scout in a Halloween costume could get it done, let alone a giant like Jones.

At first Weaver assumed that Jones had taken care of business and then wandered off to do whatever it is out-of-work actors do with their time and had just forgotten to send his report. So Weaver had prompted Jones via text. A whole string of them, one after another. A dozen in total. A single message Jones might have missed. But twelve? That seemed unlikely. Something else must be going on.

Weaver knew that Gilmour was ex-military. If Jones had spooked him – and the whole point of sending Jones was that he was so scary-looking – Gilmour could have overreacted. Gotten into a fight with Jones. Killed him, even. Or if Gilmour had caused a scene in public they both could have gotten arrested. And that would be worse. There was no way either of them would stay silent for long.

Weaver moved back to his desk and fired up his laptop. He called up the local news station's website and right away had his answer. The latest story detailed how a local man had collapsed and died on a city sidewalk a few minutes before noon that day. A heart attack was suspected. Not foul play. No mention was made of a third party being involved, which was good. No name was given, either – presumably next of kin had to be informed before that could happen – but the time corresponded and the location was a block from the coffee shop where Jones was supposed to meet Gilmour. Weaver switched to a social media site and checked which hashtags were trending. He clicked on one that sounded relevant and a photograph popped up. It was blurred and poorly framed – obviously taken on a phone, probably by someone getting jostled by a crowd – and it showed a pair of paramedics trying to lift a man's body onto a gurney at the edge of a sidewalk. The body was inert. The man was huge. Weaver couldn't see his face, but given his height and bulk, there was no doubt in his mind. It was Jones. The only question that remained was whether he had been leaving the coffee shop after dealing with Gilmour, or if he had still been on his way to meet him. If he'd been leaving, then there was no problem. The message would have been delivered. But if he'd still been on his way, Gilmour would think he'd been stood up. Nothing good could come of that. The news station's website said Jones had collapsed a few minutes before noon. That was worrying because he'd been set to meet Gilmour at noon. Worrying, but not definite. The time frame was not precise enough to draw a solid conclusion. So Weaver switched to the *Sun*'s website and found a similar version of the story. The newspaper didn't name the victim, either, but gave the time of the incident as 11:48 a.m. A date stamp on the photo that accompanied the story said the same thing. 11:48. Twelve minutes before the meeting was due to start. A substantial margin. Not what Weaver wanted to see.

Weaver switched off the phone he'd used to text Jones

and took out the battery. He would need to destroy the phone as a matter of urgency but in the meantime he didn't want the police to be able to track it if they decided Jones's death was suspicious. Next, he took out the phone he used to communicate with Gilmour, pulled up his number, and hit Call. He got dumped straight into voicemail so he hung up without leaving a message. Instead he texted:

> *My guy had an accident on his way to meet you.*
> *Not deliberate!*
> *I still want to help. Same time / place tomorrow?*
> *Lmk . . .*

Weaver sent the message and waited for a reply. None came. Five minutes crawled past. Gilmour still didn't respond, so Weaver pulled out a third phone and typed out another message. The reply came back right away: *Make it quick. I have a patient in two minutes.*

Weaver said, 'Nathan Gilmour. If he thought he'd been hung out to dry, what would he do?'

'Depends. Why would he believe that?'

'I sent a guy to meet with him, but it looks like he didn't show. Seems like he had a heart attack. Dropped dead on the sidewalk a block or so away, twelve minutes ahead of the meet. I tried to reach out to Gilmour to explain, but I can't get ahold of him.'

'Then he's going to run, if he hasn't already.'

'You sure?'

'I remember him being as jumpy as a box of frogs. And he's already spooked or he wouldn't have sent the SOS. If he thinks you've abandoned him or betrayed him, there's no way he'll stay.'

'Even without his money? He wouldn't stick around one more day if he thought he had a chance to get it?'

'Maybe. It's possible, I guess. But a guy like him could lose his nerve at any moment. So don't wait till tomorrow. Go after him today. Right now. And Zack? No more actors, okay? Use the real thing this time. It'll cost more, but you can't afford to screw this up. We still need updates from Gilmour. If the job goes south because the client doesn't have the latest information . . .'

'I get it. So where would Gilmour hide?'

The screen was static for a moment, then: *He has a safe house. A little apartment he pays for with cash. He thinks no one knows about it. I'll text you the address.*

FIVE

Nathan Gilmour changed the TV channel for the twentieth time in two minutes. He couldn't find a single thing to watch that interested him. Or that didn't actively annoy him. Not sports. Not drama. Not cooking. Certainly not home improvement shows. The only saving grace was that he wasn't paying for the garbage the cable company piped into his apartment. The first week he rented the place he had illegally tapped into the building-wide system. His main motivation was to avoid having his name or credit card attached to the apartment's address in any kind of corporate database, but saving a few bucks was a welcome bonus. Especially given how broke he had been back then. And how badly the content still sucked.

Gilmour stuck it out for another five minutes then nixed the TV and the cable box. He got up off the couch, changed into some black clothes, grabbed his go bag, and headed for the door. He knew he should get over himself and stay. He would be safer off the street and out of sight. There was no doubt about it. But he figured there was no point in staying physically safe if the price he had to pay for that was losing his mind. He decided that as long as no one was watching the building or his rental car he would drive around until it was time to head to the rendezvous with the big guy from the coffee shop. He had no particular route in mind. No specific destination. He just craved the sensation of forward momentum. The feeling reminded him of something an old friend used to say. That when she was stressed she couldn't stay still. She had to be constantly on the move, like a shark. He had thought she was being overly dramatic at the time. Now he could appreciate what she meant. For the next few hours he would be a shark, too. If the traffic cooperated. And no one killed him.

It took Reacher half an hour to walk from the hardware store to the abandoned warehouse. It sat on a corner lot with plenty of parking bays out front – all empty except for the weeds growing out of the cracks in the asphalt – and a row of four loading docks spaced out along the left-hand wall. The front part of the building was surprisingly grand. It was three stories high, all stone and red brick, and there was even some stained glass clinging on in the higher floors' windows. It could have belonged to a movie theater, Reacher thought. Or a museum or concert hall. He guessed it had been built in the days before just-in-time logistics, when torrents of merchandise were flowing into the country via the port and people believed that having supplies of valuable goods on hand was a good idea. Reacher scanned the area for security cameras. He couldn't see any, so he tried the main door. It was jammed solid. The ground-floor windows were all boarded up tight. There was no way in from that angle. Not without a sledgehammer or a crowbar.

The rear portion of the building was a whole different story, aesthetically. It didn't match the façade at all. Its walls were made of cinder block. Beige paint was peeling off them in long ragged strips. Scarred metal shutters covered the entrances to the loading bays, and the shallow-pitched roof looked to be covered with sheets of corrugated iron. The place must have been reconfigured when standardized shipping containers became a thing, Reacher guessed. The storage area had likely been rebuilt at the lowest possible cost, but the façade was retained because it was still functional. Or the owners liked it. Or were obliged by the city to keep it. Or wanted to save the money it would cost to replace.

Reacher started down the side of the building. There were no windows, and the roll-down shutters over the loading bays were all padlocked. The locks on the farthest three from the road were rusted solid but the one closest to the front was newer. It was a stout-looking item. Still shiny. Almost certainly still serviceable. If it was unlocked this would be the obvious way into the building. Reacher figured that the guy from the coffee shop must have a key. He was likely planning to get there early, unlock that shutter, leave it rolled up a couple of feet, head inside, and take up a defensive position.

Reacher returned to the front of the building and crossed to the right-hand side of the façade. The way the structure was joined to its neighbor created a kind of alcove, four feet wide and three feet deep. A metal drainpipe ran the whole way down from the roof to the ground. It was painted dark blue and was held in place by sturdy iron brackets. It was about three inches in diameter, and it snaked its way around a kind of ornamental ledge just below the level of the second floor. Above the ledge was a window. And the glass in the windowpane was missing.

Reacher tugged on the drainpipe. It felt solid. He gripped it with both hands at chest height, stretched his arms, and raised his right leg so that his foot was flat against the wall. The pipe held. Reacher leaned back and placed his left foot against the wall, eighteen inches higher than his right. Immediately the lowest bracket gave way. The pipe snapped. Reacher crashed back down and landed on one heel with a ten-foot section of pipe in his hand. He set it down gently so as not to make any noise then pressed his back against the alcove's side wall. He pressed his right foot against the opposite wall, set his left foot next to it, and pushed hard so that he was suspended above the ground. It was like he was sitting in an invisible chair. He lowered his arms to his side, below his butt, and pressed his palms against the rough bricks to take some of the strain. He moved his right foot up twelve inches, then his left. Then he slackened the pressure his legs were exerting, just for a moment, pressed down with his hands, and slid his back up the wall until his legs were again parallel to the ground. He took a breath then repeated the process: right foot up, left foot up, ease the pressure, push with his hands. He went through the routine once more and gained another twelve inches of height. He repeated the moves again and again, a dozen times in all, until the ledge beneath the window was at waist level. Then he threw himself forward, pushing against the wall with his hands, then flinging both arms out in front like a swimmer diving into a pool. He landed his forearms flat on the ledge, caught his breath, heaved himself up onto his hands, and wriggled headfirst through the broken window.

The tap on the door of the office above his bar in Harbor East was so faint that Dominic Kelleher wasn't sure if he'd imagined it. He listened for a moment, thought he could maybe hear someone fidgeting in the hallway, then said, 'Who's there?'

A woman's voice said, 'It's Mia.'

Kelleher closed his laptop, gathered up the papers that were spread across his desk, dropped them into the top drawer, then said, 'Mia? About time. Get in here.'

The door opened very slowly and the woman Reacher had prevented from ripping off the seniors at the coffee shop stepped into the room. She closed the door behind her, shuffled forward, and stopped in the center of a dusty, threadbare rug in front of Kelleher's desk. She was wearing an auburn wig now and was looking at her feet. A blind was pulled across the window behind Kelleher. Three old file cabinets were lined up along the left wall and a pair of leather armchairs sat opposite them. A small wooden table with an ashtray at its center was squeezed in between them, and the air in the little office was heavy with the scent of cigars.

Kelleher said, 'You alone?'

Mia nodded.

'Where are the others?'

'At the hospital. Mick's got a concussion. Norman's arm's messed up pretty bad. They're having trouble setting the bones. He might need surgery.'

'Someone jumped you?'

Mia nodded again.

'Who?'

Mia shrugged. 'Some guy.'

'On his own?'

'Right.'

'Three of you got jumped by one guy on his own?'

'You should have seen him. He was huge. And nuts. Like some kind of psycho. He looked like a Neanderthal.'

'You ever seen him before?'

'No.'

'Ever communicated with him?'

'No.'

'So how come he didn't send you to the hospital, too?'

'He said he wanted me to tell you what had happened. And to make sure none of us cross paths with him again.'

Kelleher's top lip curled into a sneer. 'Oh, our paths are going to cross. You can take that to the bank. No one steals ten grand out of my pocket and walks away.'

'I told him that. He said he wasn't stealing it. He said he was going to return it to the idiots we took it from.'

'Like hell. Who would do that? No way. He took it. The only question is who he's working for. We need to know. 'Cause this needs to be nipped in the bud right now.'

'He said he's not working for anyone.'

'More BS. All right. This is what we're going to do. I'm going to make some calls. See if anyone admits to hiring this guy. Or has an idea who did hire him. Or even got hit by him. You get the word out to everyone we know on the street. Spread the guy's description. Anyone spots him, I want to know. Like, yesterday.'

Reacher hit the ground shoulder first, rolled forward, then sprang to his feet. The room he had landed in was empty. There was no furniture. The floorboards were bare. There was nothing on the walls. No coverings on the three unbroken windows that faced the street. No door in the frame. Just a thick coat of dust everywhere and a smattering of pigeon droppings in one corner.

The doorway led to a kind of gallery that spanned the width of the building. It gave access to four more rooms – presumably offices – on one side and offered a view of the whole storage area below on the other. A staircase sat in the center, jutting out at ninety degrees, with flights that switched back on themselves to correspond with the height of each floor.

Reacher checked the other rooms on the same level. They were all empty, too. Stripped bare. Even the radiators had been taken, based on the stubs of copper pipe that had been cut off a couple of inches shy of the floor. He took the stairs to the third floor. The space was divided in half there, forming a pair of broader rectangular rooms. Originally for keeping files or records, Reacher guessed, given the age of the building. Next he took the stairs down to the warehouse itself. There were no goods there now. The floor was just a latticework of scuffs and scrapes carved by decades of pallets and containers being hauled in and out with varying degrees of care. The shapes were barely visible in the subdued light that filtered through from the empty offices.

Reacher took in the entirety of the space, calculating angles and possibilities, then stood with the staircase between him and the entrance to the first loading bay. The one with the serviceable lock. He nodded to himself. The staircase gave good cover, and there was no light source behind it to create a silhouette. That was where he would wait if he were planning a covert rendezvous. He figured the guy who'd left the note would do the same. That only left two questions. What kind of weapon would the guy be carrying? And how twitchy would his trigger finger be?

Reacher made his way beneath the overhang formed by the second-floor offices and crossed to the inside of the main door. It was kept closed by three planks held up by pairs of solid metal brackets. Reacher took hold of the highest plank. It was heavy. Its surface was hard and shiny. Exposure to years of polluted city air had left it feeling more like iron than wood, and time had wedged it fast in place. He pushed up at the end, but it didn't shift an inch. He tried the center one instead. It was tight, too, but it did move. Just a little. Reacher kept shoving and straining. It raised another inch. Then another. Then it popped out of the left bracket. Reacher moved and wrestled it free of the other. He set the plank down and turned his attention to the lowest one. It gave way much more easily, one end then the other. Reacher turned it and placed one of its corners on the ground, then raised it at an angle until its narrow edge was in contact with the bottom corner of the highest plank. He crouched a little, got his shoulder under it, and tried to straighten his legs. Nothing happened. He kept up the pressure for another twenty seconds, and suddenly the bracket gave up the fight. The left side pivoted up at a crazy angle. He shifted the plank to the right and reapplied the leverage. The plank groaned against its bracket, slid upward, then broke loose and shot up into the air. Reacher stood back. He let it clatter to the ground, then gathered the fallen planks and stacked them on the right-hand side of the doorframe. He needed to be sure he wouldn't trip on them in the dark. Then he pulled the ancient door open a crack, made sure no one was watching, stepped outside, closed the door, and started walking back toward the center of the city.

SIX

When Morgan Strickland bought the Kinsella limestone mine, twenty miles northwest of the city, people thought he was crazy. Geological surveys showed that the place was pretty much tapped out. And even if any limestone was left inside, no one wanted it anymore. You could barely give it away. Demand had tanked in recent years and industry experts predicted that nothing was going to change the outlook. They expected that its long downward spiral would continue right up to its final, inevitable collapse. But none of that mattered to Strickland. He wasn't planning on digging anything up. And he didn't intend to sell any raw materials. He was interested in something else altogether: the cavernous hundred-acre space that had been created as the limestone was extracted.

Aside from the access ramp the cavern was at a

consistent level seventy feet below the surface. The way it had been excavated left a series of uniform wide-open spaces between the circular pillars that supported the ceiling. The pillars were substantial. Sixteen feet in diameter. Bigger than necessary. Bigger than they would have been if computers had been involved in the design. Their bulk combined to ensure the place was secured against natural threats. And human threats, too. It was protected on all sides by residual seams of limestone, which is six times stronger than concrete. It naturally stayed at a stable temperature, sixty-eight degrees Fahrenheit, which made it cost-effective to maintain. And it was completely dry, so vehicles and equipment, plus weapons and ammunition, could be stored indefinitely without fear of degradation. But Strickland didn't regard the place as just an underground warehouse. He saw a much greater potential. The opportunity to build something no other private military contractor had. Or could have. A state-of-the-art training and assessment facility impervious to infiltration. Or espionage. Or sabotage. All in all, the cavern complex was the ideal base for his business – Strickland Security Solutions. Currently the seventh-largest private military contractor in the US. Soon to be the largest, if Strickland had his way. And already the most profitable.

The same time Reacher was heading back to town, Strickland was walking through an area that was usually full of armored vehicles. He was on his way to a walled-off space at the far end of a bay. It was nominally his office but more often than not he slept there when he was stateside. He fished a key from his pocket but before he could work the lock he heard footsteps approaching. Two sets.

Both moving fast. He adjusted the patch that covered his left eye – he had lost it to an IED, along with his left arm, when he was serving in Iraq in '03 – then turned to see who was coming. Two men hurried into view. Steve McClaren, the operations director, who was tall and rangy with a freshly shaved head. And David Moyes, VP of procurement, who was his physical opposite: short and stout with gray hair and a matching straggly beard.

Strickland waited until they were close enough to shake hands, then said, 'Steve – everything squared away?'

McClaren nodded. 'Everything and everyone is in place in Turkey. The operating base is a mile from the border with Armenia. The facilities aren't great, though. I'm hearing a few grumbles from the operators. I'm hoping we'll get the green light very soon. We're good to go the moment we do.'

'Outstanding. Anything else?'

Moyes cleared his throat and said, 'Sorry to sound contrary, but I'm hoping the green light doesn't come so soon. Issues with the accommodations aside, it turns out we have supply problems in two key areas.'

Deep creases ran the width of Strickland's forehead. He said, 'Which areas?'

'The upgrades you authorized at the last strategy session. Better body armor for the operators and hard-side kits for the Humvees.'

McClaren turned to Moyes and said, 'Wait – we don't have those yet? Why am I just hearing about this? I was told everything had been delivered pre-deployment.'

Moyes said, 'Two consignments arrived on schedule, yes. And the order numbers corresponded. But when we checked the contents, half of the armor and a third of the Humvee kits were missing. My guys are chasing the suppliers, but so far they're just running in circles.'

McClaren's face had turned scarlet. 'That's not good enough. We all know what happened last time out in Haiti, three months ago. Twenty-four men, lost. At least twenty of those deaths could have been avoided with better equipment. If this comes down to cost . . .'

Strickland stepped between them. He shook his head and said, 'No. It doesn't.' He gestured to his eye patch and his empty shirt sleeve. 'I – of all people – don't give a rat's ass about the cost of protective equipment. I signed off on the purchase orders the minute they hit my desk. Leave this with me. I'll take care of it. Now, Steve, in the meantime, what's the status with our latest class of recruits? They ready for their final assessment? We need them to be if they're going to join the deployment this time around.'

McClaren shook his head. 'The assessment is going ahead tomorrow, 10:00 hours, as planned. Whether they're ready is a whole other question. Where did you get these jackasses? I was promised vets, not donkeys.'

'They've all been through Basic at the minimum, is my understanding.'

'Been through? As in all the way through? As in passed? Or have we been stiffed with a bunch of washouts?'

'You know, some guys, their careers to date have met with mixed fortunes. That doesn't mean the die is cast. It doesn't mean they're write-offs. Maybe any bumps in the road they hit weren't their fault. Maybe the army dropped the ball. Couldn't get the job done in the training arena.

Which means we get another chance to prove we're better. So I'm hoping many of them will get through. I'm hoping most of them will.'

'I'm not passing anyone who's not fit.'

'I'm not asking you to. Just keep an open mind. Remember, we were all in their boots once.'

'We were. But at least we knew how to tie them on our own.'

The band Reacher was in town to see was even better than he remembered. The singer's voice sounded like it came from a different dimension. It was soft and powerful and confident and vulnerable, all at the same time. The guitar wailed and soared, and he could feel the bass and drums resonating in his chest. The set ended after what felt like five minutes, but Reacher didn't want to leave right away. He stayed for the next band, which was more mainstream and less bluesy. It was still good, though. They wrapped at a minute past ten and immediately the crew got to work resetting the stage for the headliners. Reacher watched them for a minute then pulled himself away. He made his way through the crowd, out of the venue, and started toward the warehouse. The note called for the rendezvous to happen at midnight, so Reacher planned to be there no later than eleven.

Two other people left the concert just ahead of Reacher. A man and a woman, neatly dressed, maybe in their late thirties. A couple. In theory, at least. Maybe they had been at the start of the evening, Reacher thought. Whether they would still be together when the night came to an end was hanging in the balance. They were walking fast, taking long, hard strides, each hugging their own side of the footpath, backs stiff, sharp elbows angled outward, not looking at each other, not talking. They made it to the street and the woman darted off the sidewalk and raced over to the first in a line of waiting cabs. She wrenched open the back door, jumped inside, and slammed the door closed before the man could catch up. He was left standing alone, stranded in the center of the street. Reacher expected the guy to take that as a cue to walk away and rethink his priorities, but after a moment he slunk around to the far side of the car, opened the other door, and slid in alongside the woman. Reacher strolled past and saw the pair staring angrily in opposite directions, each with their arms tightly folded.

The driver of the next cab in line caught Reacher's eye. Reacher half expected him to offer a ride but instead the guy suddenly looked down and started to fiddle with his phone. Reacher wasn't too surprised. He was used to drivers wanting to avoid him. Something to do with the way he looked, he thought, allied with the constant diet of horror stories people were fed by the press and online. It happened more frequently as the years went by but he usually came up against it when he was trying to hitch a ride. Now it seemed to be spreading to taxis, too. Another change in the fabric of society, Reacher thought. Another thread coming loose. Maybe social media was to blame. Maybe there was something to the article he'd read in the coffee shop after all.

Reacher could have tried the next cab but chose to ignore it. He liked being on foot in a city at night. He liked the sounds. The rhythms. The darkness. Given his height and bulk Reacher was not exactly built to blend into a crowd so night was the only time he could enjoy a little anonymity. He passed the rest of the cabs – ten in all – and kept on walking. The streets were still bustling with traffic – mainly cars, plus a couple of delivery vans, a garbage truck spewing a thick black cloud of exhaust fumes, and a solitary police cruiser – but the sidewalks were practically deserted. He only saw a dozen other people. Some were heads down, hurrying. A couple was holding hands and strolling. One guy was clearly drunk. But none of them paid him any unwelcome attention. As he walked he saw several more cabs, all with different license plates, but all from the same company as the driver who had blanked him. Rides-R-Us. Some of the cabs were heading toward him. Some were heading away. And none were carrying any passengers. Reacher wondered how the outfit could stay in business if all its employees were so averse to doing their jobs. He figured something else must be in play, like a taxi company he'd read about where it had dawned on the owner that delivering drugs was more lucrative than transporting people.

Reacher turned onto Argyle Street. No traffic was moving. No vehicles were parked. The sidewalks were empty, as far as he could tell in the gloom. All the streetlights were broken and there were no lights showing in the windows of any of the buildings. He started toward the warehouse then heard tires scrubbing across the coarse asphalt behind him, along with the growl of a rough, ragged engine. He slowed and glanced over his shoulder. A car was approaching. Another taxi. It was from the same company as before. And it had no passengers on board.

Something dubious was going on. That was clear. But the fact it was happening on every street he walked down was a coincidence too far, Reacher thought. He stepped out into the street and raised his hand like he was trying to flag the cab down. The car slowed. The driver locked eyes with Reacher, then hit the gas and swerved around him. It kept going straight for fifty yards, then coasted to the side of the road and rolled to a stop.

Reacher was tempted to circle around to a busier neighborhood and find a place where he could prevent the next empty Rides-R-Us car from escaping before he could question the driver, but he knew he didn't have time. The cab mystery was intriguing, but it was less important than getting set in the warehouse ahead of the guy who'd invited him there. So Reacher stayed in the middle of the street, clearly visible to anyone who was watching, and walked forward until he was level with the center of the next building. He headed toward its entrance as if that was his intended destination and kept moving until he was lost in the shadows. His eyes were on the stationary cab. It stayed where it was for a minute. Two. Then its brake lights went out and it pulled away. As soon as it was out of sight, Reacher doubled back to the warehouse. He found the door, heaved it open, stepped through, eased the door as near to closed as it would go without making a sound, then dodged to the side and eased back until he felt the wall against his shoulder blades. The interior of the place was pitch-dark. It was silent. The air was stale. Reacher stood still for two minutes. Three. Then he shouldered the door into its frame, took out his flashlight, held it between his teeth, and turned to the stack of planks he'd piled up earlier. He forced each one in turn into place behind its pair of brackets and checked that the door was secure. Then he made a complete circuit of the storage area. The beam of his flashlight was too feeble to penetrate all the way into the darkness so he sensed as much as saw that the cavernous space was still empty. He made his way up the stairs to the third floor and checked the filing rooms. They were still deserted. He checked the offices on the second floor. They also remained empty. Finally he picked a spot at the right-hand end of the gallery near where he had first climbed in. The only way into the building was once again the broken window in the adjacent office. Anyone who entered that way would have to walk right past him. And he was perfectly placed to see if anyone opened the shutter that covered the entrance to the first loading bay.

The clock in Reacher's head told him it was 10:52. That left sixty-eight minutes until the rendezvous unless the guy who'd left the note was cautious and showed up early. Or longer, if he was careless or disorganized or liked to play dubious mind games. Either way was fine with Reacher. Waiting was one of his strengths. It was a skill he had honed during his years in the army but even before that it had suited his temperament. Time had taught him that he had two natural states: violent, explosive action, or quiet, almost comatose inactivity.

SEVEN

The guy who had left the note turned out to be cautious.

Reacher heard a scrabbling sound, low down, on the far side of the staircase, at 11:45. Fifteen minutes before the appointed time. Someone was outside fiddling with the lock on the loading bay shutter. The sound stopped and a narrow strip of dim light appeared at the base of the entrance. It grew in a series of sharp jerks, each accompanied by a harsh metallic shriek, until it was a foot high. Then two feet. Then three. A shadow with a hunched back ducked under the solid edge and pushed it most of the way down again. Reacher heard a rustling sound, then a soft thump. A flashlight clicked to life and in the backwash Reacher saw a man dressed all in black leaning over a backpack he had set on the ground in front of him. The guy pulled out a pistol – it was on the large side, maybe a 1911 – tucked it into his waistband, closed the pack, and swung it onto his back. Reacher caught a glimpse of the guy's face. He recognized him. It was the man who had brushed past him at the coffee shop just after noon.

The guy drew the gun and held it in his right hand. He took the flashlight in his left, clamped it beneath the weapon, and made his way slowly around the warehouse's storage area. He took his time and covered every square inch of the floor. The beam of the light and the muzzle of the gun moved smoothly, in unison. He swept ten feet up all the walls. But he didn't go any higher. In the shadow on the balcony, Reacher smiled. A long time before, in Escape and Evasion training, he'd been taught that if you need to hide, you climb, because no one ever looks up. No one knows why. It's just some quirk of human nature. He had thought that was crazy at first, but over the years it had been proved right, time after time.

The guy finished his search but instead of taking a position with the staircase between himself and the loading bay door, as Reacher had expected, he continued straight along the center of the space. He stepped up onto the lowest stair and started to climb. The old wood creaked and groaned. The guy took two more steps. Four. Reacher slipped the note the guy had left out of his pocket, ready to use it to identify himself as a friend when the flashlight beam picked him out. The guy continued up four more steps. His pace was steady. Unhurried. The wood continued to complain. Then the guy stopped climbing. His head ducked down. There was a louder creak, the flashlight went out, and the guy disappeared in the total darkness.

Reacher returned the note to his pocket and strained his ears to pick up any kind of sound. His eyes searched for motion. He heard nothing. Saw nothing. Five minutes crawled past. Six. Then he latched onto another scrabbling noise. Below him and far to his right. Not metallic this time. More like pointy claws skittering across concrete. The guy's flashlight flickered back into life. The beam jerked back and forth across the floor at the distant end of the warehouse. It picked up movement. A rat, scurrying toward the far corner. The muzzle of the guy's gun flared. The *crack* of the shot echoed off the walls. A spent bullet whined as it ricocheted off the solid ground. A shell case bounced off the banister rail and rattled onto the floor, and a smell like burned hair tickled Reacher's nose.

The guy kept the flashlight switched on for another five seconds. It was a little shaky now, but steady enough to pick out a patch of blood and fur that was sprayed across the foot of the end wall. That was all that remained of the rat. The guy himself was sitting three-quarters of the way up the staircase. His backpack was by his side. His right foot was wedged securely two steps down, and his legs were crossed at the knee so that his left thigh formed a platform to support his right forearm. His body was angled to his left, giving him a perfect vantage point to cover the loading bay entrance. He breathed deeply, turned back to resume his vigil, and doused the light.

Reacher now knew where the guy was, and he had picked up some other useful information at the same time.

The guy he was watching was tactically proficient. Lowering the loading bay shutter to leave such a narrow gap had been a smart move. Anyone wanting to enter would have to roll on the ground, so even if they were armed they would be vulnerable and exposed – unless they pulled the shutter up higher and risked making a noise, which would eliminate any element of surprise. The guy was also a good shot. He had quick reactions. But he was jumpy as hell. He had gone to such lengths to set up a rendezvous where he had the upper hand and then he had blown his advantage with the gunshot. Anyone approaching or staking the place out would have heard it. And he hadn't fired because he was in real danger, but because he'd been spooked by a rodent. Reacher was ten times closer than the rat had been. He was a hundred times bigger. And he was infinitely more threatening. If he broke cover, could he rely on the guy to recognize him? To realize why he was there? The guy had seen him once, briefly, at the coffee shop. He hadn't been under stress then. Now he was freaking out. Would he hold his fire? Was there any guarantee? Reacher thought not. He still wanted to help but now he figured the risk outweighed the reward by too great a margin. So he changed his plan. He would stay where he was, safe in the darkness, and wait for it to dawn on the guy that he'd been stood up. He would leave, and after that, Reacher would head to the Greyhound station. He had done what he'd come to town to do and he saw no reason to stay any longer.

Morgan Strickland had been alone in his office for over an hour. He was sitting slumped in his squeaky chair, feet on the metal desk, eye on the monitor. He was watching the last couple of technicians who were working on the area that was going to be used the next morning for the recruits' final assessment. He was going to wait until they left before he made his move. That wasn't strictly necessary. He was the boss. He was entitled to enter the control room whenever he liked. He didn't need a reason, or an excuse. But he had learned over the years that it sometimes paid to be cautious.

The technicians were thorough. Strickland couldn't deny that. Normally he would have applauded such conscientiousness, but that night he wished they would hurry. He would be happy to see the back of them. When the coast was finally clear, he got to his feet and stretched his back the way he'd been taught two decades previously. He took a step toward the door, then paused. His phone had started to ring. The melody was 'Enter Sandman' by Metallica, which meant the caller was on his list of special contacts. He saw it was someone else who favored caution. Though in Strickland's opinion, this guy, Mark Hewson, had a tendency to let his caution tip over into cowardice. Especially since his move to the Pentagon.

Strickland answered and said, 'Mark. Have you signed?'

There was silence on the line for a moment, then Hewson replied, 'If it were up to me, I would have. You know that, Morgan. But it's not that simple. The DoD is a big ship. It takes a while to change direction.'

'How many times do we have to go over this? It's simple. Ask yourself: What do you want? Promotion and glory? Or to sit on your ass in a cubicle for the rest of your career?'

'I'm not in a cubicle. I have—'

'Focus, Mark. Fortune favors the brave. You know that. You have the chance to change history. What I'm proposing is genuinely the best way forward. The country can't afford to always be preparing for the last war. My way is the future. We can prove that.'

'I know. I'm on board all the way. But there are people I have to bring with me. People who need time to adapt to new ideas.'

'Screw those people. If you – when we – win, nothing else matters. You know how people say it's easier to seek forgiveness than to ask permission? Well, that's bullshit because you don't need either when you win.'

'I know. I get it. But there are angles I have to deal with that don't impact you. I have a major PR minefield to tiptoe through with this whole Armenia thing.'

'What PR minefield? You think the public would back Iran over whoever we pick?'

'No. But remember the Gulf. That left a stain on the careers of a whole generation. Not because of the lives lost. Not because of the money spent. But because of the weapons of mass destruction horseshit. The nonexistent threat used to justify the invasion. I can't risk starting down that road again. Not if I'm walking it alone.'

'You're worrying over nothing. For one thing, this isn't even a full-scale invasion. It's . . . Let's call it a special military operation. A proof of concept, really, that we can do a job without the army slowing us down. A better job. And for another thing, the justification is one hundred percent legit this time.'

'Are you sure it's not all a bill of goods? Because the

army's not buying it, and I'm not going to lie – that makes me nervous.'

'The army's not buying it? Give me strength. It's a classic case of *not invented here*. Come on, Mark. You've read the reports. You've seen the video. We have eyewitness testimony. It's been all over the TV. The internet. Social media.'

'Is there any way you could shore the story up a little?'

'It doesn't need to be shored up, but for you, yes, I can. The witness will be in Baltimore in a couple of days. I'll have her sit down with my community outreach guy. She can record another video. Give statements to the press. We can make as big a splash as you like. But in the meantime, don't lose sight of all the other advantages that would come with putting us in the lead role. We can move faster than the army. We're cheaper. We have fewer rules. There'd be less oversight to hold us back from doing what needs to be done. And fewer reporting requirements. Like being totally scrupulous about casualties. Meaning we would always win. We would win the media battle, anyway, and what's more important these days?'

'You have a point.'

'And that's only the *evolutionary* stuff. It hardly moves the needle next to the *revolutionary* ideas I have. Listen. Until now, war has always cost money. Imagine going down in history as the guy who made it *make* money.'

'That would be . . . something.'

'Remember the next-gen bodycams we demoed? And the shares that are sitting in a trust for you in the company that makes them? They're the game changer. The revenue opportunities are outrageous. They're limitless.

Picture this: people paying to stream footage of battles as they're fought, in real time, with surge pricing based on the level of peril. They could follow their favorite soldier. Vote on strategy. Bet on the outcome of individual actions or wholescale engagements. We could sell virtual embeds for regular civilians, not just legacy media journalists. We could call it *democratizing war reporting*. And we'd make it easy to screen-grab and post on social, so the whole thing would advertise itself.'

'People do like things to be easy.'

'Then there's sponsorship. Customized patches on uniforms, like European soccer players wear, or race car drivers. Logos on vehicles. Weapons. *Victory in Helmand Province, brought to you by our friends at Sig Sauer.*'

'That might be going a little far.'

'You've got to think big, Mark. You could have league tables. For contractors, or weapon brands. And how about this: gender. Put the whole *Should women be on the front lines* debate to bed, once and for all, with real data.'

'Real data's good, I guess.'

'And one more opportunity: competitions. *Fly a Predator Drone for a Day*. With prizes like that.'

'Morgan, you've got to promise me something. One step at a time. Slow down. If ideas like these reach the wrong ears and—'

There was a heavy *clunk* and Strickland's phone went dead. His office was suddenly fully dark. The power had gone out. The main connection to the local utility was toast. It was happening more and more frequently and it made Strickland mad. In some of the developing countries he'd served in, where modern infrastructure barely existed, or in war-torn cities where the facilities had been blown to hell, he understood. But where there was no extreme weather? No swarms of enemy drones targeting the electricity grid? There was no excuse in his book. But there was nothing he could do about it, so he shook off his irritation, counted to five, and listened as the backup generators kicked in. He'd balked at the cost when they'd been fitting the place out and had almost deleted them from the plans, but now he was glad he hadn't. The lights flickered back to life. His computer whirred and stuttered. The cave's cell booster acquired its signal again and the bars on his phone ramped back up to five out of five. He thought about hitting the call-back button but decided not to. If Hewson had been listening, his message would have gotten through. And if he hadn't been, that was a problem for another day.

EIGHT

The guy on the staircase hung on for an extra thirty minutes before he accepted the inevitable. No one was coming to meet him. He turned his flashlight back on, this time standing it upright on the step where he was sitting and switching it to work like a lantern. He set his gun down next to it, uncrossed his legs, leaned forward, wrapped his arms around his head, and started to rock slowly back and forth. Reacher wasn't certain but he thought he could hear him moaning. His mind flashed back to the last word on the note – *Please* – and all of a sudden, without a gun in his hand, the guy didn't seem like such a threat after all.

Reacher remained in the shadows and said, 'Stand up. Put your hands behind your head.'

The guy uncurled himself and stopped rocking, but he stayed sitting down.

Reacher added an extra layer of steel to his voice. 'Up.'

The guy stood. He said, 'Who—?'

Reacher said, 'Hands.'

The guy raised his hands to chest height. His palms were facing out and his fingers were quivering slightly. He shuffled around until he could see the top of the stairs. His eyes were moving wildly, scanning every inch of the balcony rail, and after a moment he said, 'Where are you? Show yourself.'

Reacher said, 'With your left foot – your left foot – kick the gun away. All the way to the bottom of the staircase.'

The guy's left leg began to move. His toe touched the gun's grip, then stopped. He said, 'Wait a minute. Let's put this together. This is an obscure place. There's nothing to steal and there's nothing to pull in tourists. We could both be here by coincidence, I guess, but I don't buy that. You're here because you got my note. Am I right?'

Reacher stepped into the dim light.

'Okay, good. So now for the important question. Did you bring my money?'

Reacher moved to the top of the staircase so that he would be close enough to react if the guy went for the gun. He said, 'There is no money.'

'Then you've wasted your time coming here. If you were going to shoot me you would have already. Beyond that, I don't care how big you are. There's nothing you can do or say that'll make me stay. Tell your boss he'll never hear from me again. He can whistle for his updates.' The guy started to turn away, then spun back around. 'And tell him he's an asshole.'

Reacher moved down one step. 'Most bosses are. But I'm not here to threaten you. I came to return your note.'

'Return it? Why?'

'You gave it to me by mistake. I figured you were in some kind of trouble so it might help you to know your message had gone astray.'

'Mistake? No. I was told to find the biggest guy in the place. That was you. I checked everyone. There's no doubt about it.'

Reacher thought for a moment, recalling the scene outside the coffee shop when he left. He said, 'Which direction did you approach from?'

'The east. Why?'

'Half a block away, to the west, a guy died. Right around the time you arrived. Looked like a heart attack. I saw him being loaded into an ambulance. He was bigger than me. Maybe he collapsed on the way to meet you.'

The guy shook his head. 'Not possible. If something like that had happened I would have been told. New arrangements would have been made. I wouldn't have been left . . . shit. Wait. And don't panic. I'm not going for a weapon.' The guy picked up his backpack, rummaged inside, and pulled out a phone. He set it on the stairs then rummaged around again until he found its battery. Then he sat, fitted the battery, switched on the phone, and waited. Thirty seconds passed then the phone let out a series of beeps. The guy studied the screen and nodded. He said, 'You were right about the dead guy. That's a relief. And a new meet's been proposed. Same time, same place, tomorrow. Well, today, as it's after midnight.' He typed out a brief message, hit Send, stood, and slipped the phone into his pocket. 'Second time's the charm, right?' He held out his hand. 'Anyway, thank you. I appreciate you taking the time, coming out here, letting me know.'

Reacher ignored the guy's hand. 'You're not going to this do-over meeting?'

'Of course I am.'

'Why?'

The guy was silent for a moment, then said, 'Listen. I appreciate you hauling your ass across town to give me my note back. But what I do and *why* is none of your business.'

Reacher nodded, stepped past the guy, and made his way down the stairs. At the bottom he turned and said, 'Planting the note on me. That was some technique. Where'd you learn it?'

The guy shrugged. 'A past life. I spent time in the army.'

'What was your MoS?'

'Intel. Sixty-sixth Military Intelligence Brigade.'

'Out of Wiesbaden, Germany?'

'Right. How do you know that?'

'Doesn't matter. But take my advice, soldier. You're in trouble. Your gut is telling you to get the hell out. Listen to it. Leave town. Today. Now. Don't stick around to collect whatever money you think you're owed. Or any possessions. Or anything else. Just go. Get out in one piece.'

Compulsive was a word that Strickland had heard many times in his life. Too many, when it was applied to him. It had started informally. The word had been thrown around by friends. Girlfriends. Soldiers he'd served with. Commanding officers. Then it had gained weight when it had been written down by the counselor he'd been forced to see during his recovery after his return from Iraq. The word seemed negative to him. Judgmental, the way others used it. Strickland saw the behavior it described differently. He felt it was a sign of thoroughness. Of logic. Just because something had turned out a particular way in the past, there was no guarantee it would again in the future. That wasn't a matter of opinion. That was philosophical doctrine, as far as he was concerned. It made sense to check important things every time you could. Which was why he didn't take the direct route from his office to the control room when he got off the phone with Mark Hewson. He took a detour to the far side of the complex, to the new storage room. It wasn't in the most convenient location in terms of geography, but it made sense from a logistical viewpoint. It had only been added three months previously, when the need to store perishable cargo suddenly arose. It needed a lot of power for its environmental equipment, so it was cost-effective to position it near the main distribution facility. That saved laying a bunch of new cable, plus a lot of time.

The room was rectangular, sixty feet long by twenty feet wide by eight feet tall. Its walls and ceiling were made of high-density foam wrapped in heat-reflecting foil and covered with steel mesh, which Strickland thought made it look like a cage. It had one door, made of hardened steel, and an electronic lock controlled by a keypad. Only two people knew the code. Strickland himself and Steve McClaren. Neither was the kind of person who would leave a door unlocked. Given its location, the likelihood of a break-in was remote. But Strickland didn't leave anything to chance. He had the door guarded by two operatives 24/7 on twelve-hour rotations. And to make sure the operatives were in position and the door was secure, he passed by whenever he got the opportunity.

Strickland thought of himself as a considerate boss, so he provided seating for the guards. He heard the chair legs scrape against the rough floor as he came closer. He turned the last corner and saw the guards standing, alert, M16s slung across their shoulders, muzzles pointing toward the ground. The guard on the right started to raise his, then recognized Strickland and relaxed. Strickland looked each guard in the eye, threw them a loose salute, then continued on his way, satisfied.

The guards waited until he'd disappeared from view, then the one on the right sat back down. His name badge said *Walker*. His buddy was named Jacklin. He said, 'Why does Strickland keep walking by like that?'

Walker said, 'Why do you care?'

'I don't. But it's weird. I wish he'd stop.'

Walker grunted.

Jacklin said, 'I hate it here.'

Walker shook his head. 'It's better than deploying. There are no bullets flying here. The food is better.'

'It's boring.' Jacklin strolled over to the storeroom door. He pressed his palm against the metal as if he'd be able to sense what was on the other side. He said, 'Ever wonder what's so important about this place?'

'No. Nor should you.'

Jacklin traced the outside of the keypad with the tip of

his finger. He said, 'Ever catch sight of the code when Strickland opened the door?'

'No.'

'Me neither. Maybe I'll take a guess . . .'

'Are you insane? What if you set off an alarm? Leave it alone. Sit down. Keep quiet.'

NINE

Two cars were waiting outside the building next door when Reacher left the warehouse. They both had their headlights on and the weak yellow beams were illuminating the entrance he'd pretended to be heading for. They were both taxis from Rides-R-Us. But these cabs weren't empty. As well as their drivers they both had two passengers in their back seats.

Reacher had emerged from the loading dock at the side of the warehouse, so he could have doubled back and avoided being seen. But he didn't do that. He had questions. So he stepped into full view and walked forward until he was level with the point where the buildings joined. The driver of the nearer cab spotted him and twisted around in his seat. Both back doors swung open and two men climbed out. A moment later the other cab's doors opened and two more men appeared. They ranged in height from five-ten to six-four, and in age from mid-thirties to late forties. They all had close-cropped hair, and they all had on the kind of overalls that construction workers wear, with all kinds of loops and straps and pockets for holding tools. They formed up into a rough line, shoulder to shoulder, and started toward Reacher. As they moved, the tallest one took a slight lead. He wound up directly in front of Reacher, six feet away, with his buddies a pace or so behind.

Reacher had his first answer. The guys had come looking for him. That was clear. He glared at each of them in turn and then focused on the tallest one. He said, 'Who sent you?'

The guy seemed surprised to be hit with a question, and he didn't respond.

Reacher said, 'I want a name. I want an address. Tell me, and you can all walk away. Refuse, and you will all go to the hospital.'

The tallest guy sniggered, then gestured toward the cabs with an outstretched thumb. He said, 'Pick one. Get in.'

Reacher said, 'That's a strange name. Are you sure?'

The guy's eyes narrowed for a moment. He said, 'What? No. I'm not giving you a name. I'm telling you, get in the car.'

Reacher said, 'When you're explaining, you're losing. You know that, right?'

Deep furrows appeared across the width of the guy's forehead. 'We never lose. Now get in.'

'Remember, you don't have to do this. Tell me who sent you and you can all walk away.'

The guy scowled. 'Get in the car. Now.'

Reacher smiled at him. 'Make me.'

'Happy to.' The guys stepped back and fanned out a little wider. Each one took a heavy leather glove from a pocket in their overalls and slipped it onto their right hand. Then each one pulled out something black and shapeless and heavy. One after another the guys raised their arms out sideways to chest height, flicked their wrists, and the objects they were holding unfurled, stretching down in dull loops toward the ground.

Motorcycle chains.

Nasty weapons, when used by people who knew what they were doing. They tore skin. Ripped flesh. Broke bones. Severed ears. Burst eyeballs. The traces of oil and grease they left behind infected the wounds they made. They wrapped around limbs, immobilizing them, preventing escape. Restricting retaliation. And critically, from Reacher's point of view, their length outweighed the advantage he usually gained from the span of his arms and legs.

The guy on the left end of the line broke away and looped around behind Reacher's back. The guy on the right did the same. The tall one waited for them to take their positions, then said, 'Not such a smart-ass now, huh? So, last chance. Get in the car. Or it'll be you going to the hospital. In pieces.'

Reacher didn't reply. He was already moving. He spun around and locked his eyes on the guy who had wound up between him and the spot where the two buildings joined. He had wanted to get to him before he had the chance to start swinging his chain, but the guy was too fast. He kept the chain down at his side, parallel to his body. He gripped it tight, working his wrist, building the speed and momentum and guiding the chain as it cut a wide, vicious circle through the dim yellow light.

The tall guy said, 'Have your fun, boys.'

Reacher heard the other three chains start moving. They made a *whoop, whoop* sound like distant helicopters and Reacher could smell the droplets of filthy oil that were shaking free from them. He was surrounded. The four guys were moving closer. Their chains were scything around like circular saw blades, slicing through the air, closing in on him. There was no way to outrun them – no one can move faster than a whirling chain – and no space to dodge between them.

Reacher pulled his flashlight out and flung it hard at the nearest guy's face. The guy flinched and instinctively raised his dominant hand – the one holding the chain – to deflect the incoming object. The chain wrapped itself around the guy's other arm and bit into his back. He screamed. Reacher launched forward. He grabbed the guy's gloved right hand with his left. He pulled, dragging the guy toward him, doubling their closing speed, and simultaneously threw a straight right that hit the guy's jaw like a bowling ball. His head snapped back and his body pivoted around and crashed to the ground like a felled tree. Reacher let go of his hand and kept going, stomping on his chest and breaking away from the other three. He continued to the alcove where the buildings came together, turned, and retrieved the section of drainpipe that had broken off when he climbed up to the missing window, earlier that day. He gripped it with both hands, held it straight out like a lance, and charged back toward the other three. The end of the pipe caught the central guy – the tallest one – square in the chest. He cannoned backward, flopped to the ground, and lay there writhing and gasping for breath. The guy to his right flailed at the pipe with his chain. It wrapped around once, twice, then got caught on itself, locking up tight.

The guy heaved frantically, trying to pull Reacher off balance. He soon realized that wasn't going to happen so he changed his plan. He tried to occupy Reacher. To leave him defenseless. That was a mistake as well. The guy was heavyset. That was for sure. But he was no match for Reacher's two hundred and fifty pounds. Or his fury. Reacher pulled back, then pivoted counter-clockwise, bringing the guy spiraling after him like a fish on a line. Reacher increased his speed and stepped to his left. The chain worked loose and the guy reeled backward. Reacher followed him. The guy staggered and fell. He tried to jump back up but Reacher was too close. He kicked the guy in the side of the head, spinning him around and dropping him face down on the ground. The guy struggled up onto his hands and knees. He was unsteady. His eyes were unfocused. Reacher kicked him again. In the gut this time. The force lifted him a couple of inches into the air. He went down flat. Reacher kicked him in the face, just to be sure, and left him bleeding but otherwise inert on the crumbling asphalt.

Reacher turned to the remaining guy. He kept him at bay with the pipe and said, 'It's just you and me now. Be smart. Give me the name. Your boss. No one will know it came from you.'

The guy snarled and spat back, 'Go to hell.' He raised the spinning chain above his head, dodged around the tip of the pipe, and rushed forward. Reacher took two long strides to his left, lowered the pipe, and swung it hard against the back of the guy's knees. His legs folded and he pitched forward onto the ground. He rolled and pushed up into a crouch, blood spurting from his nose, legs tense, ready to spring forward, but Reacher was already swinging the pipe back the opposite way. It caught the guy square in the temple and he toppled over onto his side, eyes rolled back, motionless.

Reacher glanced across the other three to make sure they were still down then started toward the pair of taxis. The driver of the closer one started his engine, dropped the transmission into reverse, pulled back onto the street, and raced away into the distance. The second driver struggled to work his key. The engine turned over but didn't start. He tried again. It still wouldn't catch. He tried a third time, but while the ancient motor was still resisting, Reacher smashed the end of the pipe through the driver's window. The guy jumped in his seat, let go of the key, and scrabbled for something fixed to the side of the transmission tunnel. A Glock 17. It looked old and scuffed. He raised it and tried to bring it to bear through the shattered glass, but Reacher leaned forward and tore it out of his hand.

Reacher said, 'Get out.'

The guy whimpered and clung to the steering wheel with both hands.

Reacher stuck the gun into his waistband, heaved the door open, grabbed the guy by the front of his shirt, and pulled him out of the cab. He said, 'Go. Run back to your boss. Tell him what happened here. And tell him I have a one-strike policy. He's had his. He sends anyone else after me, I come for him.'

The guy started moving backward then when he was ten feet away from Reacher he spun around and scampered down the street. Reacher smashed the cab's remaining windows and its windshield, put a dent in each of its body panels, then crossed to the edge of the sidewalk. He unloaded the gun and dropped it and its shells into a storm drain. Then he heard a voice from behind him. It was the guy who had left the note. He was standing over the first man Reacher had dealt with, and he said, 'Looks like you were wrong about one thing.'

Reacher said, 'What?'

'This one isn't going to the hospital. He's going to the morgue.'

Reacher shrugged.

The guy said, 'Are you okay with that?'

'I'm not delighted. I'm not upset, either.'

'You killed him. You don't feel bad about it?'

'I don't feel anything about it. He brought it on himself. He chose to come here. He was ready to hurt me. Maybe kill me. Presumably for some kind of a reward. Bad choices have consequences.'

The guy was silent for a moment, then he nodded. 'What was their beef with you?'

'I ran into some of their buddies at the coffee shop right before you showed up. I guess I hurt their feelings.'

'I guess you did.' The guy scooped up Reacher's flashlight, then moved forward and held out his hand. 'I'm Nathan Gilmour.'

'Reacher.'

They shook, then Reacher took the flashlight and slipped it back into his pocket.

Gilmour said, 'You knew about the 66th MIB. How come?'

'I've been to Wiesbaden. More than once.'

'Army?'

'Military Police. I served thirteen years. Now I'm retired.'

'Wow. I didn't see that coming.'

Reacher didn't reply.

Gilmour said, 'Do you want a hand cleaning this mess up? I know a couple of people. I could make a call.'

'No need. Whoever sent these idiots will handle the clean-up. They won't want the police sniffing around, asking questions. And they won't want their rivals to know their goons got their asses handed to them.'

'I guess you're right. So we probably shouldn't overstay our welcome. We don't need any more company.' He looked around for a moment. 'Do you have a car?'

'No.'

'Do you want a ride somewhere?'

Reacher paused for a moment, then said, 'Thanks. You can take me to the Greyhound station.'

'What, like, in the morning?'

'What's wrong with right now?'

'At this time? It's late. Are you sure?'

'Why not? Buses run all night.'

'Don't you want to get some sleep?'
'I'll sleep on the bus.'
'Are you in a hurry to get someplace?'
'No.'
'So where are you headed?'

Reacher paused for a moment, like he was surprised by the question. Then he said, 'Wherever the first bus takes me.'

TEN

Every time Strickland hauled himself up the ladder that was in the shadows at the far corner of the section of the cavern with the highest ceiling, he asked himself the same question. *Why?*

Strickland knew the answer, in theory. It was so the controller could look down at the four training zones and visually track what was happening without relying on screens or infrared sensors. But the theory wasn't everything. He couldn't help but think that the cameras would have been enough. If so, the control room could have been at ground level, and he would have been a happier man.

Strickland reached the top of the ladder and eased himself onto the gantry that ran diagonally above the border between the urban and jungle zones. He knew no one was down there but he still moved as quietly as he could.

He slid each foot along the mesh, slowly and smoothly, until he reached the control room door. He had his own code, of course, but he tapped the administrator's into the keypad instead. He stepped inside, closed the door softly, then hit the light switch. The room filled with a red glow. It was the kind of light they used in old-school photographic darkrooms. It gave him a weird sensation. It felt eerie, like he was trapped inside a fairground haunted house. He knew that the setup was necessary, though. The glass in the sloping windows was made to prevent that particular frequency from passing through so that no light could spill onto the ground below.

The equipment in the room was divided into four banks, one for each training zone: urban and jungle, which he'd passed over, along with mountain and desert. He selected urban, fired up one of the computers, clicked on the main menu, then on the option for operational parameters. He knew the correct settings well because they'd been designed to his own specifications. Partly based on his experiences in Iraq, and partly on what he had drawn from his imagination. That evening, everything was set as it should have been, under normal circumstances. He nodded to himself. His staff were well trained. Then he went to work with the keyboard and mouse. He had a feeling that circumstances the next morning were going to be far from normal.

The next bus scheduled to leave Baltimore after Gilmour dropped Reacher off outside the Greyhound station was headed to New York an hour and six minutes later. New York was as good a place to go as any, Reacher thought.

And he hadn't been there for a while. He went in through the glass door, dodged a drip from an overhead HVAC duct, bought a ticket from one machine and a cup of coffee from another, then took a seat in the waiting area. He picked the one at the far end of the last row, by the window. That gave the best view of the entrance, which was a bonus, because the ones at the end had only one armrest. That made them the only kind he could comfortably fit in.

The bus showed up four minutes early. Reacher peered through the doorway to make sure there were no Rides-R-Us cabs loitering in the area, then made his way to the bus's designated stand. No one got off. No one else was waiting to get on. Reacher was ten feet from its door when he heard footsteps behind him. Fast-moving, but not too heavy. Someone clearly in a hurry. A passenger concerned about getting left behind, Reacher guessed, but he glanced over his shoulder anyway to be sure.

It wasn't another traveler who was running down the platform. It was Gilmour. His eyes were wide and his face was bone white in the artificial light. He called out, 'Reacher, stop. I need to talk to you.'

Reacher slowed to let him catch up, then nodded toward the bus. 'Make it quick.'

'No. Stop. Please.' Gilmour glanced around in all directions then lowered his voice. 'I'm in trouble. I need help.'

'What kind of trouble?'

Gilmour shook his head. He said, 'Not here. Come back to my car.'

'There's no time. The bus leaves in three minutes.'

'There will be other buses. This is important. It's life or

death. I'll get you another ticket, if that's what you need. But hear me out first. Please.'

Gilmour's rented Chevy was on the street outside the station. It was jutting out from the curb at a crazy angle, looking more like it had been abandoned by a drunk joyrider than deliberately parked. Gilmour hurried toward it, unlocked the doors with the remote, and climbed in behind the wheel. Reacher strolled around to the other side and got in alongside him. For a minute neither of them spoke, then Reacher said, 'Are you going to talk to me or am I supposed to read your mind?'

Gilmour took two slow, deep breaths, then said, 'Okay. This is what happened. After I left you here I drove back to my apartment. I made sure no one was following. I parked a block away. But when I walked into the building, two men were already there waiting for me. One of them' – Gilmour paused and even more color drained out of his face – 'one of them showed me a photo. On his phone. It was my nephew. He's four years old. He was playing on his scooter outside my brother's house. In St Louis. The man said if I didn't do what they told me, they would blind the kid. Gouge his eyeballs out with a spoon. Send one to me and one to my brother.'

'Who were these guys?'

'I don't know their names. They were sent by the guy I'm ... involved with. The one who texted about rescheduling the meeting at the coffee shop.'

'Why send guys to your place when you already have a meeting set up?'

'One of them was pissed. He said they'd been there

since three in the afternoon. I guess the guy sent them to stake the place out when I didn't reply after the first meeting went south. Then he forgot to call them off when I finally did get in touch.'

'What did they tell you to do?'

'Stay in town. Forget about leaving.'

'Doesn't sound too difficult.'

'That's not all. They want me to keep on doing my job.'

'Doing what?'

'I work at the port. Pushing paper. Nothing exciting. Except . . . this guy I'm involved with – he wants information. I gave him some. Now he wants more.'

'This guy. Who is he?'

'I don't know his name. He approached me a few weeks back. Things kind of went from there.'

'The information he wants. It's confidential?'

Gilmour nodded. 'Commercially confidential. It's not state secrets or national security.'

Reacher said, 'What's it about?'

'Details of an incoming shipment. Its arrival date. Estimated unloading time. Storage location ahead of customs clearance. Now he wants updates because things like that can change. The ship could get stacked up outside the port. The unloading schedule could get derailed. The container could get diverted to a different holding zone. He wants to stay current.'

'Why?'

'We never discussed it explicitly. But I think it's fairly obvious.'

'He's planning to steal this shipment.'

'He never said so. Not in so many words. But yeah. I

can't see any other reason. Either he's going to steal it himself, or he's selling the information to someone who will. I kind of think he's selling it. He came off more as a fixer than a doer the one time I met him.'

'You get the information from a computer?'

'Obviously. This isn't the nineteenth century.'

'Then why does he need you to steal it? Why doesn't he hack in from the outside?'

'The port's a strategic installation. It has a top-level firewall. I guess the guy doesn't have the resources to break through it. He needs someone on the inside, old-school, hands-on, to help.'

'And you're okay with that? Helping to set up some kind of heist?'

'What can I tell you? The world's not a perfect place.'

'What's in the shipment?'

'I don't know.'

'Who owns it?'

'I don't know that, either.'

'How can you not know? You pulled a bunch of information off a computer. That must show the owner, the contents, all kinds of details.'

'Right. The manifest says it's a consignment of tables and chairs from Amritsar, India. The manufacturer is some little family-owned company. But that's not relevant.'

'The record's fake?'

'No. I'm sure it's accurate. But no one steals furniture from India. It's big and heavy and not very valuable. And if someone did steal some for any reason, the owner would claim it on his insurance. No need for any drama.'

'So what's going on?'

'My guess? Smuggling. The way it works is that a gang latches onto a legitimate shipment. They bribe a dockhand at the port of origin, or somewhere intermediate, to look the other way. They open the container, hide whatever it is they want to smuggle, and reseal it with the right kind of tags. Then, when it arrives at its destination, more money changes hands, they open the container, retrieve their contraband, and seal it up again. Depending on what they're smuggling, the whole operation could take minutes. The only anomaly is that smugglers usually pick fruit or vegetable containers. Their contents is perishable so they get priority when the ship's unloaded. The gang can get their stuff out quicker, so there's less time to get hit with a random inspection. But they can piggyback on any kind of shipment. There's no way to trace them. There's nothing in any records.'

Reacher said, 'So the merchandise this guy is setting up to steal is whatever's being smuggled – not the furniture.'

'I would think so.'

'And the information the guy wants. Is it hard to get?'

'No. It's a piece of cake. That's not the problem.'

'Then what is?'

'If I stay, I'm a dead man.'

Reacher thought back to the note Gilmour had slipped him. *Must Disappear. Life in Danger.* 'What makes you think that?'

'They've already killed someone.'

'Who has?'

'Whoever's doing the smuggling, I guess.'

'So you're getting squeezed. The smuggler will kill you if you stay. The wannabe thief will hurt your nephew if you don't.'

'Right.'

'So call your brother. Tell him to hide out someplace with the kid. Then call the police.'

'I can't. That wouldn't work. My brother's a dentist. His wife's a potter. They're not the kind of people who could act normal while they pull off a disappearing act. They'd alert the whole damn neighborhood just packing their minivan. They're being watched, remember. How else did these guys who threatened me get the photo of my nephew? And they have resources. The apartment where they cornered me? It's not my regular one. It's a bolt-hole. A complete secret. My name's not on the lease. It's not on any utilities. I have no idea how they even found it.'

'So, a rock and a hard place. You've got a tough call to make.'

'Not really.' Gilmour paused for a moment. 'Not if you stick around and watch my back.'

'Forget it.' Reacher took hold of the door handle. 'I'm not a babysitter.'

'Wait. Please. It would only be for a couple of days, max. And I don't have any other option. I saw how you handled those guys with the chains. You're my only hope of getting through this. And my nephew's only hope.'

'Leave your nephew out of this.' Reacher tugged on the handle and the door swung open. 'You got him involved. Not me.'

'I'll pay you for your time.'

'I'm not interested in your money.' Reacher climbed out of the car. 'You made your bed selling secrets to this crook. Now you have to lie in it.'

ELEVEN

Morgan Strickland hit the final key then logged off and pushed the keyboard across the desk. He slumped back in his chair. It was late. He was tired. Everything took longer with only one hand, which left him frustrated. He had planned to head back to his home in Annapolis that night but now he was no longer sure. Tomorrow was set to be a big day, with the recruits' final assessments taking place. The day after would be hectic, too, but for a different reason. He had an arrival to supervise. The eyewitness from Armenia. Her journey was not exactly straightforward, and he had a lot of moving parts to keep track of. The cot he kept in his office was beginning to seem like a very welcome option.

Again.

Strickland heaved himself to his feet. The stainless-steel surfaces in the control room were strangely disconcerting in the red light, and the air was heavy with ozone from all the electronics. He was looking forward to being back on the ground. To being able to breathe more easily. He took a step toward the door and 'Enter Sandman' started to play. It was his phone again. He checked the screen and saw the same Pentagon number as earlier. He hit the Answer key, raised the handset, and said, 'Mark. It's late. Make this quick.'

Hewson's voice came on the line. 'I've been thinking about the things you said. You made some good points. So, yeah. I'll do it. I'll sign. Go ahead. Make your preparations for Armenia.'

'I will, but I need the contract. I need a wet-ink signature.'

'You'll get one. I'll deliver it in person. On one condition.'

'What?'

'The eyewitness from the video. You said she's coming to town. I want to meet her in person. Hear her story. Look her in the eye.'

'No problem. When?'

'Tomorrow?'

'Tomorrow doesn't work. She gets here Wednesday. She has a long journey and it's not like she's in business class. Let's do it Thursday.'

'Okay, Thursday morning.'

'Ten hundred?'

'See you then.'

'Mark? One last thing. Email me a copy of the contract. I want to read it before you sign it in case anything needs tweaking.'

'It won't, but no problem. I'll send it now.'

*

The next bus out of Baltimore was bound for Boston. It was due to leave in another forty-five minutes. Reacher was okay with that, so he bought another ticket and another cup of coffee from the same pair of machines. He took the same seat with the view of the entrance and settled in to wait.

Two minutes later Gilmour appeared. His face was flushed now, and he was breathing heavily. He strode across to Reacher's corner and said, 'Two things, Mr Righteous. First, I didn't sell that information. I was caught in a bind. I was forced to get it. I had no choice. And second, I am going to stay in town and keep doing my job. For my nephew's sake. Even without your help. Even if the whole thing blows back on me big-time. So the next time you're sitting in a coffee shop reading somebody's abandoned newspaper, if there's a story about me getting murdered, you'll know why.'

Gilmour didn't wait for a reply. He turned on his heel and started back toward the door. He took three steps, then paused and looked over his shoulder. He said, 'If you're leaving town, where's your luggage?'

Reacher didn't reply.

Gilmour shrugged and continued to the exit.

The vending machine coffee was weak, and it was lukewarm, so Reacher wasn't too upset about wasting it. He set the cup down next to his seat, then got up and walked outside. Gilmour's car was still there. Its engine was running now, and it inched forward like Gilmour was getting ready to pull a U-turn. Then he saw Reacher and stopped moving. Reacher approached, opened the passenger door, and climbed in. He said, 'You were forced to steal this information?'

Gilmour nodded.

'How?'

Gilmour killed the engine. He took a deep breath and closed his eyes for a moment. Then he said, 'First of all, I want you to know that I'm not proud of any of this.'

'Don't second-guess yourself. Start at the beginning and go from there.'

'The trouble started when I got out of the army. I had a few problems readjusting. A lot of guys do. It was booze at first. I beat that. But then the gambling got me, and man, it hit me hard. I used to go to this underground card place here in the city. Once a week at first. Then twice. Then before long, every night. I was desperate to stop but I just couldn't. I tried everything. Support groups. Hypnotism. I even went to counseling a couple of times. I have to admit I was a total addict. And the debt – it just kept getting worse. The more I owed, the more I played, thinking I could win some back. Thinking my luck would change.'

'But it never did.'

'Not for long enough. In the end I always lost, and then there was the interest on what I already owed. On and on it went. Round and round. Down and down. Before long I was circling the drain. I couldn't see a way out. Except for . . . a couple of times I went to the bridge in the middle of the night. I climbed up onto the side wall. I didn't jump, though. Obviously. Then, out of the blue a guy showed up at my door. He said he had a proposition for me. Said he'd pay off all my debts. In full. All I had to do was get a job at the port, stay out of trouble, and one day before long he would ask me for some information. After that we'd be even. I'd even get a cash bonus if I kept the job and stayed away from the club. He said it would be paid in installments to help me resist temptation.'

'And you don't know this guy's name?'

'No. He never told me. But I got his picture.' Gilmour pulled out his phone, selected an image, and held it up for Reacher to see. It was a photograph of a man, early fifties, with a hard, angular face, close-cropped, graying hair, and cold, narrow eyes.

'Did he know you took that?'

Gilmour shook his head. 'I didn't plan to. Old habits die hard, I guess.'

'Did you take a picture of me?'

Gilmour looked away.

'I'll take that as a yes. Delete it. Now.'

Gilmour fiddled with the phone, then slipped it back into his pocket. 'Done. Sorry.'

'The guy knew you had debts?'

Gilmour nodded.

'He knew who you owed the money to? How much you owed?'

Gilmour nodded again.

'How did he know?'

'I have no idea. I didn't ask. You don't look a gift horse in the mouth. Not when the alternative is getting your legs broken by some psycho enforcer or throwing yourself in the ocean.'

'Okay. How did you communicate with him?'

'Text. He gave me a number. I used a different phone, of course.'

'He told you to get a job at the port. Any random job? How could he be sure you'd get hired?'

'A specific job. One with access to the information he needs. He texted me a link to an application form. Said if I applied, I'd be accepted. I did, and I was.'

'Okay. And the shipment. When's it due?'

'Day after tomorrow. Tomorrow, technically, as it's after midnight.'

'You said the owner of the shipment already killed someone. Who?'

Gilmour looked away. 'A coworker of mine.'

'He was providing information, too? Something you couldn't get? Or was he a dupe to keep you both straight?'

Gilmour's voice dropped to almost a whisper. 'Neither of those things. He had nothing to do with it. I got him killed. I didn't mean to, but I did.'

'What did you do?'

Gilmour sighed. 'I got the text telling me which shipment to track but I didn't want the search record to be tied to my log-in. Old habits, I guess. So I used his. And right after that, he got killed. Officially it went down as an accident, but come on.'

'What happened?'

'They dropped a shipping container on him.'

'They dropped a container? That doesn't sound like a surefire method of killing someone.'

'It wasn't some random thing. There was a little more to it. An hour after I did the search, a woman showed up at our office asking for him. I told her he was at a meeting. She asked where, and what time he'd be back.' Gilmour paused again. He closed his eyes and took a breath. 'And

I told her. I didn't realize in the moment but I gave her all the details she needed to plan the hit. Where to drop the container, and when. And believe me, it worked. They could have buried the poor bastard in an envelope.'

'Who was this woman?'

'I don't know. I'd never seen her before. She had an ID around her neck, so after the *accident* I called security. Gave them her name. They said she didn't exist. There was no record of her in the system.'

Reacher looked Gilmour right in the eye. Gilmour held his glare for five long seconds, then looked down at his hands, which were clasped on his lap. Reacher had questioned hundreds of people during his years in the army. Maybe thousands. He had dealt with murderers. Con artists. Thieves. Sex offenders. Scumbags of every kind. He could sense when he was being lied to. He wasn't getting that vibe from Gilmour. So he said, 'I guess I don't need to leave town this minute.'

'What?'

'I'll stay. Two days. No more.'

'That's all I need. Thank you. Thank you.' Gilmour sank back in his seat, closed his eyes for a moment, and took a deep breath. When he sat forward again his whole face was brighter. 'I'll have to interrogate the system again, which will alert the smugglers, I guess, but I'll lie low after that. Keep out of their way.'

'You're looking at this all wrong. The smugglers aren't the danger. They're a temporary threat. It sounds like they don't even know who you are. The guy who paid your debts, he's the real problem.'

'My coworker wouldn't agree.'

'Your situation is different. Think about it. This guy offered you a cash bonus to stay in your job, payable in installments. Why?'

'It's a win-win. Why not? Installments don't hurt him.'

'No. They help him. He put you in place at the port. He wants you to stay there. Stuff must get smuggled every day. This won't be his last opportunity to sell the details to thieves. The bonus was the carrot. When you lost your nerve he switched to the stick. Your nephew. But either way you're an asset to him. Do you really think he'll ever let you walk away?'

Gilmour was quiet for a moment and all the brightness ebbed back out of his face. He said, 'So what can I do?'

'Tell me, when the guys who threatened your nephew cornered you, that wasn't at your regular apartment?'

Gilmour shook his head. 'They showed up at my other place. It was supposed to be secret, for emergencies. In case I needed to disappear. I guess I wasted my money.'

'So where's your regular place?'

'Federal Hill. It's a nicer neighborhood. I'm getting a bit old for the nightlife – all the noise and the late-night drunks – but the park's good. And it's not too expensive.'

'Okay. Take me there.'

'Why?'

'The guy you sold your soul to sent his goons to your backup place and forgot to stand them down. So there's a good chance he sent another couple of them to your main address. Maybe he forgot to stand them down, too. If we're lucky they'll still be there.'

TWELVE

Gilmour pulled up outside a square yellow-brick building. It was three floors high with a flat roof and was set back six feet farther from the sidewalk than its neighbors. The space was taken up by a raised flower bed. It was crammed with bushes and shrubs. None were in bloom. Reacher didn't recognize any of them, but he did spot a couple of empty Keystone Light cans that someone had shoved among the foliage.

Gilmour locked the car and led the way around the side of the building. He took the gun out of his backpack, held it down against his leg, and continued to a pair of glass doors. He unlocked them and stepped through into an entrance lobby. The floor was covered with black and white tiles, and six brass mailboxes were lined up along the left-hand wall. Reacher scanned the row of names.

Gilmour's wasn't on any of them. Gilmour saw what he was doing and said, 'Old habits. I don't want to advertise where I live. And there's no point leaving one blank because that's like doing the same thing.'

'Which one are you?'

'3F.'

'David Cruikshank?'

Gilmour said, 'He was a buddy of mine at grade school. He died when we were twelve.' Then he stepped forward and unlocked a second pair of glass doors. Reacher followed him into a hallway. The floor was oak. The planks almost glowed from years of polish. The stairs and banister rail were also oak, and wood panels rose three feet up the walls. The whole place smelled faintly of wax with a hint of some kind of spicy food. There was a door at each end, painted white. The one at the front of the building was labeled 1F. The one at the back, 1B. Gilmour led the way up one flight of stairs then paused. Reacher saw that someone had stuck a couple of handwritten notes on the door to the front apartment so that instead of 2F, it read *NOT* 2 *B*. There was no sound from the floor above, so Gilmour gestured to Reacher to be quiet and continued to the top floor. He moved slowly, placing his feet at the edge of the stairs, and craned his head to peer along the full length of the landing.

Gilmour whispered, 'No one's there. They must have gone. If they were ever here. Unless they're inside . . .'

Gilmour crept up to the door marked 3F. He slid a key into the first of five locks. He started to turn it. Then he heard a sound behind him, from the far end of the corridor. The door to 3B was opening. Gilmour spun around, started to raise the gun, then tucked it down and behind his leg. A woman stepped out onto the landing. She was maybe five foot six. Mid-thirties. She was wearing yoga pants and a long-sleeved running top. Strands of orange hair were escaping from a scarf that was tied around her head. And she was brandishing a fire iron in her right hand.

The woman said, 'Oh. Nathan. It's you.'

'Who else would it be?' Gilmour said. 'You're up late.'

'I couldn't sleep. I thought maybe it was your friends coming back. I told them I'd call 911. I warned them. You need to have a word with them. They can't just trick one of those idiots downstairs into buzzing them in and then loiter around outside your door for hours on end. If it happens again I'm putting in a formal complaint against you. The landlord will kick you out.'

Reacher stepped to the side. He had no interest in getting in the middle of some neighborly squabble.

Gilmour held up his left hand, palm out. He said, 'Gretchen, slow down. What friends? What are you talking about?'

'The two guys who were here. This afternoon. Banging on your door and calling for you. One of them had a keg. I asked what they were doing and the taller one said you were going to watch a game together. Some streaming thing. I told them to get out. They didn't, until I lost my patience and threatened to call the police on them. Then I think they lurked around outside for a while.'

'They're no friends of mine. I don't know anything about this.'

'Yeah, right. Don't be an asshole.'

'I'm not. I don't even like sports. But don't worry. I'll find out who it was. I'll make sure it doesn't happen again.'

'You better.'

She started to back away into her apartment but Gilmour called after her. He said, 'What did they look like, these guys?'

The woman shrugged. 'They were tall. They had on black suits. White shirts. No ties. Kind of unshaven. Menacing somehow. The sort of people you'd cross the street to avoid. I suggest you get better friends.' She glared at Reacher. 'Starting now.'

'What time did they show up?'

The woman narrowed her eyes for a second. 'A little after three in the afternoon, maybe. Definitely before three-thirty, 'cause that's when my Pilates class starts. Online.'

'All right. Well, thanks again, Gretchen. Leave it with me. I'll handle it.'

Gilmour waited for the woman to retreat into her apartment then finished unlocking his door. He flicked on the light and stepped inside. Reacher followed him into a corridor. There were two doors on the right, both closed, and a rectangular kitchen/living room straight ahead. The room was practically empty. There was a darker patch on the floor where a rectangular area rug had been, and scuffs on the hardwood where a couch and an armchair had sat on either side of it. There was no TV. The bookshelves were bare. On the kitchen side there was no oven. No stovetop. No microwave. No fridge. The only piece of furniture was a folding chair in front of a window, and there was a distinct chill in the air. Reacher figured the heat was turned off.

Reacher didn't speak but Gilmour could tell what he was thinking. He looked down at the floor and said, 'I had to sell a few things. A while back.' He stepped into the center of the space and spread his arms out wide. 'Why gambling is a crap idea: exhibit A.'

Reacher didn't reply.

Gilmour dropped his backpack then sank down and sat cross-legged on the floor. 'Sounds like you were right. Some goons were here looking for me. But we missed them. I guess the pair that found me reported in, jogged the main guy's memory, and he stood them down. So. What now?'

Reacher said, 'We need to figure out what connects you with this guy. How he identified you. Start with the gambling debt. How did he find out about it? The specifics. Who you owed. How much.'

'I have no idea.'

'Think. Did you tell anyone?'

'No. Absolutely not. Why would I? It was embarrassing.'

'You said you went to a support group. What about someone there?'

'It wasn't that kind of group. It was about being an addict. Not about being in debt.'

'You saw a hypnotist?'

'Again, that was about addiction. It was supposed to reprogram my brain. Break the habit. Make gambling feel unpleasant.'

'What about friends? Maybe you were at a bar. Had a couple too many. Let something slip.'

'I don't have any friends. And I don't go to bars anymore. I have no time. And no money. Because I spent it all playing cards. I can't see how anyone could have found out.'

'What if they didn't have to find out, because they knew all along?'

'I don't follow.'

'Whoever you owed the money to. He knew.'

'Right. But he wouldn't pay himself. That makes no sense.'

'What if he approached it like a bank does? He figured you were a deadbeat. You couldn't pay even if he set his heavies on you. So he sold the debt to someone else for cents on the dollar. He gets something, which is better than nothing. And whoever bought it gets leverage. It's a win-win, for everyone but you.'

'I guess. I hadn't thought of that. But . . . shit. You know what that would mean? I'm going through hell to get rid of the debt, I got my coworker killed, and whoever bought it didn't even pay full price. I hate this guy.'

'Then let's even the score. Come on. Get up.'

'Why?'

'We need to talk to whoever you owed the money to. Find out if we're right.'

'Now?'

'Why not? Card games go on all night, don't they? The sketchy ones especially.'

'Yeah, but we can't just walk into the place and confront the guy.'

'Why not?'

'For a start, they won't open the door unless you know

the special code. And it's not the kind of door you can bust down. Not even you.'

'But you used to go every day. So you know the code.'

'They might have changed it.'

'So that returning customers from out of town can't get in? Big spenders? I doubt it.'

'Okay. Suppose they open the door. I'm persona non grata there. They'd probably kill me for just showing my face.'

'Don't worry. You can stay in the car. I'll take care of the rest.'

'How? Although ... It's all about money, right?' He rummaged in his backpack and pulled out a bundle of cash held together with a brown strap. He held it out to Reacher. 'Maybe he'll sell you a name, the same way he sold mine.'

Reacher took the cash. He said, 'Or maybe he'll tell me out of the goodness of his heart.'

'You haven't been in that place or you wouldn't joke like that.' Gilmour stood up and walked down the corridor. He disappeared through the first door, then returned a minute later. He was carrying a phone. He held it out to Reacher.

Reacher didn't take it. He said, 'I'm not planning on calling anyone.'

Gilmour pressed a couple of buttons on the phone, then took out his own and pressed a couple more. He held it out again and said, 'Take it. You can't call anyone with it. But I've copied the picture of the guy who approached me onto it. Maybe you can use it to get a positive ID.'

THIRTEEN

Gilmour pulled over in front of a dry cleaner and left Reacher to walk the final block alone.

The door Reacher needed was not hard to find. It was plain black, with no name or number, sandwiched between a vegetarian restaurant and a cocktail bar, just as Gilmour had described. What Gilmour hadn't mentioned was the paint. It was gleaming like it was still wet, and a red rose was flowering in a pot on either side of the doorway, despite the season. The overall impression was a world away from what Reacher had been expecting. His experience of underground gambling clubs was based on dragging AWOL soldiers out of dingy basements or tracking down suspects in sleazy back rooms, but he knocked, anyway. A moment later, a slim stainless-steel intercom crackled to life and a disembodied metallic voice said, 'We're closed.'

Reacher glanced around, hoping no passers-by were in earshot, and quietly recited, 'The laurel shall wave and form a bright wreath for the brows of the brave.'

The intercom was silent for a moment, then the voice said, 'Who sent you?'

'My friend Ulysses.'

'Get lost.'

'Really?' Reacher took the bundle of cash Gilmour had given him out of his pocket. He held it up to the pinprick lens at the top of the intercom, riffed through the stack, and ended up with the engraving of Ulysses S. Grant clearly visible on the final fifty-dollar bill.

The voice said, 'Stay there.'

Reacher put the money away. Nothing happened for twenty seconds, then the door clicked several times and swung smoothly inward. That revealed a guy standing in a kind of narrow vestibule with pale wood on the floor, soft yellow walls, and a slender crystal chandelier hanging from the ceiling. The guy was maybe five foot six, and he was easily sixty years old. He was wearing a gray suit the exact same shade as his shoulder-length hair, and a white shirt with a red-and-blue-striped tie. He moved back and gestured for Reacher to come inside. The guy was a world away from the bulked-up bouncer Reacher had been expecting. And given the way he seemed to glide rather than step, Reacher would have bet the whole stack of fifties that he had years of training behind him. More than enough to outweigh a gut full of steroids and too many pointless hours in the gym.

Reacher stepped inside, the door swung closed behind him, and the gray-haired guy gestured to a velvet container on a waist-high wooden table. He said, 'You can leave any weapons here.'

Reacher said, 'No weapons.'

'You can collect them on your way out. No one will interfere with them. You have my word.'

Reacher said, 'No weapons.'

'Perhaps you would like to double-check. You see, weapons are not welcome here. None are permitted inside at all. If you were to attempt to bring one in, even inadvertently, the results could be quite . . . unfortunate.'

Reacher said, 'No weapons.'

'Very well.' The tone of the guy's voice made it clear that he wasn't convinced, but he moved back anyway, ducked into a shallow alcove, and left the way clear to a carpeted staircase. 'Enjoy your evening.'

Reacher stepped forward. The light changed as he moved, and his eyes picked up a band of plaster with a different texture, four inches wide, running vertically up one wall, across the ceiling, and down the other. It concealed a metal detector, he thought. Farther ahead, level with the foot of the stairs, something else ran across the ceiling. A slight ridge. A hinge concealing the opening for a security screen that could slam down. Reacher estimated the distance between them. He wondered if a person could sprint fast enough to get through the detector with a gun or knife and dive under the screen before it dropped. He decided it was impossible to be sure. And even if someone got through, they'd have no idea who or what would be waiting for them at the top of the stairs.

It turned out that a woman was waiting that night. She

was much younger than the guy in the hallway. Probably in her mid-twenties, Reacher guessed. She had chestnut-brown hair, braided and coiled on top of her head. She was wearing a black cocktail dress with a short, asymmetric skirt and plunging neckline. The tail of a glittering snake-shaped necklace descended almost out of sight. And without her four-inch heels she would also have been around five feet six. She slipped her arm under Reacher's and smiled like she was genuinely happy to see him. She said, 'You're new here? I don't think I've seen you before.'

Reacher said, 'This is my first time.'

'Well, I'm glad to meet you. You're going to have a great time tonight. It's my job to make sure of that. My name's Amy, by the way. And yours?'

Reacher said, 'Engle.' It was an old habit of his, using a cover name, and he always liked to have a theme. He'd gone through several over the years – vice presidents, Yankees second basemen, astronauts from the Mercury, Gemini, and Apollo programs – and now he was working his way through space shuttle commanders.

Amy lowered her voice and leaned in a little closer. 'Just to let you know, we're going to need some valid ID if you want us to set you up for any credit, so if you'd like to try that name again for any reason . . .'

'No.' Reacher patted the wad of cash in his pocket. 'I'm good.'

'Fantastic!' Another smile lit up Amy's face. 'In that case, what's your pleasure?'

The room was long and narrow with pale-green carpet and walls that were painted a similar shade. Reacher had read a study that claimed green was a calming color. Probably why the owner had chosen it, he thought. To reduce the number of punters who freaked out and tried to smash the place up when they lost all their money. There was a small bar to the left. Nothing fancy. Just a counter with four stools in front and a shelf behind holding a bunch of bottles of spirits, plus an ice bucket and all shapes of glasses on top. Another smart move. Money flowed faster with the right lubrication, Reacher had always noticed. Although fists were quicker to fly, too. Four square tables took up the rest of the space. Each had a half-dozen chairs around it, but only two tables were occupied. One had three people plus a dealer playing some kind of a card game. The other had a single guy plus a dealer.

Amy said, 'It's late and we're winding down a little, so we just have poker and blackjack on the go right now. Which one sounds good to you?'

Reacher said, 'Neither. I'm looking to spend my money a different way.'

Amy let go of Reacher's arm and took a half step away. 'I don't know what you mean, Mr Engle. What kind of place do you think this is?'

'I know exactly what kind of place.' Reacher crossed his arms. 'I'm here to buy some information. From Mr Horner. Please ask him to join me. In the meantime, the house can buy me a drink.'

Reacher moved across and took the end stool.

Amy hurried after him. 'Mr Horner? We don't have any customers by that name. Whoever told you—'

Reacher leaned in close to Amy's ear and dropped his

voice to a whisper. 'Horner is the owner. You know that. Go get him.'

Amy's mouth opened but she didn't speak, and she didn't move.

Reacher kept his voice as quiet as he could make it. 'Get Horner now. You don't want me to have too much time on my hands. I might get bored. I might decide to relieve your blackjack dealer over there. Take a look at the deck. Show your customer why it is he can never seem to land a break. Maybe move on to the poker table. See where all the picture cards are . . .'

'Fine.' Amy crossed her arms. 'I'll get him. You stay here. Don't move. Don't go near those tables.'

Amy made her way to the far corner, moving quickly, all stiff-legged and awkward in her heels. She shimmied around the final empty table, pressed her palm against the wall, and a concealed door swung open. She hurried through and the door closed silently behind her. A moment later Reacher heard muffled footsteps on the stairs. Someone was coming up. They were in a hurry. A man appeared, also in his mid-twenties, with a mess of fair, curly hair and a leather apron over black pants and a white shirt. He paused, seeming startled to see someone sitting at the bar, then scurried across and dodged behind the counter. He said to Reacher, 'Good evening, sir. What can I get you?'

Reacher said, 'Drop the *sir*. What can you make that uses a lot of ice?'

The bartender looked confused. 'Anything you like. A martini? A margarita?'

'Either of those. Whichever's quicker.'

He gave Reacher a sideways glance as if he thought he was being tricked or tested, then took a cocktail shaker from a shelf beneath the counter. He opened it, set it down, grabbed a pick, and set to work chipping away at the big block of ice in the bucket.

The guy hadn't made much progress when the concealed door at the far end of the room opened again. A man stepped into the frame. He had a shaved head and was wearing a tuxedo. The suit looked too tight for him, which was no doubt deliberate. The guy wasn't especially tall, but he was surprisingly broad, and to emphasize the fact, he stood still, silhouetted for a moment in an awkward, exaggerated stance. Some kind of body-building pose, Reacher thought. The guy certainly had the physique for it. He was all puffed up and bulky. The opposite of the gray-haired guy downstairs. Reacher was happy that the older man had stayed down there. There was something about him that he'd liked. His gracefulness, perhaps, or his politeness. Reacher had been hoping he wouldn't have to hurt him.

There was nothing graceful about the guy who'd just appeared. He broke out of his pose and lumbered across the room, heading directly toward Reacher. And as he grew closer, he showed no signs of politeness, either. Instead he barked, 'You. Out. Now.'

FOURTEEN

Reacher leaned back to avoid the specks of spittle that were flying from the tuxedo guy's mouth, but he didn't stand. He made no move to leave.

The bartender carefully set his tools down and crept to the opposite end of the counter. The card players stopped their games and turned to gawp.

The tuxedo guy stepped closer, put his hands on his hips, and bellowed, 'Are you deaf? I said get out.'

Reacher pretended to suppress a yawn, then said, 'Stop talking. Turn around. Fetch your boss.'

The guy began to raise his right hand and stretch forward but he froze when Reacher said, 'Stop.' Reacher's voice was louder than before and had an added edge of steel. 'Do not touch me. Turn around. Walk away while you still can. Bring your boss here.'

The guy didn't move for a moment, then rocked slightly back and forth.

Reacher said, 'What's the problem? Too many thoughts to handle all at once? Want to try again, one word at a time?'

The guy roared and shot out his hand. His fingers were curled into a claw and he was aiming for Reacher's throat. Reacher watched the fist coming. He matched its movement with his left hand. He matched its speed. Then at the last moment he grabbed the guy's wrist. He wrapped his fingers underneath, planted his thumb on top, and whipped his arm all the way around so that his palm was facing up. He kept pulling, using the guy's momentum against him to keep him off balance, and when he was close enough, he slammed the back of the guy's hand down on the counter. Empty glasses rolled and fell. The guy roared louder. He struggled and heaved and tried to pull his hand back, but Reacher held it tight. He leaned over the counter, grabbed up the abandoned ice pick, and drove it down through the palm of the guy's hand. It buried itself deep into the wooden surface. Blood spurted out around the shaft like a crown. The guy's roar turned to a howl. He dropped to his knees. His howl turned to a whimper and he knelt there shaking, overwhelmed by the pain, not knowing whether to pull his hand free or hold it still to avoid further damage.

Reacher heard a crash behind him from the center of the room. The guy who had been playing blackjack had jumped up and knocked over his chair. Now he was standing almost on tiptoe, craning his neck to catch every detail. One of the other card players was grinning like he'd just been dealt the hand of a lifetime. The other one looked like he was going to be sick. The dealers were both on their feet, fidgety and anxious. Behind them all, Amy was standing by the wall, to the side of the hidden door, mouth open, eyes wide.

Reacher looked at each card player in turn, then said, 'Show's over. Time to go home. You can settle up tomorrow. Right, Amy?'

Amy managed a strangled 'I guess so. Sure. Why not?'

The card players headed for the stairs. The blackjack guy lingered and took a long last look at Reacher and the bouncer, then made his way down. A moment after the top of his head disappeared from view, the hidden door opened again and a man stepped through. He was tall. Maybe six feet six, with gray hair neatly trimmed, and a tidy goatee. He was wearing a black three-piece suit that was baggy and loose. It made him look like a small-town undertaker who was down on his luck. His eyes darted around the room, then settled on Reacher. He said, 'I'm Horner. You want to talk to me?'

Reacher gestured to the next free barstool. 'Come. Sit.'

Horner said, 'Sit? No. Give me one reason I don't have you dragged outside and beaten to death.'

Reacher said softly, 'I'll give you two. But I'm not going to yell across the room.'

The dealers glanced at each other then looked down at the floor. The bartender shuffled on the spot. Amy looked like she was trying to press herself into the wall. Horner stood quietly for a moment, then tipped his head to one side. He said, 'Everyone, give us the room.'

Amy was first through the hidden door. The dealers

were hard on her heels. Reacher took hold of the ice pick and wrenched it free from the bar. The bouncer shrieked and fell backward. He rolled into a ball, clutching his hand, blood soaking his jacket. The bartender scuttled around him and hared after the dealers. The bouncer hauled himself upright and started to follow. Horner met him halfway and blocked his path. He shook his head and pointed to the stairs. He said, 'You leave that way. You're fired. And you're paying for the damage.'

Horner waited until he heard the downstairs door slam shut, then strolled across to the bar and stood next to Reacher. He said, 'So. Two reasons. These better be good.'

Reacher said, 'You're not going to drag me anywhere because one, you can't.' He gestured to the blood that was pooled on the bar and the spotty, erratic trail that led to the staircase. 'Two, you're not stupid. This is a successful operation. Well run, aside from your security staff. It takes brains to stay afloat in this world. So you figure, maybe whatever I'm here to talk about will have mutual benefit. You want to hear what I say before you do anything.'

'I have other security guys. Raymond, for example, who you met when you came in. He's very experienced. It would be a mistake to underestimate him.'

'I'm sure it would. I'm sure he is. And I'm sure he knows his Sun Tzu. Which is why he didn't come up here when he heard his buddy break a nail.'

Horner raised an eyebrow.

'Sun Tzu. Never use force unless you're certain you will win. Is Raymond certain? Shall we ask him?'

'No need. Because you're right about the second part. Your proposal. I do want to hear it.'

'You give me a name. I solve a problem for you.'

'I'm a fortunate man. I don't have any problems for you to solve. Unless you're volunteering to work the door.'

Reacher shook his head. He said, 'You do have a problem. You just don't know it yet.'

'All right. I'll bite. What name do you want? What problem do I have?'

'I ran into a couple of guys not long ago. They were trying to fleece some seniors. I may have cooked that goose for them. Seems that their boss was upset. He sent some more guys after me, with bicycle chains. They won't be making that mistake again, but that's not the point. I object to that kind of behavior. I started asking around. People were cagey about putting a name to the guy, but I kept hearing one rumor. His next move is into cards. Your turf. So, you tell me who he is. Where I can find him. And I make sure that move never happens.'

'I haven't heard these rumors.'

Reacher shrugged. 'I have. You know what they say. No smoke . . .'

'Who's saying this?'

Reacher shrugged again. 'You know. People.'

'Sounds like BS. My ear's to the ground. Believe me.'

'Fine.' Reacher stood up. 'If you're sure. I mean, this is a classy place. I bet your clientele is loyal. Not the kind of people who'd be tempted by somewhere newer. Shinier. With tables that are a little . . . straighter.'

Reacher took a step toward the stairs.

Horner said, 'Wait.' He was silent for a moment, then

a thin smile crept across his face. 'All right. The guy you want. How's he fleecing these seniors?'

'He has a whole dog-and-pony show. Three guys and a bunch of BS about some hotshot investor making an overnight killing on the futures market. Desperate people want in, looking for a slice of the action. I caught it at a coffee shop, but a dollar gets a dime he's running it other places, too.'

Horner's smile grew broader. 'The name you want is Dominic Kelleher. The guy thinks he's some kind of Irish mafioso. Runs his operation out of a bar in Harbor East. A dump called the Butcher's Dog. But listen. Don't think for a minute I believe you. I know you're shining me on, but I respect the effort. Kelleher's a dumb son of a bitch, but he's not stupid enough to try to run with the big dogs. He's a nuisance, is all. You want to take a swing, be my guest. Hit, miss, doesn't matter to me.'

'This Kelleher sounds like a treat. Is he the one you sold Nathan Gilmour's gambling debt to?'

'What? Don't be ridiculous.'

Reacher held up the ice pick. Its shaft was black with blood. He said, 'Are you sure?'

Horner said, 'Certain.' He stood up a little taller. 'Understand this. I don't sell debt. I collect. Every penny. Every time.'

'You sold Gilmour's.'

'What are you smoking? Gilmour paid his debt. In full. With interest.'

'He did not.'

'Not in person, no. He sent someone to hand over the money. Same difference.' Horner tried to step around

Reacher. 'And none of your business. Conversation over. You can keep the pick.'

Reacher moved to block his path. 'This person who you think Gilmour sent. How did he know how much to pay? You just give out information like that to anyone who asks? You get lots of fairy godmothers showing up in this business?'

Horner slowed his speech right down, dragging out the syllables as if he were talking to an idiot. 'I didn't tell him how much. Gilmour did, before he sent him. Obviously.'

'Who was this guy?'

Horner shrugged. 'How would I know? Some asshole shows up with a sack of cash. He gives it to me. That's all the bona fides I need.'

'You'd never seen him before?'

'Or since. Now, this is getting old. It's time for you to leave.'

'One more question.' Reacher set the ice pick down on the bar, took the phone Gilmour had given him from his pocket, and fumbled through a couple of menus until the photograph appeared onscreen. 'Is this the guy?'

Horner glanced at the display. He nodded. 'He's the one. Now beat it. We're done.'

FIFTEEN

Morgan Strickland stepped down with his left foot, then his right, then slid his hand down the outside of the ladder's vertical rail. He kept up the routine, step, step, slide, over and over, slow and steady, until he was six feet from the bottom. Four feet. Then there was a heavy *clunk*. His world went instantly dark. He hung in the pitch-black, swearing to himself, and counted to five. The generator coughed back into life, the light returned, and he swiftly covered the rest of the way down until he was standing gratefully on solid ground.

Strickland had been debating whether to sleep at home or in his office, but the conversation he'd just had with Mark Hewson tipped the balance. Hewson wanted to meet Violeta Vardanyan, the eyewitness from Armenia. He needed to be convinced by her testimony. The meeting was vital to Strickland's plans, but it was going to happen the day after Vardanyan arrived in the United States. It would be her first time in the country. He had no idea how long it would take for her to get over the journey. Or to adapt to a new culture. Or how cooperative she would be. It was a while since he'd last seen her. All these factors left him feeling like there could well be a need for some serious diplomacy in his future, and for him, diplomacy called for energy. Energy required sleep. So he settled on his office, as it was so much closer. He started to move and, late as it was, a familiar word floated back into his head. *Compulsive.* Right away he changed direction and made for the storeroom.

Strickland heard the chair-legs scrape on the ground again as he approached, but there was something different about the sound this time. It was quieter. That struck him as odd, as the guards wouldn't have changed shifts yet. He came around the corner and immediately saw what the issue was. There was only one guard present. Not two. He felt the rage start to flare in his chest. Hot bubbles rose within him like magma in a volcano. He picked up speed until he was almost running, and he stopped a pace away from the solitary guard. Walker. He was standing as still as a statue and as straight as a die, as if he were on a parade ground and expecting an appearance from the commander in chief.

Strickland said, 'Where's your buddy Jacklin?'

Walker said, 'I don't know, sir.'

Strickland's voice rose to a shriek and spittle sprayed from his mouth. 'Don't lie to me!'

'I think he's in the storeroom, sir.'

'Bullshit. That's not possible.'

'I think it is, sir.'

'How? Explain.'

'He's always been fascinated by what could be inside there, sir. He keeps going over and putting his hand against the door like he can commune with the contents. I told him not to, over and over. But he always ignored me. He was doing that, pressing the door, when the power went out just now. I heard a click, like the lock had released. A squeak, like the hinge was moving. Then the lights came back, the door was closed, and Jacklin was gone. So either he's in there, sir, or he disappeared into thin air.'

Strickland paused for a moment to think about what he'd been told. Then he heard a sound coming from inside the storeroom. Someone was tugging at the door and rattling it against its lock. A futile effort. There was no doubt about that. Then Strickland heard Jacklin's voice. It called out, 'Walker, where are you, man? Get me out of here.'

Walker turned to Strickland and said, 'Do you want me to get him out, sir?'

Strickland put out his hand and said, 'Give me your cuffs.'

Walker unclipped the holster on his belt and passed his handcuffs to Strickland.

'Key.'

He dug in his pants pocket, pulled out a small silver key, and handed it over.

'You're dismissed.'

'Sir.' Walker double-timed it toward the exit. He knew better than to slow down or look back.

Strickland tucked the cuffs into his waistband and drew his sidearm. He crossed to the storeroom door, extended his trigger finger far enough sideways to work the keypad, entered his code, then stepped to the side. The door burst open. Jacklin rushed out. He was shivering hard. His face was pale and his eyes were wide.

Strickland said, 'Stop. Do not turn around.'

Jacklin stopped. He was panting.

Strickland said, 'Put your hands behind your back, wrists together.'

Jacklin was almost sobbing. He said, 'I'm sorry, sir. I'll forget what I saw. And I swear I won't ever go back in that place.'

Strickland raised his voice. 'Hands behind your back. Wrists touching.'

Jacklin did as he was told. Strickland swapped the gun for the cuffs. He stepped forward, secured Jacklin's hands, and said, 'Never say never.'

Reacher figured that if you could power a car with nervous energy, Gilmour's rental would run forever. He was practically vibrating when Reacher got back into the passenger seat. He couldn't sit still. Couldn't focus. Reacher had dealt with meth heads who were more composed.

Reacher started to fasten his seat belt, then paused and said, 'Are you okay to drive?'

'Of course I am.' Gilmour tried to start the engine. He got it going on the second attempt. 'So? Did you get a name?'

'No.'

Gilmour slammed the steering wheel with his palm. 'So it was a waste of time.'

'Not entirely. The guy who came to you with the proposition did pay your debt. He did it himself. That's confirmed. Horner didn't sell your details to anybody.'

'But we don't know who the guy is?' Gilmour pulled away from the curb. 'You couldn't make Horner tell you?'

'Horner didn't know. The guy delivered a bag of cash. No names were required. But here's the weird thing. He knew how much you owed. Independently. Horner didn't have to tell him.'

'That's impossible.' Gilmour slowed for a truck to pass in the opposite direction, then pulled a tight U-turn. 'I'm telling you, there's no way he could have known.'

'He knew.'

'How?'

'Did you write the total down somewhere? Maybe doing calculations, figuring out your budget, where to scrape the money together from. How fast the interest was building up. On a scrap of paper. The back of an envelope. A notebook. Something someone could have found in the trash.'

'You think I had a budget?' Gilmour spotted a cop car lurking in a side street and lifted off the gas a little. 'The way I was living? A closet full of space lasers would have been more useful. So no. I never wrote the number down. I didn't need to. It was all I could think about. It was front and center in my brain, twenty-four seven.'

'Did you apply for a loan anywhere, looking to pay it off?'

'What kind of bank would have touched me? I had no

job back then, remember. And I was acting like a basket case.'

'So a loan shark? Plenty of backstreet operations out there. Those guys have no scruples.'

'I'm not insane. Out of the frying pan, into the runaway nuclear reactor? No, thank you.'

'So how did he know?'

'I'm telling you, he couldn't have.'

'All right. We need another angle. Some other way to connect him to you.'

'Like what?'

Reacher thought for a moment. 'He told you to apply for the job at the port. There must have been a process. How did that work?'

'He texted me a link. It led to a form – an application. I completed it. An HR person got back to me. She sent me an email. Invited me for an interview. I went. I passed, by some miracle. I started the next week.'

'The HR person who emailed. Did she handle the interview as well?'

'Yes.'

'Alone, or with someone?'

Gilmour glanced across at Reacher. 'Alone. She actually apologized. Said it was policy to have an ops representative there, but whoever she'd lined up was out sick. She offered to postpone if I wasn't comfortable. I said hell no, I was there, I wanted to get it over with. I didn't think I had a snowball's chance, anyway. Why waste time coming back?'

'Did she send the offer letter? The same woman?'

'The offer email. Yes.'

'And did she handle your induction, or orientation, or whatever they do at the port?'

Gilmour nodded. 'It was all her. I was happy about that. I liked her. She was kind of cute.'

'Were you qualified for the job?'

'Hell no. Not even close. I had no experience, at that point. No qualifications. I was unemployed. I had a massive gap in my résumé. I had no references. My clothes looked like I stole them from a scarecrow. I wasn't sleeping or eating, so I looked like a heroin addict. My hair hadn't been cut for months. Birds could have been living in it for all I knew. And I probably stank.'

'So—'

'I get it.' Gilmour pulled a quick left under the wheels of an oncoming sports car, causing the driver to honk and flip him off. 'No need to hammer it home. The fix was in. The guy had a hook in the HR woman, too. Or someone working with him did. Damn! I didn't put that together before. I'm an idiot.'

'Is she still with the company?'

'I think so. I'll find out in the morning.' Gilmour pulled over. 'You must think I'm stupid. I don't know. Maybe I am. The job offer came and I was so damn grateful I didn't question it. I didn't connect the dots between getting it and the guy telling me to apply. I know I sound ridiculous, but back then it didn't seem like he was using the debt against me. It seemed like he was saving me. Like an angel or something. Imagine you're in a pit, and it's pitch-black, and it's filling up with water, and you know you're going to drown, and suddenly a flashlight appears above you. Then a pair of hands, stretching down. You don't ask questions. You don't wonder why one's there, and then the other. The light lets you see. You let the hands pull you out. And afterward, when you're warm and dry and safe, you don't look back. You just accept the freedom. I don't know. It's like some kind of emotional self-preservation mechanism, I guess.'

'Whatever it is, don't beat yourself up. What happened, happened. What's the woman's name?'

'Sabrina Patten.'

'All right. We'll talk to her in the morning.'

'The hell *we* will. No, I'll talk to her. Like I said, she's cute.' Gilmour killed the engine and opened his door. 'Come on. This is it. My other place. The one no one's supposed to know about. We'll sleep here tonight. What's left of it.'

SIXTEEN

Gilmour was happy to spend the rest of the evening at his secret apartment. He felt it was a less predictable move, if anyone had watched them leave his regular place. And it had the advantage of having a couch as well as a bed. That took away the obligation to sleep on the floor, which he would hate to do. Partly because it was uncomfortable, and his bones were less forgiving than they'd once been. But mainly because it would make him feel like a loser for having needed to sell most of his furniture when he was totally broke. There are some things in life you don't need to be reminded of.

Reacher was happy to spend the night at that apartment, too, but not because of the sleeping arrangements. Because the place had a coffee machine, and he needed a decent mug before he turned in, given the ups and downs of the day. He found an unopened pack of grounds in one of the cupboards. It was long expired but he used it, anyway. The brew came out stale, like dissolved cardboard, but Reacher didn't mind. He wasn't much of a connoisseur. He went with strength over flavor every time.

Gilmour had offered to let Reacher have the bed, but Reacher refused. He was sure the couch would be fine. He waited for Gilmour to close the bedroom door, used the bathroom, then settled down, using his new coat as a pillow. His legs hung over the couch's arm from his knees down, and beneath him the rips in the cushions grew longer and deeper, but he didn't care. He had slept in worse places over the years. Much worse, many times. And he had a knack for dropping off to sleep pretty much at will. He could usually count on being under within thirty seconds of lying down, but that night it took him longer. The events of the day had left him with a lot to think about. He shifted positions and felt the phone Gilmour had given him in his pocket. He took it out and managed to get the photograph to come back onto the screen. The picture of the man who had approached Gilmour. The link to whatever else was going on. Reacher studied his face. The sharp angles of the guy's skull were showing through his dusting of gray hair. His nose had been broken more than once. That was clear. And his eyes looked cold and bleak. Reacher imagined staring into them in real life. He imagined what lay behind them. The mind of a person who took advantage of vulnerable veterans. Who moved people around like pawns on a chessboard for his own advantage. Who made hideous threats against little children. Reacher didn't know if the guy would follow through with blinding Gilmour's nephew if Gilmour defied him. His gut told him it was probably a bluff. But in the moment that didn't matter. Reacher felt his heart start to beat faster. The hairs on the back of his neck began to stand upright. A rage was building inside him. It wasn't a thing he could control. It was an unconscious response hardwired into him like an allergic reaction to a toxin. He liked Gilmour. He sympathized with him. But Gilmour barely moved the needle compared to this other guy. This abuser. This bully. There was no question. Reacher was going to stop him. That was for damn sure. He would see to that personally.

Reacher shifted his position again, eyes closed, and then another thought intruded on his rest. There was a second part of the equation. The smuggling operation. He turned the details over in his head. Some faceless gang inserting their wares into other people's cargo containers like parasites. Maybe they were bringing drugs. Maybe guns. Or off-label medicine. Cigarettes. Electronics. Stolen art. Any number of possibilities. Whatever it was, it needed to be stopped. So did the people behind it, and everyone who helped them. That was important. But somehow Reacher felt less invested in that side of things. He figured he would make sure that Gilmour's nephew was out of danger, then dial 911. The police could deal with the smugglers. Or the Coast Guard. He didn't need to handle that aspect himself.

At two a.m. outside, the contours of the world were lost in the soft darkness of the night. The area around the entrance to the former Kinsella limestone mine was barely visible in the few gentle rays of moonlight that reached it. There was an occasional hum of traffic on the distant highway. The hoot of an owl. Scurrying claws as a fox or badger hurried by, careful to keep clear of the infrared beams that crisscrossed the approach to the mine's gate and threatened to flood the area with harsh artificial light.

At two a.m. inside, the level of brightness in each of the zones could be set to whatever Morgan Strickland wanted it to be. For the desert terrain he chose dusk, made a few other arrangements, then returned to the storeroom. He entered his code, opened the door, stepped inside, and approached Jacklin. He was standing near the bottom of a metal-framed cot, one wrist cuffed to its rail, shivering uncontrollably.

Strickland said, 'Turn sideways. Put your free hand behind your back. Try anything and I'll shoot you in the spine.'

Jacklin turned. He said, 'Hurry, please. This place is as creepy as hell. I thought I was going to freeze to death or die of fright.'

Strickland ignored him. Thirty-five Fahrenheit is no picnic, but it's not life-threatening. Not for a few minutes in the dry with no wind. A healthy man should survive for a few hours. He'd learned that theory on a training exercise. And he'd experienced the reality in the desert in Iraq one night after a snafu with his unit's supplies. Strickland shook the memory away, removed the cuff from the bed rail, snapped it around Jacklin's free wrist, then marched him out of the room. He paused to slip an eye mask over Jacklin's head. Jacklin was reluctant to move after that, so Strickland had to prod him at the base of his skull with his pistol.

Strickland kept Jacklin stumbling along at a reasonable pace until he was satisfied with their position. He said, 'You have a fifteen-minute head start. Use it well.' Then he unlocked one cuff and stepped into the empty central area between the four training zones. He took an iPad from the cargo pocket in his pants and looked into its camera to unlock it. Then he used his thumb to prod a button on its screen. A second later a heavy, barred gate came crashing down. It blocked the archway nearer to Jacklin, shutting him in.

The crash of the gate shook Jacklin out of the trance he'd fallen into. He pulled off the mask and stood for a moment, blinking in the dim light. He was shivering. He was hungry. He hadn't eaten for ten hours. He had no idea where he was. He looked around and saw nothing but sand. A broad swathe of small, fine grains in front of him and on either side. A swooping rise farther ahead, like a wave on a frozen, tan-colored sea. And behind that, dunes. Tall, steep, rising, and disappearing into the gloom.

Jacklin forced himself to think. He wasn't in a real desert. That was obvious. He was still inside the cave. In the training area where he'd done his assessment when he first joined Strickland Security. He turned around and saw the metal gate. That helped orient him. He was on an exercise. He had screwed up at the storeroom and needed to redeem himself. To prove he was still worthy of his place in the company. Important, but not life or death. Although, after what he'd seen behind that locked door ... He pushed the thought aside. It was decision time – he had to at least try. The goal had not been stated, but presumably it was to avoid getting captured for a period of time, or to find a way to escape. The alternative was to stay where he was. Get caught. And presumably get kicked out. He shook his head. He couldn't believe that a little earlier he'd been complaining to Walker about his situation. Now that he was faced with having to leave, he realized he liked it in the cave. He liked his job. He decided to try to keep it.

He tossed a mental coin and decided to stay low, on the flatter, more even expanse of sand. He tossed another and decided to start out to his left. He moved quickly, scanning the area ahead. He caught sight of something. A shape, vague and brooding, fifty yards away. He kept going, but more slowly. He closed in and realized the shape was a tent. It was tall. Made of pale canvas. Not the backpacking kind. It was more like a mess tent. He crept closer. Made it all the way to the front. He pulled up the flap and looked inside. He saw a slatted wooden table with four folding chairs around it. There was an enamel mug on the table and a camp stove on the ground with a kettle perched on it.

Jacklin shivered. The cold from the storeroom was still deep in his bones. He thought about the kettle. About hot coffee. Maybe even a mug of soup. He pushed the rest of the way into the tent. Reached for the kettle. Then stopped. An alarm was chirping in his brain. He stepped back, took out his wallet, and threw it at the kettle. He hit the target. The kettle toppled. And as it fell, its base erupted. Flames shot out. Smoke billowed. Pieces of the handle broke off and spun through the air. The explosion wouldn't have been big enough to kill him, even if he had picked the kettle up. He was fairly sure of that. But it would probably have taken a few fingers off. Maybe his whole hand.

Jacklin shivered again, but he was no longer cold. He retrieved his wallet then backed out of the tent and headed right this time. After a couple of minutes he picked up a set of tire tracks. They were narrow. Almost certainly a bike. He wondered where it was. Whether he could steal it. But the tracks grew fainter and finally disappeared. Jacklin was finding it harder to walk now. His feet were sinking deeper into the sand. It reminded him of the beach. He hated the beach, but at least here there was no sun to burn him. No bugs to bite him. He pressed on and felt himself sinking a little more. Then a lot more. His ankles were buried. So were his legs, halfway to his knees. Then instinct kicked in. He flung himself onto his back, arms and legs spread wide like a starfish. He caught his breath, then started to pull down with his arms and push with his legs in a kind of awkward swimming motion. It was exhausting and extremely inefficient, but he did move. And he didn't sink. He kept it up for four feet. Six. Then he risked rolling over. He scrambled to his feet and hurried back the way he had come.

Jacklin had regretted a lot of things in his life, but at that moment, nothing more than opening the storeroom door.

Both ventures along the flat sand had proved nearly disastrous, so Jacklin decided on a change of tack. He went up. He thought he could maybe climb all the way over the dunes and escape at the far side. Or that he might find a maintenance hatch in the wall or in the ceiling if he got high enough. He started out walking normally, but pretty soon the incline increased to the point where he had to lean forward and scramble on all fours. The farther he went, the harder the sand became. Soon he was able to walk upright again. He could sense victory. Freedom. He was getting closer. He pushed himself to go faster. To take longer strides.

The sand beneath one foot fell away and Jacklin stumbled to the side. He heard a *crunch*, then a *crack*, then the entire top layer of sand sheared away. It was probably three feet thick. It slid, and a crust of sand from above careened down to take its place. More sand poured down from all directions. Jacklin tried to ride it like a scree runner but couldn't keep his balance. He fell. He rolled and tumbled and spun until he couldn't tell which way was up. He was inside a roiling cloud of sand. It was in his eyes. His mouth. His nose. He couldn't stop himself. He couldn't see. Couldn't breathe. He kept going, lower, faster, growing dizzy, until he slammed into solid ground. The last of the air was knocked out of his lungs. He was choking. It was dark. He was buried. The weight of the sand was pressing him down. He tried to stand but couldn't. The sand was too heavy. His mind started to drift. He thought he was done. Then, from out of nowhere, a thought hit him. He drew in his arms and legs. He tucked them under himself. Then, with one last giant push, he launched himself toward the sky. His head broke through the surface. He wriggled until his chest was free. He gulped air, then scrambled up and out and clear of the sand. He turned once, twice, until he was sure which way led back to the starting point. Enough was enough. He was giving up.

Jacklin stumbled back toward the entrance. His shoulders were hunched. His arms hung down at his sides. He wasn't looking where he was going. His steps were erratic. He was weaving one way, then the other, as if he were drunk. Then, as his right foot fell, he felt something give beneath it, hidden by the sand. He heard a *click*. He stopped dead. He'd heard that sound before in training. He had stepped on a mine. He told himself it couldn't be real. It was safe to keep going. It had to be. But his legs wouldn't move. The sand avalanche had been real. The explosive in the kettle had been real. He didn't know what to do. He was stuck. He felt the cold fingers of despair take hold of his soul, but he cast them off. Then he heard a harsh, metallic clattering: the sound of salvation. The gate was opening. He looked up and saw Strickland heading toward him.

Strickland was carrying something. He drew closer, then held it up for Jacklin to see. It was a pistol. An unusual one. A CZ 52, from the former Czechoslovak Socialist Republic. He said, 'It's not pretty, but it's effective. It's from my personal collection. I've been told it was used in three separate assassination attempts. But that's beside the point. No long guns for me anymore, obviously. And the beauty of this baby is that it's chambered in 7.62. Shorter than the round the AK uses, but no one's going to be able to tell that from the hole it blows in you. So, body or head?'

Jacklin stood staring at the pistol. His mouth hung

open. He didn't reply, so Strickland shot him in the chest. He watched Jacklin fall, then slipped the gun into his waistband and pulled out his phone to call for help with the clean-up. He finished that conversation, then paused. It struck him that the conflict hadn't even started yet, and he already had a twenty-fifth KIA. There was no point letting it go to waste.

SEVENTEEN

Reacher was awake before Gilmour appeared. He started the coffee machine and left it wheezing and hissing while he hit the bathroom. He rummaged in the closet until he found a towel. He guessed it had once been blue. Now it was gray, almost transparent, and as rough as sandpaper. He showered quickly, using the shriveled remnants of the only bar of soap he could see, then dried himself, used his fingertips to scrape his hair into some sort of order, dressed in the same set of clothes, and returned to the kitchen.

Gilmour had emerged from his bedroom. He was wearing an Orioles shirt with a pair of baggy orange shorts and was stomping around, grumpy and disoriented. He grunted a half-hearted greeting, refused Reacher's offer of coffee, and managed a grudging apology for the lack of breakfast food. Then he retreated to his room. He reappeared five minutes later dressed in the previous day's work clothes, though now he had an ID card slung around his neck on a royal-blue lanyard.

Gilmour led the way to his rental car then drove in silence to his regular apartment. When they arrived, he explained that they needed to switch to his personal vehicle because it had a permit for the port's employee parking lot affixed to the windshield. Reacher didn't respond. He had no need for permits, for parking or anything else, and he was happy about that. It was as if Gilmour had picked up on his line of thought, because as they climbed into the second car, he said, 'Do you have a car stashed away somewhere? Or a truck? I can see you more in a truck. Or a decommissioned Humvee.'

Reacher shook his head. 'My days of riding in Humvees are long gone. I don't need a truck. And I don't want a car.'

'So how do you get around?'

'I take the bus. I hitch rides. I fly, on occasion, if there's no way to avoid it.'

'You have a license?'

'No. But I can drive. If I have to.'

'You can drive but have no license. You travel but have no luggage. What do you do for a home?' Gilmour started the engine, then looked across at Reacher. 'Don't tell me. You have an RV. You live off-grid somewhere remote. Somewhere that looks great in photographs but is actually a pain in the ass to spend time in. Hence the travel.'

Reacher shook his head again. 'The clue's in the name.

RV. Recreational *vehicle*. Too much like a car or a truck. Not for me.'

'Okay, then. A houseboat.'

'Also a kind of vehicle. Also a no.'

Gilmour pulled away from the curb. 'All right, I give up. Where do you live?'

'Live? Everywhere. Anywhere. Wherever I want.'

'I don't follow. Wait. I'm sorry. I shouldn't have pushed. Are you saying you're – what's the correct terminology these days – unhoused?'

'Terminology? Right. That gets to the heart of it. You asked where I *live*. That doesn't make sense to me. But I knew a guy from Scotland a while back. Over there they say, "Where do you *stay*?" And that does make sense. If you have a house or whatever else, you have to stay in it. Or near it. Most of the time, anyway. And I don't want to do that. I don't want to stay anywhere. Not permanently. Not for more than a day or two.'

'You don't? Why not?'

'It's just the way I'm wired.'

'I guess you liked the army, then. In the right unit you're never in one place very long.'

'But with a twist. The army tells you where to go, and when. Now I get to pick.'

Gilmour set off driving in the opposite direction to what Reacher had expected. It felt like they were heading back toward the card club rather than to the port, which he knew was near the coffee shop. He was surprised about that but he wasn't too concerned. He figured it was Gilmour's idea of an evasive maneuver, and if that made him feel better, Reacher was happy to roll with it. It wasn't his paycheck that would get docked if they showed up late.

Gilmour did pass the card club, then he took a right at a doughnut store. He took a left at a pizza place, then another left at a bakery. For a moment Reacher felt like they were navigating by food outlet. Gilmour kept going straight after that, then slowed for no apparent reason, missing the next green light. A figure darted out from the entrance to an apartment building. A man. He was tall and skinny, wearing jeans and sneakers and a hoodie with the hood pulled up, hiding his face. He scurried around the front of the car like a panhandler, then approached the driver's door. Gilmour lowered his window. Reacher thought he was going to give the guy some money, but he had it backward. The guy handed something to Gilmour. A brown envelope, letter-sized, folded in half. Gilmour took it and hit the window button, and before the glass was all the way up, the guy had disappeared into the nearest alleyway.

Gilmour passed the envelope to Reacher. He said, 'It's for you. Go ahead. Open it.'

Reacher tore the top off the envelope and shook out its contents. It was an ID card, identical to Gilmour's, except for the name, the photograph, and the color of the lanyard, which was green and interspersed with the silhouettes of various Disney characters.

Gilmour caught Reacher's expression and said, 'What? It's not a problem. Lanyard choice is left up to the employee. There's no set protocol. I guess that was the best my guy could do. We didn't give him much notice. And a big teddy bear like you?' A cheeky grin spread across Gilmour's face. 'Be honest. It suits you. Go ahead. Put it on.'

Reacher pointed to the front of the card. He said, 'My photo. I told you to delete it.'

'I did delete it. You saw me do it. But you didn't tell me not to retrieve it later. And you're lucky I did. I had my guy meet me in the car when you were in the club last night. He cloned the chip in mine and I gave him your picture. Otherwise you'd have to meet him yourself later so he could take one of his own. And who knows what kind of crazy dive that would have been at. He won't let anyone near his place. He's paranoid. We've been tight since we were kids and I don't even know where he lives these days.'

Reacher held up the card and examined it in the light. 'This is good enough to fool the guards at your work?'

'It should be. I had him put a short expiration date on it. Two weeks. That'll match the cover story we're going to use. We'll say you're a temp, and you're covering for the guy who got killed. We'll say you're shadowing me while you do your orientation. That way you can go wherever I go and watch my back.'

Gilmour parked in the most isolated corner of the port's lot. He slipped his old, basic phone into his pocket, locked his backpack in the trunk, then led the way to the security hut. Inside, the setup was pretty basic, like the kind of thing Reacher would have expected at a remote thirdworld airport. There was a reception counter to the side. Its pale laminated surface was wearing thin in places. A guard was sitting behind it wearing a faux paramilitary uniform complete with all kinds of badges and patches and emblems. There was a metal detector arch in the center and a scarred conveyor belt feeding an X-ray machine on the other side. Beyond that, another uniformed guard sat and stared blankly at a screen. Gilmour dumped his keys, phone, wallet, and loose change in a rubber tub, sent it on its way to be scanned, and stepped through the arch. Reacher still had the borrowed phone in his pocket. He wanted to see how well the system worked, so he walked through the arch without removing it. No lights flashed. No alarm sounded. The guard didn't seem to notice that anyone was there. Gilmour retrieved his things and tried a cheery 'Morning, Bob.' Some kind of sound escaped from Bob's throat but Reacher couldn't tell if it was a reply or a random grunt.

Reacher followed Gilmour across a courtyard and through a set of double doors leading to a larger brick building. The doors were wooden with round windows near the top, and they were painted a jarring shade of turquoise. Institutional buildings always had the worst colors, Reacher thought. He didn't know whether that was because they were the cheapest, or if it was to discourage thieves from raiding the supply closets.

The office Gilmour had shared with the dead guy was up one flight of echoey concrete stairs and along a bleak, dimly lit corridor. Inside, the air still carried a hint of rotting vegetation, but the flowers were gone. Gilmour guessed the cleaners must have finally taken them. He was happy about that. He had hated those flowers. He could have dumped them in the trash himself, but some irrational, superstitious part of his brain had stopped him. He had feared that would seem like an admission of guilt.

Gilmour offered Reacher his own chair, then sat down at his coworker's desk and picked up the phone. He hit zero for the switchboard and asked for Sabrina Patten in HR. She answered after two rings. Gilmour asked if she could spare him five minutes sometime that morning. Reacher could only vaguely make out her side of the conversation, but that was enough to tell that she was reluctant to meet him. She mentioned something about leaving work early, then being stuck with back-to-back interviews for some new IT position over the next couple of days, but Gilmour stuck to his guns. He said he was feeling depressed. That he needed to explore some sensitive issues in a safe and supportive environment for the sake of his mental health. It sounded like nonsense to Reacher, but it did the trick. Patten said she could make time for a brief chat in twenty minutes.

Gilmour hung up the phone and turned to his coworker's computer. He pulled the keyboard a little closer, then looked at Reacher and said, 'Ready?'

Reacher said, 'You're not expecting me to operate that thing?'

'No. Of course not. But I'm going to check the shipment. The smugglers will notice. That's what led to . . . the accident last time.'

'What are you expecting them to do? Bust in through the windows?'

'No. But I don't want to end up as a stain on the sidewalk the minute I step outside. I need you to be alert.'

'I am alert.'

'You look half asleep.'

'Appearances can be deceptive.'

'Okay, if you say so. Now, wish me luck. I'm hoping IT hasn't deactivated it yet. I don't want to have to use my own.'

Gilmour went to type, but before he could, he froze. His hands hovered over the keyboard, fingers outstretched, immobile. He had caught his reflection in the monitor. Just his silhouette – the glass wasn't shiny like a mirror – but for a second he thought he'd seen the outline of his coworker's face floating there. He closed his eyes and felt a shiver dance down his spine.

Reacher said, 'What's wrong? Did you forget the password?'

Gilmour shook the image away. 'Of course not. I was just thinking, do you ever wish you could go back in time? Change something you did?'

'No.'

'Never?'

'Why? It would be a waste of time.'

'Even if you did something that had a bad outcome? Even if you hadn't meant for it to?'

'If you made a mistake, learn from it. Sure. But at the right time. After the action. Not during. Otherwise you lose focus. One mistake becomes two. Two becomes four. And then what will you want to do? Go back to before you were born?'

'Right now I'd take that deal.' Gilmour laced his fingers together and cracked his knuckles. 'But there are no do-overs in life, I guess.' He lowered his hands and his fingers began to dance across the keys. He checked the screen, then nodded. 'Good. I'm in. The day's the same for the shipment. The time's the same. The holding zone is the same. We're all good. Now let's get out before anyone... Unless...' He grabbed the mouse and started to click and scroll. 'Wait a minute. This could... Hold on.' He clicked again and a small square printer that was balanced between the two desks coughed into life. A single sheet of paper crawled out into its tray. 'Right. Now I'm done.'

Reacher retrieved the paper. It was an image of the screen before Gilmour had shut it down. Nothing spectacular. Just a form with about eighty percent of its fields filled in. He said, 'What am I missing? What are you seeing here?'

Gilmour said, 'I'll have to check. But if I'm right, I'm seeing a whole heap of trouble.'

EIGHTEEN

Dominic Kelleher didn't consider himself to be a flashy kind of guy. He had money and he appreciated the finer things in life, but he didn't draw attention to those facts. His choice of car was a case in point. He drove a Mercedes S560, which was a regular model, not the sportier AMG. It was five years old, in sober Lunar Blue, and he'd had the model designation badge deleted the first time the car went to the shop for an oil change. He didn't have vanity plates, either. He didn't feel the need to advertise that the car was his. Everyone in the neighborhood knew whose it was and therefore wouldn't mess with it. But he did worry about strangers and dumb kids who were off their heads on drugs. People like that didn't necessarily make wise choices, so he always parked in a reserved spot around the back of his bar. That provided security.

And it was convenient. It was close to where he lived and worked, so he didn't have to walk to whatever curbside spot he'd been forced to use. He could be certain he'd get in and out without delay whenever he had an appointment to get to.

Except for that day. He stepped out of the rear entrance to the Butcher's Dog after a late breakfast and saw that his driveway was blocked by a line of cabs. Three of them, all from Rides-R-Us. They weren't parked. All had drivers on board, and the one at the front – the newest and shiniest – was also carrying a passenger. Kelleher approached, ready to read the riot act, and the cab's rear door opened. A man climbed out. Fyodor Gorbolevski. The owner of the cab company. Kelleher knew him. He was in his mid-fifties, six feet tall, and he looked to be about the same size across the chest. His head was shaved, and a jet-black goatee added some straight lines to his otherwise pudgy face.

Gorbolevski stepped up close to Kelleher and said, 'Dominic, what the hell is going on?'

Kelleher forced a smile and said, 'Top of the morning to you, too.'

'Last night I did you a favor. I did you two favors. I put my drivers on alert for that Neanderthal you were looking for. And when they found him, I gave four of your guys a ride so they could settle whatever kind of score you two have.'

Kelleher nodded. 'I appreciate that. I thanked you.'

'Maybe you do appreciate it. But do you know what I do not appreciate? I now have one cab off the road. One handgun missing. And four of my drivers have quit.'

Kelleher was silent for a moment. Then he said, 'I didn't know that. I'll replace the gun, of course. And I'll pay for the damage to the cab.'

'Damn straight you will.'

'And the drivers? Don't worry about them. Guys are lining up to work for you. They always have been, since you first got here.'

'They won't be for long if word gets out that I hang with losers who can't protect their own operations.'

Kelleher didn't reply.

Gorbolevski lowered his voice and said, 'Seriously, Dominic. Take care of this lunatic. He's your problem now. I've talked to the others. We all agree. You deal with it, or one of us will. And we'll deal with you at the same time. Are we clear?'

Kelleher stepped back and said, 'There's no need—'

'Are we clear?'

Kelleher nodded. He said, 'Yes. We're clear.'

Gorbolevski climbed back into the cab and his driver started the engine. He pulled away and the others followed slowly, one at a time. Kelleher stood by the trunk of his Mercedes breathing their fumes. He put his hand in his pocket and fiddled with his keys. Then he turned and went back into his building. The errand he was going to run could wait. He had a new priority now.

Gilmour took the paper from Reacher and ran his index finger over a series of boxes down the right side. He said, 'I think I was wrong about the smuggling. I don't think that's what's happening here. I think it's something else altogether.'

Reacher said, 'As in altogether better? Or altogether worse?'

'As in, we could altogether be screwed seven ways till Sunday. Or I could be, anyway. You haven't done anything. You're not involved. Not really. You should walk away. No. You should run. Like now.'

'Explain?'

Gilmour took a breath, then let out a long, slow, exaggerated sigh. 'Suppose you have something you want to bring into the United States. Something sensitive. You can't bring it on a plane. And it's on another continent, so you can't get a truck and drive it over the border. So what do you do?'

'Put it in a container. Load it on a ship.'

'Right. Only you can't just rock up with your own container. You can't buy them at Walmart. There's a worldwide shortage, and every one is marked with a special code to identify it. And track it. So you rent a container from a legitimate owner, or you rent space in one, and you load in your cargo. And when you do that, you need a thing called a bill of lading, plus a couple of other documents. They're basically a record of everything to do with your cargo. What it is. Where it came from. What it's made of – because a lot of things, certain kinds of wood, animal products, lots of chemicals, are prohibited due to being endangered or hazardous in some way. The container doesn't get on a ship without these forms. And God help you if you lie when you fill them in, because they go straight to Customs and Border Protection. They take this shit seriously. They put every detail under the microscope. And you can't submit the paperwork yourself because it has to be done electronically using bespoke software. You need an agent to do it. A specialist. Now, theoretically you could buy the software, but it costs an absolute arm and a leg, and it wouldn't actually help you. Because to submit the forms you need to be registered with CBP ahead of time, and you need to post a bond. A bond with a lot of zeroes at the end to guard against failure to pay duty, or in case the importer gets fined for having illegal merchandise or breaks some other rule. Which is another reason you need to go through an agent.'

'Sounds like a tight system.'

'It is.'

'So where's the back door?'

'Who says there is one?'

'There's always a back door.'

'There's not one that you or I could use. But you're partly right. If you were with the CIA. Or a deniable operator working for the CIA. Or Military Intelligence. What do those guys do if they need to bring something in? Something so secret they can't admit it exists? They follow the same process. Rent a container, load it, get an agent to file a bill of lading along with all the other paperwork. But here's the crucial part. The shipper provides the information that goes on the bill. And the way it's designed, certain fields can be completed in a particular way. Certain words can be combined, like a code. It tells CBP that the shipment is officially unofficial, so they don't inspect it. They don't go near it. And it tells the handlers at the port to take the container to a specific location, and then leave it alone so the cargo can be recovered.'

Reacher tapped the screenshot. 'The codes are in here?'

'I need confirmation. It's been a while. But I'm pretty sure.'

'So the guy who paid your debt. Whoever he's working with, they're not just going after some random smuggler. They're looking to rip off the CIA.'

'Right. Think about that. What could the cargo be? Maybe weapons. Advanced ones. Prototypes stolen from China. Chemical weapons smuggled out of Russia. New kinds of drones from Iran or North Korea. Next gen. Electronics. AI stuff. Shit that definitely shouldn't wind up in the wrong hands.'

'That's for sure.'

'And you know what else? It shows I was right about me getting my coworker killed. For a random smuggler, a cold-blooded murder like that would have been extreme, I admit. But the CIA? Or a contractor? They'd assume anyone snooping was working for a hostile power. By definition. And eliminating that kind of threat is business as usual for those guys.' Gilmour's back stiffened, then he jumped out of his chair and snatched up the screenshot. 'And that's not all. I just snooped again. They'll know the log-in is bogus this time. It has to be. They already killed its owner. So they'll trace the terminal. That's the next logical step. And it'll lead them right to us.'

Gilmour logged out of the computer, stretched across to his own desk, and opened the top drawer. He grabbed a tub of alcohol wipes, pulled one out, cleaned the computer's power switch, then moved on to its keyboard and mouse. Reacher watched him work. He figured Gilmour was wasting his time, so he shifted his focus to rearranging the pieces of the puzzle in his head. When Gilmour had told him his coworker had been murdered, he'd been dubious. Dropping a shipping container on a person was an unreliable method of assassination. There were too many variables. Too many factors that could not be controlled. Reacher crossed to the window and looked down at the tent that covered the scene of the accident. Or maybe, crime. It was at the edge of a broad, open area. There was no guarantee that any target would pass through that spot. In fact, it was more likely that they wouldn't. And there was no way to be certain that they'd be alone, so the killer would need the stomach for collateral damage. An unknown number of extra deaths. Potentially multiple casualties. All of that struck Reacher as too much for a bunch of smugglers. If Gilmour's friend had been shot in the back in a dark alley, he might have believed it. Or if he'd been knifed in the gut in a bar fight. But if Gilmour's new theory held water and the CIA was bringing in some critical, top-secret item and they believed foreign agents were making a move to steal it? Lethal force wasn't so far-fetched. It was to be expected. Maybe even required. Especially if the operation had been farmed out to a private contractor with little oversight. If any.

If Gilmour's theory held water.

Reacher turned back and saw Gilmour drop the tub of wipes back in his drawer, then line up the screenshot in the center of his desk. He said, 'You need to confirm the contents of that thing?'

Gilmour said, 'I'm doing that now.' He took out his

phone, scanned the piece of paper, then prodded away at the little keyboard on the screen for a moment. 'I'm sending it to a buddy in Wiesbaden. He can check the entries. And don't worry. Our email is secure. It's a service we use out of Switzerland.'

'If I was in the mood to worry, it wouldn't be about your email.'

Gilmour shrugged, then took his old basic phone out of his pocket. He rummaged for its battery, assembled it, waited for it to come to life, then typed a message. He double-checked that it had sent, then dismantled the phone again. He said, 'I figured I better send an update on the shipment. Confirm the intel's still good. I'm putting my ass on the line here, so if that guy harms my nephew after all this, I'll kill him.'

There was hope for Gilmour yet, Reacher thought.

Gilmour checked his watch, then turned to leave. He said, 'Come on. It's time we weren't here.' He opened the door but stopped before he could step through. He turned and looked around the little room. 'This is the second time I thought I was leaving for good. Let's hope I'm right this time.'

NINETEEN

Steve McClaren knocked on Morgan Strickland's door and opened it without waiting for a reply. That was a serious breach of etiquette on his part, but it was done with intent. Partly because he was annoyed. But mainly because he wanted Strickland to have no doubt about just how annoyed he was.

Strickland was sitting at his desk reading a printed copy of the proposed contract that Mark Hewson had emailed him. He had a pen in his hand and was about to make some alterations to one of the clauses. He pretended not to notice McClaren, crossing out a word here, adding a phrase there.

McClaren stepped forward, right up to Strickland's desk. He had an iPad in one hand. He held it out and said, 'Have you seen this?'

Strickland glanced up. The screen showed an image of

a man in his twenties. He was wearing a plain olive-drab battledress uniform. He was standing in the shell of a ruined kitchen with an M16 in his hand. The weapon was aimed at nothing in particular. Behind the man a robotic terrorist figure was pointing a pistol at a point between his shoulder blades. Strickland said, 'Looks like footage from an assessment. This morning's?'

'You say *assessment*. I say *abomination*.' McClaren swiped the screen sideways and a video began to play. It showed another man. He was a similar age. He had the same kind of generic uniform. He crept into a dusty living room. He was holding a pistol. It was pointed to his right. He was looking to his left. Another robotic figure emerged from behind a couch to the side of the door. The robot had a shotgun. The guy didn't notice it was there for fully six seconds. 'Impressive, huh? Would you want him watching your back?' McClaren swiped again. The next guy to appear was in a backyard. A robot popped out from behind a child's playhouse. It was dressed as a woman in a bright yellow sundress. It was holding a baby. The guy shot it in the chest and again in the head, covering its mechanized frame with sticky red paint.

Strickland said, 'I'm guessing this isn't the highlight reel?'

'There are no highlights.' McClaren killed the screen and tossed the iPad onto the desk. 'There are only low-lights. *Disaster-lights*. The only thing that saved us from a giant cleaning bill is that the system wasn't working right. The paintball guns only fired about ten percent of the time. And do you know what was even worse than the jackasses' performance out there? The automated system passed all but two of them.'

'All but two? Was there—'

'But don't worry. The scores don't stand. I overwrote them manually. I failed the whole damn class.' McClaren turned and made for the door but paused before exiting. 'Morgan, seriously. We need a new process. We can't keep wasting time and money like this.'

Strickland waited for McClaren to close the door behind him, then spun the iPad around and switched it back on. The video of the robotic mom was frozen on the screen. He tapped an icon at the top-right corner and a menu replaced the image. He used a PIN to access a hidden level. A new list of options appeared. He selected the one that gave him the ability to view the candidate's score. McClaren had rated the guy at 39 out of 100. The overall rating said *FAIL* in heavy red letters. Strickland dragged a slider up the screen. The guy's score increased to 50. 60. 70. And when it hit 71, the rating changed to *PASS*. Strickland repeated the process for all the recruits that McClaren had failed. He gave some 71. Some 72. One got a 100 because his finger slipped on the shiny glass. But whatever number they ended up with, he made sure each recruit got switched to a passing grade. Then he checked the two that the system had failed. One had gotten a 12. The other, 22. Strickland thought for a moment, then passed both of them, too.

The Human Resources department was housed in the farthest building from the docks. It was a dozen years old, and when it was built, the company's accountants had the upper hand over its architects. That was clear. It looked like the runner-up in a cost-cutting contest for a particularly unimaginative budget hotel chain, Reacher thought. There was nothing actively offensive about it. The place was just utterly bland. It was as if any feature that could have brought a hint of visual interest or discernible style had been shaved off, watered down, or deleted. Reacher had heard of sick-building syndrome, where workers' health suffered as a result of being incarcerated in sixties or seventies brutalist bunkers. He figured that if boring-building syndrome was a thing, this place would be a prime example.

Reacher followed Gilmour inside and up a flight of stairs that led to a wide rectangular office suite. The layout reminded Reacher of a bookstore he'd visited in an old railway town out west somewhere a couple of years before. That place had started life as a brothel. The reception area was in the center, and the perimeter was lined with a whole series of smaller rooms where the business had been taken care of. This place seemed similar, only the rooms had desks and computers rather than beds.

Gilmour pointed Reacher to a couch in the center of the reception space, then continued toward an office with an open door in the middle of the row on the left-hand side. A woman saw him coming and stepped out to greet him. Sabrina Patten, Reacher assumed. She was around five feet ten with straight black hair pulled back in a ponytail. Despite being tied up, it stretched halfway down her back. She was wearing a bottle-green pencil skirt that just covered her knees, black pumps with three-inch heels, and a crisp white blouse that was cinched in at the waist and pulled tight across her chest. She shook Gilmour's hand, arm straight, keeping her distance, and gestured for him to come inside. She closed the door behind them. It was solid, and the walls facing the reception area had no windows. Reacher couldn't hear what was happening inside Patten's office. He couldn't see. She could be murdering Gilmour, for all he knew. Then Reacher smiled to himself. He shook the thought away. He was spending too much time with the guy. Paranoia must be infectious.

Reacher settled down on the couch and kept an eye on the entrance. Three people entered the reception area while he was there. The first was a man who looked to be barely out of his teens. He was wearing a suit a size too large. It was made of some kind of dark, shiny material. Reacher guessed it was the first one he'd ever owned, probably bought specially for that day's visit. A woman came out of the office next to Patten's, greeted him, and herded him inside. He was probably there for an interview. Reacher wondered if he would be successful. And if he was, what kind of path that would start him on.

The next two people walked in together. A man, in his fifties, also wearing a suit, only this one was creased and worn. Almost ready for the trash. He was with a woman. She was younger and had smarter clothes. She was carrying a briefcase, and she had a deep-seated scowl carved into her face. A union rep, Reacher thought. Or a lawyer. Either way it suggested a career heading in the opposite direction to the first guy's. Or maybe a glimpse into the first guy's future.

No one paid the pair any attention for five minutes.

Neither of them sat down. The man stood still, head bent, arms hanging slackly at his sides like a deactivated robot. The woman prowled back and forth like she was looking for someone to yell at. Eventually a man came out of a corner office. He looked tired and belligerent. He glared at them for a moment, then ushered them through his door and out of Reacher's sight.

Sabrina Patten's door opened sixteen minutes after it had closed. Gilmour emerged on his own. He looked the same as when he went in. There was no sign of any improvement in his state of mind. He nodded to Reacher, then made for the exit. He led the way outside and into a narrow passage that ran between the HR building and its neighbor. He pressed his back against the wall, body rigid, fists clenched, and said, 'She was hiding something. I'm sure of it. But I just couldn't make her give it up.'

Reacher said, 'Want me to try?'

Gilmour shrugged. 'I tried charm. Tried to make her laugh. Make her feel sorry for me. Nothing worked. Maybe if you could frighten her . . . I don't know. Something's got her good and scared already. She's dug in. I spun a good story but she wasn't buying any of it.'

'What did you tell her?'

'I said I was depressed. Struggling with imposter syndrome, like I wasn't qualified for my job. I told her that if I could understand why she hired me it would help. Give me some validation. She could tell I was angling for something, I guess, because right away she went into corporate robot mode. Nothing like when I first met her. She said I got the job because I was the best-qualified candidate, which we both knew was a load of crap. I said that with all the stress I was under I couldn't remember who I'd used as a reference. I asked her to remind me. Said it would help to know who had a good opinion of me. She said she'd have to check the file, but really there was no point because references these days are basically just confirmation of employment dates. She said people are scared of getting sued in case they praise someone who turns out to be an ax murderer or whatever. More BS, obviously. But I couldn't shake her.'

'We need another angle.'

'Right.' Gilmour pulled a phone out of his pocket. It was in a bottle-green case. 'This might help.'

'Hers?'

Gilmour nodded. 'I'll get into her email. Her messages. Her calendar. Something in there will give her away.'

Dominic Kelleher had three piles of papers lined up in front of him on the desk in his office at the Butcher's Dog. He'd put them there thirty minutes ago but had hardly looked at them since. He couldn't focus on anything. He couldn't hold a train of thought. The papers wound up so far from his mind that he almost forgot to scoop them up and hide them away when he heard a gentle knock on his door.

Kelleher called out, 'Who's there?'

A woman's voice replied, 'It's Mia. And Mick. And Norman.'

'Get in here now. All of you.'

The door opened and a woman walked in, followed by two men. The woman, Mia, was wearing a shoulder-length black wig. One of the men, Mick, had a bandage wrapped around his head. The other, Norman, had one arm in a sling. Kelleher gestured to the pair of leather armchairs at the side of his shabby rug. The men sat. Mia hung back, then perched on the arm of the chair that was farthest from the desk. She said, 'What do you need from us?'

Kelleher said, 'Ideas. The ape who jumped you all in the alley? Do you know the trouble he's causing? I need to make an example out of him. Fast. But out of my go-to guys, one is dead, one's in witness protection, and the others are in jail or on the lam. So I need you to think about who you know. I want someone who's filthy. Nasty. No – disgusting. I want someone who makes your scrotum shrivel when you think of his name.'

Mick and Norman shifted in their seats.

Kelleher said, 'That's not all. They need to be dependable. And available. And I don't care how much they cost.'

The men swapped glances. They had never known their boss to not care about the bottom line before.

Kelleher said, 'Well? Talk to me.'

Mick said, 'What about the bike chain brothers? I thought you were sending them last night.'

Kelleher's top lip curled into a sneer. He said, 'Those pussies are about as useful as an ashtray on a Harley. And do you think I'd be asking you now if they'd already gotten the job done?'

There was silence for a moment, then Norman said, 'If you want the asshole to disappear, I know a good guy. Very creative.'

Kelleher slammed his palm down. 'Did I say I wanted to disappear him? No. What good would that do? No one knows this guy. If he drops off the radar right away, even people who've heard of him would forget him in twenty minutes. I need a visual reminder. Something long-lasting. I want pictures in the papers. On TV. Online. Maybe of him in the hospital. With tubes sticking out of every orifice. Or him staggering around on crutches, then falling on his face in a pile of dogshit. Or sleeping in Saks's doorway, soaked in piss, unable to walk. Get it?'

There was silence again, for longer this time, then Mia said, 'What if he winds up in a wheelchair? Permanently?'

Kelleher said, 'Go on.'

'I know a couple of guys. I've seen them work. And I tell you, if I had a scrotum, it wouldn't have shriveled. It would have turned itself inside out and fallen off.'

'A couple of guys? Is that enough?'

'They can handle it.'

'Are you sure? This freak got the better of the three of you. And the four brothers.'

'With these guys it's quality, not quantity. They have special equipment. They start out by immobilizing their ... subject. They strap him down. Then they go to work with a drill. They're thorough. They can handle him. Do you want me to call them?'

Kelleher thought for a moment, then nodded. He said, 'Do it.'

TWENTY

Gilmour didn't want to go back to his office and Reacher didn't want to waste time in traffic driving to either of Gilmour's apartments, so they wound up at the coffee shop where they'd first crossed paths the day before. The location was convenient. It was full of witnesses, which set Gilmour's mind at ease. And there was a good supply of caffeine, which made Reacher happy. They took the table next to the one they had both used previously, as it was larger and almost as well positioned. Gilmour ordered a decaf cappuccino. Reacher, his regular straight black. Gilmour used some kind of back-door hack he'd learned in training at Fort Huachuca to unlock Sabrina Patten's phone. Reacher scooped up another abandoned newspaper from a nearby table. Gilmour started in on Patten's emails. Reacher picked up on another article about the situation in Armenia, where the US contractor was massing its operators near the border. It had evolved into an ongoing saga. *Countdown to Conflict*, some hack had named it. This installment included a series of maps. Reacher liked maps. These charted the changing fortunes of a region called Nagorno-Karabakh in the Arabian Peninsula, going right back to the fall of the Russian Empire. The region had been claimed by each of two new states, Armenia and Azerbaijan; fought over; absorbed into the Soviet Union; and fought over again after the Iron Curtain collapsed. It had claimed independence in 1991, but then it had been invaded by Azerbaijan in 2020. And that lay at the heart of the current problem. The group accused of helping Iran wanted its independence back. Reacher could sympathize.

Gilmour leaned over and nudged Reacher right as he was finishing the article.

Reacher said, 'Did you find something?'

'Not yet. But my buddy just replied to my email. He's taken a look at the screenshot. He says the combinations of keywords are totally consistent with the cover for some kind of black op.'

'Run by the CIA? Or a contractor?'

'He can't say. Could be either.'

Reacher thought for a moment. 'Ask him who we should warn about the planned theft. I'm guessing it's outside a 911 operator's comfort zone.'

Gilmour rattled out a message and a reply came back almost immediately. 'He says don't warn anyone. Leave the whole thing well alone.'

'Really?'

Gilmour read a follow-up message, then nodded. 'He says first, it would be pointless. Ops like this are untraceable by design. There'll be no trail of breadcrumbs for any other agency to follow, even if they wanted to help. And they're run by experienced guys with unlimited budgets. They'll be expecting to be attacked by professionals. Nothing these amateurs can pull will get close to them.'

'We don't know they're amateurs. We don't know who the guy who set you up is working for. Or with.'

'It doesn't matter, honestly. You wouldn't believe the kinds of things that have been tried in the past. Foreign operatives camping out on the docks in containers taken from maintenance depots and using them to launch their attacks. Or kidnapping refugees and throwing them overboard out at sea to get the host ship to slow down so it can be boarded. The point is, CIA or independents, they'll be prepared. We don't have to worry about them.'

'Prepared is good. Forewarned is better.'

'Maybe. But there's a second reason to let it drop. My buddy says there've been times when foreign operatives have called in speculative reports as an attempt to verify if an operation was under way. They could think we were doing the same thing. We could wind up getting ourselves thrown in jail. Or worse.'

Reacher found nothing else interesting in the newspaper, so he set it down and began to run through some songs in his head. He had just finished 'Waitin' on the Night Train' by Junior Wells when he felt a prickling sensation spreading up from the base of his neck. It was a product of his lizard brain. A remnant from the times when humans depended on their instincts to survive. An ancient warning that someone was watching him. He scanned the room and it only took a moment to identify who had his eyes on him. The kid behind the counter. The *barista*. Kevin, his name tag said. He had a gap in his stream of customers and was leaning on his elbows on the service counter staring at Reacher. Reacher stared right back. Kevin couldn't handle the intensity for long. He looked away, then shuffled around the end of the counter and scurried toward Reacher and Gilmour's table. He glanced around the room, then bent down and said to Reacher, 'I'm sorry to interrupt your coffee.'

Reacher said, 'Then don't.'

Kevin looked baffled. He said, 'What?'

'Interrupt my coffee. Why do something you don't want to do?'

Kevin paused. He shook his head, then said, 'It's just that, I thought you should know, the guys you argued with yesterday? Who tried to rip off those old folks who were here? I saw them out back a minute ago. There's another old couple with them. I think they're going to steal their money, too.'

Reacher glanced around the room, then leaned forward and said, 'You think they're going to commit a crime?'

Kevin nodded. He said, 'I think so. Yes.'

Reacher stood up, sending Kevin scuttling back. He said, 'Then call 911. Me? Not my problem. I'm out of here.'

Gilmour looked up, surprised. Reacher gestured for him to stay put, then crossed to the door. He went out into the street. Walked a block to the east. That was the opposite direction from the alley he'd followed the scam artists into the day before. He made a left, then cut back along the narrow street behind the building that housed the coffee shop. He identified its fence. It was made of wood, six feet high. Reacher crept toward it. He peered over and saw two guys. One was around six feet six, skinny, with long blond hair. The other had to be no more than five feet six, with broad swimmer's shoulders and a shaved head. They had their backs to Reacher and were watching the building's rear entrance. The one employees would use when they needed to take out the trash. A wheelchair was parked at the tall one's side. It was a heavy-looking thing. Sturdy. Hard to break. Extra bars had been welded to it. Thick leather straps had been attached to the bars. One pair at thigh level. Another at ankle level. The guy shifted his position and Reacher saw he was holding something. It was like a handgun, but bright orange. A taser. There was a tool chest on the ground by the shorter guy's feet. A black cube with drawers and wheels and a handle. A yellow cordless drill was sitting on top of it with a long, wide bit.

Reacher stepped back and examined the fence. He needed to know if it would be strong enough to take his weight if he climbed on it, or vaulted over it. He figured it wouldn't be. Its panels were thin. The grain was coarse. It looked like it had been years since it had seen any maintenance. Its posts were slender and most were far from vertical. If he even leaned on it he figured there was a good chance it would collapse, so he backed away. He moved to the far side of the street. Planted his feet for maximum grip. Then hurled himself forward like a sprinter at the starting gun. He picked up speed. Closed in on the fence, aiming right at its center panel. He turned his shoulder a moment before impact. The wood shattered. Fragments flew all around. One post was pulled out of the ground. Another snapped a couple of inches above its base. Ahead of him, the two guys were just starting to turn as Reacher powered away from the gap he had made. He kept up his speed. He spread his arms wide like a preacher. The tall guy reacted faster, so Reacher's right forearm caught him square in the chest. His left arm slammed into the short guy's shoulder. They both went down like bowling pins. The tall guy scrambled onto his hands and knees, trying to stand. Reacher kicked him in the side of the head. He was aiming for the guy's temple but misfired slightly and hit him in the jaw. The hinge shattered and his mouth sagged open. He howled like a dental patient with no anesthetic, then flopped onto his side. He rolled back and stopped, slack and silent and still.

The short guy was trying to heave himself upright, too, so Reacher said, 'Stop, or I'll kick your head clean off.'

He stopped.

Reacher said, 'What's wrong with you guys? Can't you count?'

The guy grunted.

'There are two of you and just one chair. What's the story?'

The guy said, 'The chair's not for us, wiseass.'

'Who's it for?'

The guy was silent.

Reacher raised his voice. 'Who's it for?'

'You.'

'What makes you think I need it?'

The guy didn't answer.

Reacher pointed at the drill. 'What's that for?'

'Yard work. We were going to fix the fence.'

'Why are there extra straps on the chair?'

The guy shrugged. 'It came that way.'

Reacher tried a conspiratorial tone. 'That's not true, is it?'

The guy turned his head away.

Reacher said, 'Let me ask you something. Are you a fan of rules?'

'Not in general. No.'

'That's a shame. Rules bring order. I'll give you an example. If someone pulls a knife on me, I break their arm. I recently shared that with someone you might know.'

The guy shook his head. 'Never heard it.'

'Here's another. This one's new. I just made it up. If someone tries to kneecap me with a power tool, I break their legs. What do you think of that?'

'Are you crazy?'

'Maybe. I like rules, and a lot of people do think that's crazy.'

Reacher darted forward and drove his right fist into the guy's gut. He doubled over, wheezing and gasping for air. Reacher pulled back and brought up his left fist in a tight, fast arc. It caught the guy below the chin and lifted him right off his feet. He fell back and slammed into the ground. He was winded. He had double vision.

Three of his teeth were broken. He began swallowing blood. But he was still conscious. For another second. Then Reacher crashed his heel down onto the guy's leg, just above his knee. The bone shattered but there was no other sound. The guy had passed out before he could even scream. Reacher stomped on the guy's other leg in the same relative position. He moved over and stomped on both the tall guy's legs. Then he took the drill and the toolbox and threw them in the dumpster at the rear of the building. He picked up the tall guy and dropped him into the wheelchair. He loaded the short guy in on top. Looked around to see if anyone was watching. No one was. So he stepped through the gap in the fence and looped around to the coffee shop's front entrance.

Reacher walked in, crossed to their table, and took a seat next to Gilmour. Kevin the barista was back at his post. There were no customers. Reacher stared at him. He looked away. He glanced back after a few seconds and saw that Reacher was still there, still staring. He shuffled on the spot for a moment, then slunk out from behind the counter and made his way to Reacher's side.

Reacher said, 'How did you know I had an argument?'

'What?'

'You said I argued with some guys yesterday. How did you know?'

'I heard about it, I guess. Customers talk in the line. All the time.'

'Someone told you. Not a customer.'

Kevin didn't reply.

Reacher said, 'The same person told you to send me out back.'

Kevin looked down at his feet. He said, 'Don't hurt me. Please.'

Reacher said, 'I'm not going to. Here's the deal. Call this guy back. Tell him his handymen need a ride to the hospital. Stat. And he owes the coffee shop for a new fence.'

TWENTY-ONE

Gilmour spent the next two hours focused on Patten's phone. His eyes were locked on the screen. He clicked and scrolled, over and over, in a constant, unwavering rhythm, like a human metronome.

Reacher drank coffee. He skimmed through the rest of the paper. He scanned the coffee shop, assessing the other customers. He watched the entrance, alert for killers or con artists or their marks. The whole time Gilmour clicked and scrolled. Clicked and scrolled. Only his eyes and fingers moved. It was as if they had been grafted onto a statue. Reacher refilled his mug for a second time. A third. He was about to fetch his fourth refill when Gilmour flung Patten's phone onto the table. He raised his arms above his head. His eyes narrowed. The tendons in his neck bulged through his skin and he looked like he was struggling for breath.

Reacher was worried that Gilmour was having some kind of a fit. He leaned forward and said, 'You okay?'

Gilmour said, 'I need a moment.' He managed to gulp down a lungful of air, then retrieved Patten's phone. 'It's okay. I'm all right. But this is it. I've found the connection.'

Gilmour slid the phone across so Reacher could see it. The screen showed an entry from Patten's Contacts app. The name was Dr Alyssa Martin, and on the next line, it listed her employment as *Owner: Holistic Wellbeing Solutions – Complete Counseling and Psychotherapy Services.*

Reacher pushed the phone back. He said, 'This Dr Martin. She's the connection?'

Gilmour was scowling. 'She has to be.'

'Why?'

'There are no emails or messages or appointments in her calendar, but why else was Dr Martin in Patten's contacts? She must have been seeing her.'

'So?'

'Remember I told you I tried counseling? When I was trying to quit gambling? Dr Martin was the shrink I went to see. She didn't help, obviously. But she was the only one who knew about my debts. The specifics. How much I owed. Who I owed it to.'

'Gilmour, you said you didn't tell anyone. You swore up and down.'

'She isn't *anyone*. She's a shrink. They're like priests. They have rules. They aren't allowed to tell anyone anything they learn about their patients. The sessions are totally confidential.'

'This whole enterprise you're caught up in. Does it

sound like it's run by people who pay attention to the rules?'

Gilmour looked down at the table. 'No. But that's why I didn't think of her. Not till now.'

'Dr Martin took information she learned in your sessions. She gave it, or sold it, to someone she could exploit. You think she did the same thing to Patten?'

'She must have. I bet the guy who paid my debt got something to hold over Patten, too, and manipulated her into hiring me.'

'That sounds possible. It's worth a closer look. That's for sure.'

Sabrina Patten had told Gilmour that she was leaving the office at noon, so he looked up her own entry on her phone. It gave a home address in Roland Park. That was too far to walk, so Gilmour led the way back to his car and fired up his mapping app. His phone's robot voice gave directions that brought them to a broad street with large houses on both sides. They were well set back from the road with neat lawns, lines of mature trees, and flower beds overflowing with plants and shrubs. The houses all had garages – at least two stalls each – as well as long driveways, but there were still plenty of cars parked on the street. BMWs. Audis. A couple of Jaguars and a few others that Reacher assumed were expensive, fashionable brands.

Patten's house was smaller than her neighbors'. It had a porch to shield its front door; white-framed windows pierced its sky-blue wooden siding, and a rooster-shaped weathervane rose from the apex of the steeply pitched roof.

Gilmour knocked on the door. There was no answer. He turned to walk back to the car, but Reacher stepped in front of him. He knocked the way he had when he was an MP. Not a tentative *Is anyone there?* but a command: *Come out. Now.*

Light footsteps padded along the hallway inside the house and the door swung open, just a little. The gap was held at six inches by a gold-colored chain, pulled tight. Patten peered out at her visitors. She looked part curious, part surprised.

Gilmour pushed past Reacher and held up Patten's phone. He pulled a smile, which he hoped looked friendly, and said, 'Hi. We've come to return this.'

Patten's expression became instantly suspicious. 'Where'd you find it? How did you know it was mine? And where did you get my address?'

Gilmour held up his hands in mock surrender. 'I can explain.' He took out his own phone, pulled up the picture of the guy who'd paid his debt, and showed it to Patten.

The color drained from her face. For a moment it looked like she was going to be sick. She said, 'I don't understand. I did everything he told me to. Why—'

Gilmour said, 'He blackmailed you into hiring me?'

'How did you find out?'

'You're a patient of Dr Alyssa Martin?'

'I don't want to talk about that.'

Patten started to close the door, but Gilmour blocked it with his foot. He said, 'I'm not asking you to. I'm not interested in the details. But listen, please. I've been blackmailed – kind of – by the same people you have. I'm a victim, too. And on top of that, something serious is happening. Something that puts my little nephew in danger. Horrible danger. So can we come in for a minute? Can we talk? I really need your help. And who knows? Maybe we can help each other.'

Patten was silent for a moment. She didn't move. Then she nodded, unhooked the chain, and opened the door. She flattened her blouse over her stomach then turned and led the way down the hallway and into the kitchen. It was at the back of the house with a view of the yard, which was full of grass and more trees. French doors opened onto a stone-paved patio. The cabinets were gloss white with gray granite countertops and the appliances were all stainless steel. Patten opened the dishwasher, took out three glasses, and filled them with water from a dispenser on the door of a giant fridge. She set the glasses down in a line at the edge of the island in the center of the room, looked Reacher up and down like he was a specimen in a zoo, and said, 'Who are you?'

Reacher said, 'A friend.'

Patten shook her head and turned to Gilmour. 'The charade this morning. All your questions. You were fishing. Trying to find out if I was in touch with the guy in the photo?'

Gilmour nodded. 'Do you know his name?'

'No.'

'How'd you meet him?'

'He showed up here out of the blue, just like you did. He knew things about me. Private things. He said he'd post them all over social media if I didn't do what he told me. That would be the end. I'd have to kill myself.'

'The things he knew—'

'I'm not telling you. Forget it.'

'I'm not asking you to. My only question is, did he get the information from Dr Martin?'

Patten took a mouthful of water. 'I can't see it any other way. I feel so betrayed. If you can't trust your therapist, who can you trust?'

Reacher said, 'Are you certain the information came from Dr Martin? Could this guy who threatened you have found out from anyone else?'

Patten set her glass back down. 'Definitely not. How could he? I didn't tell anyone else.'

'Not your friends? Your family?'

'If I had, half of them wouldn't be my friends anymore. And my family would disown me.'

'Do you keep a diary?'

'Not since I was thirteen.'

'Did you check any research books out of the library about . . . whatever your situation is? Or buy any from a bookstore?'

'No. I didn't google it, either. And I didn't ask Siri or Alexa.'

Reacher glanced at Gilmour, eyebrows raised. Gilmour shook his head. Reacher said, 'You quit therapy when this happened?'

Patten said, 'Before, actually.'

'How did you settle on Dr Martin?'

'My brother had seen her a year or so ago. The court sent him for evaluation. He'd gotten into some trouble with drugs, the idiot. The doctor didn't help his defense any, but he said she made him feel better about himself.

Less likely to backslide if he could ever get himself clean. So I figured I'd give her a try.'

'So you quit therapy, then sometime later this guy, whoever he is, showed up and told you to hire Gilmour?'

'Right.'

'Was that the first time he contacted you?'

'Yes.'

'Do you have a way to get back to him?'

'No. No name. No number. No email. Just a threat and an instruction.'

'Has he been in touch since then?'

Patten paused, then said, 'One other time. A couple of days later. He made me hire somebody else as well as Gilmour.'

'For the same role?'

She shook her head. 'No. A security guard.'

'Another train wreck with no experience?'

Patten glanced an apology to Gilmour, then said, 'No. This guy was well qualified. I remember thinking, why bother with the strong-arm shit? He would easily have gotten hired on his own.'

'What's his name?'

'Arlon James.'

Gilmour thought for a second, then shook his head. 'I don't know him.'

'He's part-time. Usually works nights, I think. At the Seagirt Terminal.'

Reacher said, 'We should talk to him. Find out what he's been told to do. Presumably he's there to let people and equipment in and out, off the books, but we should make sure of that.'

'You can do that. Not me.' Patten turned to Gilmour. 'What do you have to do for them?'

Gilmour said, 'Provide information.'

'About?'

'An incoming shipment. Arrival details.'

'Why?'

Gilmour didn't reply.

'Oh. Someone's planning a heist?'

Gilmour said, 'It looks that way.'

'What's in the shipment?'

'We don't know.'

'Who owns it?'

'Don't know.'

'Are you going to try to stop the robbery?'

'That's the plan.'

'You said your nephew was in danger. How's he involved in this?'

'I tried to bail on them. Threatening him is their way of stopping of me.'

Patten was quiet for a moment, then she said, 'Listen. I know this sounds wrong, but hear me out. Individual containers aren't guarded. No one will get hurt when they steal whatever's in it, especially if they have their own guy at the gate to let them in and out. The owners will have insurance. They won't lose any money. If we call 911, the police might not be able to stop it from happening anyway, so there's probably no upside to doing that. But there's definitely a downside. Because the police will investigate. They'll look at each one of us. They'll say we're accessories or something. And they'll dig into our lives. Which means they'll find out what the guy was using to blackmail me with, and I really, really don't want that to happen. Plus, there's your nephew to think about, if he's in danger. So, here's what I suggest: We do nothing.'

Reacher said, 'That's not an option.'

'Why isn't it? Think about it. You'll see it makes sense.'

'It's complicated. We can't ignore what these guys are doing. But we'll do our best to keep your secret from coming out. I promise. In the meantime, thanks for the water, and thanks for your help. We should be on our way now.'

Reacher moved toward the hallway. Gilmour started to follow him.

Patten said, 'Wait.' She thought for a moment. 'You're going to see Dr Martin next?'

Reacher didn't answer.

'You must be. She's the link to the guy who blackmailed us.'

Reacher nodded. 'You're right. We need to talk to her.'

'Give me one minute. Let me grab my purse.'

'Why?'

'I'm coming with you.'

'No you're not.'

'I am.'

'You've already helped with—'

'I'm coming. There's a good chance my life is about to go up in flames because of Dr Martin, so before that happens I'm going to hand the bitch her ass on a silver platter.' Patten looked Reacher up and down again, with a different kind of appreciation on her face. 'Or at least I'm going to be there when you do.'

TWENTY-TWO

Patten insisted on driving. Gilmour was happy about that. He didn't want his own car to be spotted anywhere near Dr Martin's office in case anyone was watching, and there wasn't time to switch to his rental. Reacher didn't care either way. He climbed into the back of Patten's car – a silver Lexus with all the dings and scrapes that come from five years of driving and parking in the city – stretched out sideways, and saved his energy for whatever was coming next.

No one spoke for the first few minutes, then Patten glanced at Gilmour and said, 'Should we have called first? To make sure she's there? We could be wasting our time.'

Gilmour shook his head. 'It's better we didn't call. She's got to assume we've realized she's the one who sold us out. She'd never agree to see us.'

'I guess.'

'And we don't want to spook her. She could disappear. Or tell the people she's working with that I'm not cooperating. That could put my nephew in danger.'

'So how do we handle getting to see her? We should have thought this through. If she recognizes us – which she's bound to – she could lock her office door. Call someone. Raise the alarm.'

Reacher leaned forward. He said, 'I'll go.'

Patten said, 'You? Impossible. No offense, but she'd take one look at you and hit the panic alarm, if she has one. Or dial 911, if her receptionist hadn't done that already.'

'I'll act like I'm a new patient.'

Gilmour said, 'She won't buy it.'

'Why not?'

'You don't exactly come across as a therapy-friendly person.'

'I don't need to. She works with criminals. And addicts. And vets.'

'So?'

'So she won't want to risk losing referrals from the courts or the VA. She'll see me.'

'I hope so. We can't let her skate on this. After what she's done . . .'

'If she's guilty, we won't let her skate. That's for sure. But let's not get ahead of ourselves. We don't know how she fits into the picture. Maybe she's another victim. Maybe she's getting blackmailed, too.'

'I doubt it. She sold us out. But . . . okay. I'll keep an open mind. For now. Until we've spoken to her.

But she's going to need a damn good story to convince me.'

Dr Martin's practice was in Canton, just north of the Patapsco River. A park ran the whole length of one side of her street. It was narrow, full of grassy patches and kids' play areas, and it was separated from the traffic by an ornate iron fence. Buildings were lined up opposite it. They were mostly three stories and looked like they'd been built around the turn of the twentieth century, given the intricate brickwork and prominent keystones that ran along the top of their walls. Most were painted soft pastel colors. The first floors were mainly taken up with bars and restaurants and boutiques. Bright awnings jutted out, with bold white lettering that stated the businesses' names. Dr Martin's office was at the end of one block, on the second floor above a real estate broker. Patten pulled over fifty yards farther on. Reacher opened the door, unfolded himself, and climbed out. He said, 'Back soon.'

Reacher was back very soon. He was only gone for three minutes. He came out of the building, walking fast, and headed toward the car. He stopped by Gilmour's door. Gilmour rolled down his window and said, 'Was she not there? Or was she already with a patient? I don't hear any sirens . . .'

Reacher said, 'Do you have a picture of Dr Martin?'

'I don't know. Why?'

'You take pictures of everyone. Do you have one of her? Yes or no.'

Gilmour took out his phone and started to scroll through his photo library. 'Yes. Found one.'

'Let me see.'

Gilmour handed Reacher the phone. Reacher took a look, then passed it back.

'Why'd you need her picture?'

'For confirmation.'

'Of what?'

'That it's Dr Martin who is lying on her office floor.'

'Why's she doing that? Does she do meditation now? Yoga?'

'She doesn't do anything anymore. She's dead.'

Reacher climbed back into the car and locked eyes with Patten in the rearview mirror. He said, 'You should go now, Sabrina. We're about to cross a line. Dr Martin was shot to death. We should call 911 right away. But we're not going to do that. We're going to search her office. If we get caught we're going to be hit with some very difficult questions. The kind that could lead to serious jail time. You don't need to be part of that.'

Patten swiveled around in her seat and said, 'I can't believe she's dead. Are you sure?'

Reacher nodded.

Patten bit her lower lip. 'I feel awful. I was just saying such horrible things. When I said I wanted her ass handed to her—'

'Bad thoughts don't get people killed. This isn't on you.'

'I guess.'

'But you should go. Right now. The longer we wait, the bigger the risk.'

Patten shivered. 'Dr Martin's body's still there? You saw it?'

Reacher nodded.

'Is it, like, all bloody and gross?'

Reacher said, 'She's been shot . . .'

Patten's face turned another shade paler. 'I can't be involved with that. I'm sorry.'

'There's no need to be sorry. But you do need to leave. Now. When the police show up you don't want to get dragged into this.'

'I'm already in this, right up to my ass, no dragging required.' She closed her eyes for a moment and struggled to control her breathing. 'I can't go into her office. Not with her body in there. But I can help. I can stay out here. Keep my eyes open. Watch the street. Cover the entrance to the building. If the police arrive before you get out, I can warn you.'

Reacher thought that through, then said, 'That would be good.'

'And I can drive you wherever you need to go afterward. There's just one thing, though. One favor. The doctor kept records. She made notes during our sessions. No one can see mine. Not the police, the press, no one. Could you find them while you're in there? And bring them to me? Just don't read them. You have to promise me that.'

Reacher shook his head. 'I can't get your file, Sabrina. If the police find that a file's missing, that person becomes suspect number one. You'd have cops crawling all over you. But don't worry. This is a big city. The doctor must have had hundreds of patients. There'll be all kinds of things in their files. And whatever you did, the police will have come across it before.'

'Maybe . . .'

'Trust me.' Reacher turned to Gilmour. 'You ready?'

Gilmour opened his door. 'I need two minutes. Wait here. I'll be back.'

Gilmour disappeared into a drugstore halfway down the next block. He emerged six minutes later with two plastic shopping bags in each hand. He got back in the car, took out two shower caps, and handed one of them to Reacher. Then he emptied the rest of the contents onto the floor.

Patten said, 'What is all that stuff?'

Gilmour said, 'Shampoo. Shower gel. Toothpaste. Things like that.'

'Why are you dumping it in my car?'

'Because I don't want it. I'll put it in the trash later. Unless you want it?'

'I – I don't. Why did you buy it?'

'As cover. I only need the shower caps, but two of them on their own? That would be too specific. Too memorable, if the police question the clerk later. But a bunch of regular bathroom stuff? That doesn't stand out. And I also needed four bags. It would look weird if they weren't all full.'

'How long were you seeing Dr Martin for?'

'I gave it two sessions. Less than a week.'

'Maybe you should have stuck it out a while longer.'

A slim white security camera was mounted at head height in the corner of the entrance lobby in Dr Martin's building, covering the door leading to the street. A thin wire was dangling down behind it. Gilmour tugged Reacher's sleeve and pointed to it. He said, 'Did you do that? Disconnect it?'

Reacher shook his head.

'It's a cheap piece of shit, anyway. A DIY webcam. You don't even have to unplug it. You can just knock out the Wi-Fi. Take out all the cameras on the network in one go.'

Reacher believed him but figured that if he was up to something secret, he'd still rather pull a physical plug.

They continued up the stairs and Gilmour pointed to another camera that covered the length of the corridor. 'Also disconnected.'

Reacher led the way toward Dr Martin's office, but when they got close to the door, Gilmour stopped. He pulled on his shower cap and gestured for Reacher to do the same. Then he gave Reacher two of the plastic shopping bags. He said, 'For your feet. Step into them.'

Reacher slipped the bags over his shoes one at a time, taking care not to rip them. They only just fit.

Gilmour took a roll of duct tape from his backpack. He tore off a long strip and handed it to Reacher. 'Tape the bags in place. And the cap. It'll hurt taking it off, but that's better than *life without* if you leave a bunch of hairs behind.' Gilmour rummaged in his pack again and pulled out two pairs of latex gloves like surgeons use.

Reacher tried to pull on one of the gloves, but it tore immediately. The second glove did the same.

Gilmour shrugged. 'Just don't touch anything, I guess. Put your hands in your pockets.'

Reacher opened the door with his elbow and stepped

into Dr Martin's reception area. There was a desk with a phone and a computer, and an empty chair behind it for the receptionist. A pair of narrow couches with textured beige cushions sat facing each other across a woven area rug. A glass-and-steel coffee table filled the space between them. The furniture was lined up symmetrically in front of the window, and two paintings of the English countryside hung on the walls on either side. The blinds were closed and some kind of artificial floral scent hung in the air.

Reacher said, 'Was the receptionist usually here when you came for your appointments?'

Gilmour said, 'She was both times. You couldn't get in without her checking your ID, and you couldn't get out without her trying to fleece you for another session.'

'We need to talk to her. Find out why she wasn't here today.'

Reacher moved to an inner door. He leaned down and worked the handle with his elbow. Gilmour rummaged in his backpack, took out his gun, and followed Reacher inside.

TWENTY-THREE

Dr Martin's office had a line of tall windows running the length of one wall. There were eight altogether. Each was covered with a venetian blind, angled upward but not closed, so that all the light wasn't blocked, but anyone trying to peek in from the sidewalk or the building across the street would only get a view of the ceiling. The space was set up to form two distinct areas. The part farther from the door was the business end. It had a dark-blue rug covering the floor, a chrome desk with a glass top, an office chair, and a row of two-drawer file cabinets against the far wall. Four framed diplomas were hanging above them. A couple of dog-eared folders were sitting on the desk between Dr Martin's computer and her landline phone, and a half-empty coffee mug had been left on a coaster.

The space nearer the door was laid out to be more friendly and casual, like a living room. The rug was sky blue. Two teal-colored couches made from soft fabric faced each other across another coffee table – this one made of wood, with a selection of magazines scattered across it – and there was a well-worn leather armchair on one side. The wall behind it was lined with tall bookcases. The shelves were full, mainly with novels and collections of poetry, but there was also a smattering of ornaments and statuettes. Reacher saw a box of Kleenex peeping out from behind a Greek-style urn. It was within arm's length of the chair. He wondered how often it got used.

Gilmour glanced at the seating and said, 'The couches are for the patients. You can take your pick. The chair is for the doctor.'

The doctor's body was lying on its back beneath the line of windows, feet toward the desk, head toward the door. Her hair was deep auburn. It looked like it had been tied back originally but had come loose when she fell, and it was now spread around her face like a ragged, rusty halo. Her eyes were closed. Her arms were down by her sides and her legs were stretched out straight. She was wearing white sneakers, pale high-waisted jeans, and a navy blazer. Her blouse was white. A rough hole maybe three inches across had been torn out of the center of her chest, and a ragged one-inch margin around its edges was stained crimson. The air was heavy with a hard, coppery residue. Reacher and Gilmour stood by the body for a moment, looking down, not speaking. It was like they felt some unspoken obligation to pay their respects. To a fallen enemy, in Gilmour's mind. Reacher's mental jury was still out.

Gilmour tucked his gun into his waistband and said, 'Damn. If we'd gotten here an hour earlier . . .'

Reacher said, 'But we didn't. Where's her purse?'

Gilmour looked all around. 'There's no sign of it. The killer must have taken it. Let me check something.' He moved to the far side of the desk and hit the space bar on the keyboard, then brought it over to Martin's body. He crouched down and pressed her right index finger against a sensor built into a key at the top corner. Then he hurried back and checked the screen. He clicked a couple of times and said, 'There's nothing in her calendar. She wasn't with a patient. At least no one who had an appointment. So, did her husband do it? A boyfriend? Was it a robbery gone wrong?'

Reacher said, 'She's not wearing a wedding ring. It could have been a boyfriend or a burglar, but I doubt it.'

'Why?'

'Have you heard of William of Ockham?'

'No. Who is he?'

'Was. He was a philosopher. Born in the thirteenth century, died in the fourteenth. His claim to fame is a principle he came up with. People call it Occam's Razor. It says that if there are multiple possible explanations for something, unless you have proof to the contrary, you go with the simplest one. Medics use it to help with diagnoses. Their version goes, "If you hear hoofbeats, think horses, not zebras." So, what do we have? The doctor was betraying her patients. Exploiting them. Potentially ruining their lives. In other words, she was providing an ironclad motive. That's why we came here. Ockham would say that whoever killed her came for the same reason.'

'We didn't come to kill her.'

'Whoever did it didn't plan to, either.'

'How do you figure?'

'Look at her chest. That's an exit wound. She was shot from behind. Whoever did it was farther from the door than she was. If she'd been at her desk or in her chair, I could see someone walking in and executing her. But this person had moved past her. He or she was on the far side of the room. Maybe searching for something in the desk or the file cabinets. Dr Martin either walked in on him then turned and tried to get away, or he was trying to make her cooperate and she saw a chance and tried to run. Our guy panicked and pulled the trigger. Then he rolled her over. Probably to check her vitals to see if she could be saved. And when it was clear that she couldn't be, our guy closed her eyes. That suggests remorse. Or at least that murder wasn't the intention.'

'I guess. Okay, so we're looking for a patient of hers. How do we figure out which one?' Gilmour checked his watch. 'And how do we do it quickly?'

'We start with the files. See if there are any obvious gaps between the files that are left in the drawers. Whoever did this was organized. He disabled the cameras, and look at the wall.' Reacher pointed to a spot by the side of the door. A chunk of plaster was missing, the size and shape of a boiled egg. 'He retrieved the bullet and the shell case. He made no attempt to dispose of the body, which means the police will find it and investigate. So the obvious move would be to remove anything else that could tie him to the victim.'

'I'm on it.'

Gilmour started with the *A* drawer and worked his way down and to the right. Reacher grabbed a wad of Kleenex from the box on the bookshelf to cover his fingertips and began with *Z*, moving up and to the left. They met at *G*.

Reacher said, 'How many missing on your side?'

'Four.'

'I found three spaces.'

Reacher turned to the folders on the desk. He picked up the top one and checked the name on the cover. *Yungblut*. He said, 'This is one of mine.'

The other folder was for a patient named Andersen. Gilmour pointed to it and said, 'That one's mine. Which leaves five. How do we narrow them down?'

'Do computers have address books in them like phones?'

'Some do. Why?'

'Patten had Dr Martin's details. Maybe Dr Martin kept her patients' details. For correspondence. Billing. That kind of thing.'

'Good call.' Gilmour opened one of the file drawers. 'The first gap is between Carragher and Charles.' Then he turned to Dr Martin's computer and clicked on Contacts. The app opened to Dr Martin's personal entry, so Gilmour scrolled back to the *C*s. A moment later he said, 'Found him. James Chaplin. There's no one between Carragher, him, and Charles. There's a note that says . . . Oh. Chaplin's off the hook. He died. Okay, who's next?'

Gilmour repeated the process four more times and

accounted for three more of the missing files. One patient had moved to Cincinnati. One had changed therapists. And one had quit therapy altogether. Dr Martin's note made it clear she thought that was a mistake.

Gilmour let go of the mouse, straightened up, and said, 'There's one name I can't trace. There's a gap in the drawer between Jung and Kay. And there's nothing in the computer between them. So either there isn't a missing file at all – just a hiccup in the layout of that drawer – or whoever we're looking for is very clever. They could have guessed there'd be an entry in the doctor's electronic contacts and deleted it as well as stealing the physical file. And there's no way to know which it is.'

'You deleted my picture, then recovered it. Can't you recover an address book entry if there was one?'

'Not here. Not without special software. We could try the doctor's phone – only there's no sign of it. It must have been in her purse.'

'What—'

Gilmour's phone began to ring. He pulled it out and hit Speaker, and right away Patten's voice blurted out, 'Police! They're outside.'

Gilmour said, 'Stay on the line.' He hurried after Reacher, who was already halfway to the door. 'Tell us what they're doing.'

TWENTY-FOUR

Reacher paused in the doorway and turned back to check the room. Satisfied, he stepped through to the reception area. Gilmour glanced back, too, then stopped. He grabbed Reacher's arm, pointed toward Dr Martin's desk, and said, 'Look!'

Reacher said, 'At what?'

'The computer. See the wire coming out the back? It goes to a little box, like a pack of cigarettes.'

'We don't have time for—'

'It's an external hard drive.' Gilmour was talking soft and fast, like a low-rent auctioneer. 'They're used for backups. Computers like Dr Martin's have a thing called Time Machine. It saves changes automatically at set times every day. But here's the thing. When it saves a new version of something, it doesn't delete the old one. It saves both. So imagine you're working on a document.

Something long and complicated. You keep making changes. Then one morning you decide you don't like what you did yesterday. You prefer the version from the day before. Or the week before. With Time Machine you can switch back to it.'

Reacher felt the seconds ticking away. 'Does it work with the address book?'

'It should.' Gilmour lifted the phone. 'Sabrina, what's happening?'

Patten said, 'Another cop car's arrived. It pulled in behind the first one.'

Gilmour turned to Reacher and said, 'What do we do? This could be important.'

Reacher said, 'I'll get it.' He started back into Dr Martin's office.

'You can't just grab the box.' Gilmour pushed past Reacher and ran to the desk. 'It's more complicated than that.'

Patten's voice came back over speakerphone. 'The cops from the first car have gotten out. Two of them.'

Gilmour dropped into Dr Martin's desk chair then jumped straight back up like he'd sat on a tack. He said, 'Damn thing! It's gone to sleep.'

Patten's voice: 'The cops from the second car are out. Two more.'

Gilmour grabbed the keyboard. He dodged around the desk, ran to Dr Martin's body, pressed her finger against the sensor, and raced back.

Patten: 'They're on the sidewalk. Moving your way.'

Gilmour sat again. He grabbed the mouse and started scrolling and clicking. Reacher moved back into the reception area. He eased the edge of the blind aside and looked down.

Patten's voice was louder: 'They're ten yards from the door. Five. They're coming in.'

Gilmour jumped up and ran for the door. He almost crashed into Reacher, steadied himself, and turned to the exit. He said, 'Come on. The police are in the building. We can't go down. It's too late. We've got to go up.'

Reacher grabbed him by the shoulder and pulled him back. 'No. We stay.'

Reacher worked the lock on the outer door, turned out the light, and pushed Gilmour back into Dr Martin's office. He eased the inner door into place, trying to make no noise.

They heard footsteps thumping up the stairs. Two people. Heavy, purposeful, but not in a hurry.

Gilmour hissed, 'Are you insane? Do you want them to catch us in here with the body – dressed like this?' He gestured to the bags on their feet, his gloves, and their shower caps. 'Do you want to go to jail? Because I—'

Reacher pressed his finger to his lips. Gilmour stopped talking.

The footsteps clomped along the corridor.

Patten's voice crackled through the speaker: 'Two cops are still outside. Blocking the entrance. They just stopped a woman from going in.'

Reacher drew his finger across his throat. Gilmour hit the End button on his phone.

The footsteps drew closer. Closer. And stopped. They sounded like they were right by the outer door.

Gilmour closed his eyes and started to rock back and forth. His lips were moving but he didn't make a sound.

The footsteps began to move. They clattered up the next flight of stairs, climbing steadily. There was silence for a minute. Two minutes. Four. Then the footsteps started again. They were coming back down. Going more slowly now. It sounded like a third set had joined them. These ones were lagging a little. They seemed stiff. Reluctant. All three got to the second-floor corridor. They approached the outer door to Dr Martin's suite. Gilmour closed his eyes again. He held his breath. But the footsteps didn't stop. They didn't pause. They kept on moving, traveling along the corridor and down the lower set of stairs, growing quieter, more distant, until they finally passed out of earshot.

Gilmour whispered, 'How did you know?' Then he opened his eyes. 'You did know? You weren't guessing? Because—'

Reacher shook his head and pointed at the phone. Gilmour pulled up Patten's number and called her back. She answered almost immediately and said, 'Where'd you go? Wait. Something's happening. They're bringing someone out. It's not Reacher. It must be . . . Hold on, who is this? How did you get this phone?'

Gilmour said, 'Sabrina, it's okay. It's me.'

'Oh. Right. Yeah, I can see now. It's some other guy they're bringing out. He's got cuffs on. I think he's crying. Is he the killer?'

Gilmour said, 'We don't know who he is. No one

connected to Dr Martin. You sit tight. Let us know when the cops get clear and we'll come right out.'

There was a short pause, then Patten said in a quieter voice, 'Is it awful in there?'

'I've been to better places.'

'The doctor's really dead?'

'She won't be billing any more hours, that's for sure.'

'Did you find anything?'

'We'll fill you in when we get to the car.'

Gilmour lowered the phone and turned to Reacher. 'So how did you know? I'd have run right into those cops if you hadn't stopped me.'

Reacher said, 'Think about it. No one found the body and called it in, or the police would have been here before us. The doctor's not been dead long enough for anyone to report her missing. So if the police had been coming to her office, it would be because the killer had made the call. For some kind of tactical advantage, or after a crisis of conscience. Either way, he wouldn't have said, *I did it an hour ago and now I'm somewhere safe.* He'd have just hinted at the crime and given the location. I've responded to a hundred anonymous calls. That's how it always goes. The officers who came would have assumed the killer could still be on the premises. They'd have been alert, weapons drawn, with both sides of the building covered. But these guys? Their guns were in their holsters. I could see from the window. They were relaxed. They were serving a two-bit warrant or something like that. They probably knew the guy they were looking for. Knew he wasn't dangerous. They weren't expecting any trouble.'

'I guess. I wish I'd known. I nearly had a heart attack.'

Patten's voice came through the speaker stronger this time. 'The coast is clear. They've gone. Both cars.'

Gilmour said, 'Thanks. On our way.' Then he hung up, turned back to the file cabinets, and opened the drawer containing the *G*s.

Reacher said, 'What are you doing now?'

'Checking my file.'

'There's no time.'

'Come on. I can't be this close and not see what she said about me.' Gilmour pulled out a folder. It was thin. Its cover was stiff. It hadn't had time to fade or pick up any marks or creases like the other ones they'd seen. He opened it, leafed through the pages, then turned to Reacher and said, 'The bitch. Get this – she wrote that I was unstable. Paranoid. Prime for manipulation. It's unbelievable. I knew she was no use as a shrink.' He dropped the file back in its place and pointed at the frames on the wall. 'I bet those diplomas aren't even real. I bet she bought them on the internet. She was a total charlatan.'

Gilmour closed the drawer, stepped to his right, and opened another one.

Reacher said, 'What are you doing now?'

Gilmour didn't answer. He selected a folder and started to pull it free.

Reacher saw which drawer Gilmour had opened – *P* – and said, 'Stop.' The hard edge was back in his voice.

Gilmour's hand froze. He said, 'Come on. Sabrina won't know. What harm can it do to take a peek?'

'Put it back.'

'Don't you want to know what's up with her? It must be something juicy. She's acting so secretive. And if she's vulnerable in some way, she could be a threat. In which case we ought to know.'

'Drop the file. Close the drawer. Step away.'

Gilmour was still for a moment, then he caught the expression on Reacher's face. He let go of the file, nudged the drawer into place with his hip, and started to slink toward the door. He muttered, 'Who made you her guardian angel? You only just met her.'

'When I met her makes no difference,' Reacher said. 'You don't break your word. You don't betray a confidence.'

'Clearly you never worked in Intelligence.'

Reacher took a step toward the door, then stopped. He said, 'Wait. Go back. You still have gloves on. Get Arlon James's file.'

'Who?'

'The security guard Patten was forced to hire. Let's see what his story is.'

'So it's okay to read his file, but not Sabrina's? What's that about?'

'Just do it.'

Gilmour shook his head but went back to the cabinets, anyway. He opened the drawer holding the *J*s, rifled through the files, but didn't pull anything out. He said, 'It's not here.'

'It's missing? No. I would have noticed the gap when we checked. Look again.'

'There's no point. It's not missing. There's no space for it. It looks like it doesn't exist. I'll check the doctor's address book, too, just in case.' He turned to the computer, then went through the ritual with the keyboard and Dr Martin's finger. He clicked and scrolled, then shook his head. 'No. Nothing. Maybe Sabrina remembered the name wrong.'

'Did you check the backup drive?'

Gilmour nodded. 'Nothing there, either.' He took out his phone and redialed Patten. When she picked up, he said, 'What was the name of the security guy you had to hire after me?'

Reacher could just about hear her muffled response: 'Arlon James.'

Gilmour said, 'Are you sure?'

'Certain. Why?'

'We can't find his file here so I wanted to check that we had the right name.'

'You're reading our files? Stop! You can't—'

'Don't worry. I looked at my own but I haven't gone near yours. Neither has Reacher. Right?'

Gilmour held the phone at arm's length and Reacher called out, 'Right. And we won't.'

Gilmour moved the phone back to his ear, listened for a moment, then said, 'Because we've met you. We know how we're both involved, and why. But we don't know this James guy. It would help to see how he fits into the picture, and reading it in his file would be quicker than tracking him down in person. That's all. I swear.'

He hung up, exhaled loudly, and got to his feet.

'Are we done with the backup drive?' Reacher said. 'Or do we need to take it?'

'We're done with it.'

'What about the other missing person? The fifth file.

The name you were trying to match when the police arrived.'

A thin smile crept across Gilmour's face. 'Oh yeah. I found that entry.'

'Was it useful?'

'Define useful. If you mean finding the killer's name and address, then yes, I'd say it was.'

TWENTY-FIVE

'Kathryn Kasselwood,' Gilmour said when he and Reacher were back in Patten's car. 'She killed Dr Martin.'

'Are you sure?' Patten said. 'How do you know?'

Gilmour talked Patten through the process they'd followed in Dr Martin's office. He told her about the missing files, the deleted entry in the computer's address book, and how he'd recovered it when he spotted the doctor's backup drive.

'Kathryn Kasselwood?' Patten said, as if trying the name on for size. 'Who is she?'

Gilmour said, 'We don't know much about her, aside from her address and her birthday. It looks like she hasn't been in the city for long. She only moved about six months ago. Her previous address was just "care of the VA," so I guess she's a vet. That's about it.'

The whole time Gilmour and Patten were talking, Reacher could feel a wave of unease washing over him. An uncomfortable scratching sensation was growing at the back of his brain. It was tugging at him. Telling him something was wrong. Something to do with Dr Martin's computer. Images from their search flashed and flickered in his head like scenes from a magic lantern. They were moving fast. Blurring together. He knew one of them had to be the key, but they were spinning too rapidly for him to figure out which one would unlock the problem. Whatever the problem was.

Patten took a moment to think through what she'd heard, then said, 'So Dr Martin sells out this Kasselwood, like she sold us out. Kasselwood reached the end of her rope. She killed Dr Martin and took her file to hide her secrets and keep off the cops' radar. But what about the guy?'

Gilmour said, 'What guy?'

'The guy who fronted the blackmail. Why would Kasselwood kill the doctor and stop there? Wouldn't she finish the job? Take down the blackmailer, too? That's what I'd do.'

The flurry of images in Reacher's head started to slow.

Gilmour said, 'I guess she would do that. She'd go after him next. Maybe kill him. We can't allow that. We have to get to him first.'

Patten said, 'How will we find him? If Kasselwood made Dr Martin talk before she killed her . . .'

'We have to get to Kasselwood. Make her give up whatever the doctor told her.'

'How will we find her?'

'I have her address. It was in the record I got from Martin's computer.'

The images in Reacher's head slowed further, then stopped.

'Excellent.' Patten started the engine, then picked up her phone and opened Maps. 'Give it to me.'

One of the images floated to the front of Reacher's mind. It was bright and clear, but for a moment he couldn't see its significance.

'It's—'

Then Reacher could see it. He said, 'Hold on. Kasselwood deleted her entry in Dr Martin's address book, yes?'

Gilmour nodded.

'What happens when you delete an entry?'

Gilmour said, 'Nothing. It just disappears.'

'So what does the screen do? What do you see?'

'The next entry alphabetically. Just like if you tore a page out of a physical book.'

'Which should have been Kay. That was the name on the file after the space left by Kasselwood's.'

'Right. Kay. I saw that on the computer as well, the first time I cross-checked.'

'So why was the address book open on Dr Martin's own entry when you first woke the computer up? Why wasn't it open to Kay's?'

Gilmour was silent for a moment. Then he said, 'You're right. It was open to the doctor's entry. I have no idea why. Or how. It shouldn't have been.'

Patten said, 'Presumably Dr Martin didn't need to look it up. She knew her own address . . .'

Gilmour said, 'Maybe there was some kind of software glitch? Maybe she hadn't updated—'

'Maybe Kasselwood wanted Dr Martin's info. Maybe she thought that if she sent the doctor an email after she was dead, it would make her look innocent. Or if she showed up at the doctor's house and made sure all the neighbors saw her. Because who emails a person they know is dead? Or drives across town to visit them?'

'I think Kasselwood did want the doctor's information,' Reacher said. 'Trying to build an alibi is possible. Sure. But this is what I think happened: Dr Martin admitted that whatever links her to the blackmail guy is hidden at her house. Not at her office. Kasselwood demanded her address. Dr Martin balked. She tried to run. Kasselwood shot her. Probably not intentionally. More of an instinctive thing. Then, when Kasselwood turned Dr Martin's body over, it wasn't to try and save her. It was to see if she could still talk. When Kasselwood saw the doctor was dead, she probably thought she was screwed. Then she remembered the computer. She'd already used it to delete her own record, so she realized she could get Dr Martin's address from it, too. That's why Dr Martin's record was still showing. Finding it was the last thing Kasselwood used the computer for.'

Gilmour said, 'That's possible. The pieces fit.'

Patten said, 'If you're right, Kasselwood won't go home. She'll go to Dr Martin's house. And if she finds the link to the blackmail guy there, she'll go after him. And we'll have no way to find either of them.' She picked up her phone. 'What's the doctor's address? We need to hurry.'

Gilmour said, 'We're too late. Kasselwood killed Dr Martin an hour ago.'

'We still have to try. Maybe Kasselwood won't go straight to the doctor's house. She just killed the woman. Maybe she's in shock. Maybe she needs a drink. I would.'

Reacher said, 'There's only one way to find out.'

'I guess.' Gilmour took hold of the door handle. 'I'll run back inside and get the address.'

Reacher said, 'There's no need,' and gave Patten an address in Fells Point.

Patten keyed the details into her phone. Gilmour swiveled around, clearly surprised. He said, 'How did you remember that? It was on the screen for like one second. Do you have a photographic memory or whatever?'

'No. Nothing like that,' Reacher said. 'But the street number – 10301 – is a palindromic prime.'

'A what?'

'A prime number that reads the same forward or backward. It's the kind of thing I notice.'

Reacher was expecting Dr Martin's home to be in a neighborhood like Patten's. He imagined something picturesque and elegant with a manicured yard and enough space for a couple of fancy cars. What they found was very different. Martin's address was at the center of a group of old industrial buildings, now converted into houses. Hers was the only one that was still fronted in brick. The others had been painted white, like they were pretending to be in London or Paris. The buildings extended right to the sidewalk, front and back – there was no yard space at all – and the lot they were on was triangle-shaped due to the layout of the adjoining streets. That made one side of the building straight but the other cut at an angle. An optimist would think the building had gained space, Reacher thought. A pessimist would think it had lost some.

They risked one drive-by along the straight side of the buildings. That seemed to be where the main entrances were. The door to Dr Martin's house was wide and high, like it had been designed to accommodate sizeable pieces of machinery or other kinds of equipment. There were two large windows on either side, classically proportioned with eight leaded panes each, and there were six more windows on both of the floors above.

Patten looped around and found a place at the curb to pull over where she'd have a view along both sides of the triangle. Reacher and Gilmour had fleshed out a rough plan as she drove. Patten would be on lookout duty. Gilmour would take the front of the house. Reacher would take the back. Gilmour would knock on the door. If anyone was home, he would try to talk his way inside. If the house was empty, he'd join Reacher and they would break in at the more sheltered side. It was a simple course of action, but it should be effective. They hoped.

Reacher paused with one foot out of the car. He said, 'Sabrina, you don't have to stay here. If we have to force our way in and the police arrive . . .'

Patten said, 'I'm staying.'

'If Kasselwood shows up, it could get nasty. She doesn't take prisoners. We've seen that.'

Patten turned and stared at Reacher. She said, 'I'm staying. So don't waste time. She could be in there already.'

TWENTY-SIX

Reacher took the angled side of the building, as there wasn't a traditional backyard. The street was narrower there. It was more like an alley. There were clusters of garbage cans dotted around, and all the first-floor windows had their blinds drawn for privacy. The door to Dr Martin's house was smaller on this side. More suited to people than machines. There was an alcove next to it. Reacher couldn't tell what its original purpose had been but he wasn't too concerned about that because it gave him an ideal place to wait.

Gilmour appeared after less than two minutes. He came along the alley, not through the house. He was breathing hard and the corners of his mouth were curled into a hard frown.

Reacher stepped into the open and said, 'The door looks solid. One of the windows will be our best bet.'

Gilmour shook his head. 'Forget it. We're not going in. It's too late. She's already been here. Kasselwood. We need to leave right now.'

'She's been here? How do you know?'

'Someone was home.'

'You spoke to them?'

'I couldn't. Because whoever he was, he's dead. If there was anything linking the doctor to the blackmail guy, Kasselwood must have found it.'

'You saw this dead guy?'

'I did. His feet, anyway. I looked in the window on my way to the front door and saw them sticking out through a doorway. Now come on.' Gilmour turned and took a step toward the main street. 'Time to go.'

Reacher grabbed Gilmour's arm. 'Go where?'

'Kasselwood's house.'

'She won't be there.'

'I know. But we might dig up something with her picture on it, and hopefully something with her license plate. If we don't find her, we'll never find the guy who's threatening my nephew. Let me go. We need to hurry.'

Reacher didn't let go. He said, 'How many people live in Baltimore? How many cars are there? You think you'll magically spot her driving down the street?'

Gilmour stopped straining against Reacher's grip. He was silent for a moment, then said, 'I could call my buddy in Wiesbaden. See if he knows anyone at the Pentagon who knows anyone in the Baltimore Police Department.

Or how about whoever you pissed off, with the eyes in the taxis? We could find him. Make him help us.'

Reacher released Gilmour's arm. 'Those are kind of last-ditch ideas, don't you think? Kasselwood might not still be in the city. But we are. We're here. We should look inside first. It'll take five minutes.'

'You think Kasselwood found the link to the blackmail guy and left it behind? Does she seem that stupid to you?'

'I think we don't know for sure that the guy you saw through the window is dead. He could be unconscious. He could be down to his last breath, but perhaps he can still talk. He could tell us something useful. And if he can't, maybe there'll be something else to find. Something Kasselwood overlooked. Like there was on the backup drive in Dr Martin's office.'

Gilmour didn't reply.

Reacher moved to the window next to the door and checked its lock.

Gilmour said, 'We should see how Kasselwood got in. Go in the same way.'

'She went in through the front door.'

'How do you know?'

'She had a key.'

'She did?'

'That's why she took the doctor's purse.' Reacher glanced back at Gilmour. 'Do you have any credit cards?'

Gilmour grunted and took out his wallet. 'What if there's an alarm?'

'There is an alarm. I can see sensors on the inside of the frame. And look up there.' Reacher pointed above his head. There was a siren mounted on the wall between the third-floor windows. 'But it's not switched on.'

'How can you tell?'

'Someone was home when Kasselwood showed up. Alarms are for when a place is empty, or at night when people are in bed.'

'She could have showed up first when the place was empty. The guy could have walked in on her.'

'Then either it was switched off all along, or she switched it off.'

'She could have turned it back on when she left, to screw with anyone who was on her tail. Like us.'

'If she did, I'll be impressed.' Reacher held out his hand. 'Better get ready to run . . .'

Gilmour opened his wallet. He took a moment to select a credit card, then passed it to Reacher. 'Are you sure a card will work with that kind of lock?'

'It won't if they tightened it properly,' Reacher said. 'But most people don't. Let's see.' He took the card and slipped it vertically into the gap between the lower and upper window panels, dead in the center. It moved easily at first, then caught tight after a quarter of an inch. He pushed upward and wriggled the card back and forth. It slid in another quarter inch. Reacher pressed his face close to the glass. He guided the card between the two halves of a latch that spanned the top horizontal rail of the lower panel and the bottom rail of the upper panel. It slid farther, then pressed against the arm that joined the two halves of the latch together. There was a bell-shaped piece at the end of the arm. If it had been screwed in tight, there was no way the latch would open. But if the arm had just been dropped into place . . .

Reacher tightened his grip on the base of the card and pushed. Hard. The arm didn't move. Even if the latch wasn't done up tight, Reacher knew that physics was working against him. The arm was like a lever and he was pressing against it right at the fulcrum. The least beneficial spot. He turned his hand so that the edge of the card pressed against the side of his finger. He pushed again. The arm moved. Just an eighth of an inch. Another eighth. Then the bell at the end of the arm caught against the curved edge of its receiver. For a moment there was equilibrium – the friction balanced the force – then the force took the advantage. The arm sprang up. It banged against the glass, and the credit card shot up and got jammed between the window rails.

Reacher moved to grab the base of the lower panel, but Gilmour tapped him on the shoulder. He had put on another pair of latex gloves. He said, 'Let me. You don't want to leave prints.'

Reacher stepped back. Gilmour took his place and peered through the glass to locate the alarm sensors. He eased the lower panel up an eighth of an inch. He glanced up at the alarm. It stayed silent. Its strobe light remained dark. There was no sound from anywhere. No light. He heaved the panel up another eighth of an inch. There was still no sound. Nothing flashed. He held his breath and wrenched the panel up a full inch. The credit card rattled as it came free and fell to the ground. Gilmour jumped back. He retrieved the card, then continued to struggle with the panel until the gap was wide enough for him to climb through. He pulled his gun out of his backpack, turned to Reacher, and said, 'Let's make this quick. Be careful. We don't have anything to cover our hair or feet. I don't want to be inside a second longer than we have to be. And for the love of God, don't touch anything.'

TWENTY-SEVEN

Gilmour sat on the windowsill, swung his legs over, and ducked in through the gap. Thirty seconds later the back door swung open. Reacher stepped through into a deep rectangular space. It stretched all the way to the front of the building. The ceiling was supported by six ornate iron columns. Each was painted a different color of the rainbow, from red to indigo. The floor was polished concrete. The walls were brick, with coarse patches of their original surface peeking through a tired, flaky layer of whitewash. To the left was a dining area. There was a long, narrow table made of weathered wood. It was surrounded by eight transparent polycarbonate chairs, and beyond it, three chrome-and-leather couches were grouped around a fireplace that was hanging from the ceiling by its own stainless-steel chimney pipe. To the right, a kitchen area was set into a broad alcove – a horseshoe of shiny lemon-yellow cabinets and matte-black appliances – and a textured concrete wall extended the rest of the way to the front. It was broken by two doorways with the kind of doors that hung on exposed horizontal rails. The nearer one was standing open and Reacher could see a half bath on the other side. The farther one was three-quarters closed. It had been prevented from sliding all the way home by a pair of men's feet. They were lying prone, bare toes pointing at the ceiling.

Reacher was first to the door. He nudged it open with his elbow and stepped through into a square study. He looked down at the body. There was no chance of this guy telling them anything. He was dead. That was clear. He'd been shot in the temple at close range. The skin around the entry wound was scorched and stippled with flecks of powder. The opposite side of his skull was missing altogether. Parts of it were stuck to the side wall, and a trail of drying blood and brains had been sprayed across the desktop and the laptop that sat on it. The guy didn't need to be able to speak for Reacher to identify him, though. He'd seen his angular face and cold, narrow eyes before. But not in person. On the screen of Gilmour's phone.

Reacher heard Gilmour approaching across the hard floor and stop abruptly in the doorway. He turned, and for the second time that afternoon they stood in silence and gazed at a corpse.

When Gilmour finally spoke, there was a note of disbelief in his voice. 'What the hell is he doing here?'

'Looks like he lived here.' Reacher leaned down and

pulled the dead guy's wallet from his jeans pocket. He opened it and took out his driver's license. 'His name was Zachary Weaver. And yes. This was his address.'

'That explains a lot, I guess. They were a couple. This guy Weaver and Dr Martin. No wonder she wouldn't give up her address to Kathryn Kasselwood.' Gilmour stepped into the room. 'Dr Martin mined the information. Weaver exploited it. I wonder how they got together. A therapist and an extortionist. Not a typical love match.'

Reacher pointed at Weaver's right wrist. It was ringed with a tattoo. An unbroken strand of barbed wire. Not a terrible representation artistically, but the edges were blurred and the blue color of the image was pale and washed out. 'Looks like prison ink. He was probably referred to her by the court. But that's not what's important here, is it?'

Gilmour was silent for a moment, then his eyes grew wide. He said, 'Holy hell. With this guy dead, the chain's broken. Dead men can't follow through on their threats. My nephew's in the clear. I'm in the clear.'

'You're as free as a bird. You can fly away right now.'

Gilmour stood still for thirty seconds. A minute. Then he backed out of the room and said, 'You're right. Come on. Let's get back to the car and give Sabrina the news. And then go . . . I don't know, anywhere I want.'

Reacher listened as Gilmour's footsteps tapped away toward the back door. He shrugged, then crouched down to check Weaver's other pockets. He found a phone but nothing else. From his position closer to the ground he could see farther under Weaver's desk than when he was on his feet. And also farther under a leather armchair, which was shoved at an awkward angle against the wall by the door. Something was stuck beneath it near its front right leg. Something soft and fluffy, like a chunk of lint that had been missed by a vacuum cleaner. If the rest of the first floor had been a mess, Reacher might not have thought twice. But the whole place was immaculate. It could have been used as a commercial for a top-dollar cleaning service. He reached under the chair and fished out . . . a clump of hair. It was the color of rust. One set of ends looked slightly uneven, like they'd grown that way. But at the other end, the strands were uniform. They'd been cut. Recently. There was no doubt about that.

Reacher straightened up, and from the main room he heard Gilmour turn and head back. He waited, and a few seconds later Gilmour appeared in the doorway. He said, 'What are you doing? Come on.'

Reacher shook his head and said, 'You go. Take Patten with you. I'm not done here.'

'What do you mean?'

'Like you said, the chain is broken. I need to find out what connected this guy to whoever's trying to steal the shipment.'

'Why?'

'We don't know what's in it. Not exactly. But a dollar gets a dime it's nothing good. In which case I don't want it getting into the wrong hands.'

'That's not your problem, is it? The CIA's responsible. Or a contractor is. Leave it to whoever decided to bring it to this country. They can handle it.'

'Maybe they can. Maybe they can't. But I'm not a gambling man.'

Gilmour spun away. He took two angry steps toward the exit, then stopped and crept back. He said, 'Nor am I. Not anymore. All right. How do we do this?'

'We think like Kasselwood.' Reacher opened his hand so Gilmour could see the hair he'd found. 'This was under the chair.'

'Distinctive color. I've seen it before, somewhere.' Gilmour was silent for a second. 'It's Dr Martin's. Kasselwood must have brought it for leverage. Made out like the doctor was still alive. She probably told Weaver he had to cooperate if he wanted her to stay that way.'

'Meaning Kasselwood didn't just come to kill Weaver. She wanted something from him.'

Gilmour thought for a moment. 'She took her file from Dr Martin's office. Maybe she found out that the doctor kept a copy here.'

Reacher said, 'Or that Weaver had a copy.'

'Either way works. Because then she'd want to take it for the same reason as before. To stop the police from tying her to the murder. Murders now. And maybe to keep whatever secret she'd told Dr Martin from getting out as well.'

'And to avoid any liability if the conspiracy she'd been forced into came to light.'

'What conspiracy had she been forced into?'

'There's no way to know unless we find the file. Or Kasselwood, herself.'

There were no file cabinets in the office, so Reacher moved around behind the desk. It was a giant thing, way too big for the space. It was made of mahogany with green leather set into the top. The leather was scratched and scuffed and worn all the way through in places. The wood was intricately carved, but chunks had been knocked out, and large sections were dented and scarred. The old thing had seen better days, even before Weaver's blood and brains got sprayed across it.

The desk had one large drawer in the center section and three in each pedestal. The lower one on each side was tall enough to hang files in. Each side had a keyhole at the top. And lying on the floor, roughly in the center, was a bunch of keys. The fob was shaped like a baseball bat, three inches long, and there were at least a dozen keys attached to the ring. Reacher glanced across to check that Gilmour still had his gloves on, then beckoned him over. Gilmour hurried around, then looked at Reacher and said, 'Where do you want to start?'

Reacher pointed to the right. He said, 'There. More scratches around the keyhole. He used it more than the other side.'

Gilmour tried the bottom right-hand drawer. It slid open easily. The inside was divided into three sections. Each divider had a handwritten label attached to it. At the front, *On Deck*. In the center, *At Bat*. And at the back, *Struck Out*. Behind each divider was a bunch of files. Maybe twenty at the front, all pretty thin. Two in the center. And at least twenty more at the back. Gilmour took one from the front section. A name was scribbled on the front. In it there was just one sheet of paper. He held it up so Reacher could read it at the same time. It was written by hand. The same name was at the top, followed by what they both guessed was a summary from Dr Martin's full file. The subject was a local judge. He had started seeing Dr Martin due to his attraction to a certain kind of girl. A kind he described as being *a little on the young side*. Gilmour snorted with disgust and shoved the file back into its space. He pulled out another. This one gave details of a businessman who liked to expose himself in the gardens near the statue of Mayor Schaefer. Gilmour sighed and put that one back, too.

Reacher said, 'Move on to the central section. Those should be the live ones. You and Patten should be in one of them. Arlon James, too. See if Kasselwood's in the other.'

Gilmour pulled the first file from the center. A company name was written on the outside of this one. *Maryland Wholesale Fashion, LLC.* Inside were summary pages for three people. A welder. A fitness instructor. And a truck driver. Gilmour scanned each one, then said, 'What do you think? Someone's ripping off a bunch of clothes? Seems a little boring.'

Reacher said, 'Very boring. Assuming clothes are all the company sells. Maybe they store something else in their warehouse.'

'I kind of hope they do.' Gilmour switched to the second file. *Safe Harbor Retirement Homes.* There were four summaries inside this one. A nurse. A taxi driver. A doctor at an inner-city practice. And a claims clerk at an insurance company. 'It's not hard to connect these dots. But here's my question. There's no mention of Kasselwood, or us. Why would she take both of our files?'

'Maybe she didn't. Check the rest of the desk. Maybe there's more.'

Gilmour looked in each drawer in turn. There were no

other files, but he did find three cellphones, all switched off. He lined them up on the green leather, taking care to avoid the smears of drying blood, and said, 'Burners, would be my guess. Let's see what Weaver used them for.' He picked up the phone on the left and prodded a button on its side. The screen came to life after a moment, and an image of a numeric keypad appeared. Gilmour ignored it. He carried the phone to Weaver's body and held it near his face. The phone didn't respond. Gilmour straightened up and said, 'Okay, he had Face ID disabled. No problem. I can get around the PIN number. Give me two minutes. I'll check his computer as well. There were no dates in those files. Maybe they're old. Who knows? Maybe he moved into the twenty-first century.'

'Go ahead,' Reacher said. 'I'll try the rest of the house. Maybe he kept the newest files somewhere else.'

TWENTY-EIGHT

Steve McClaren knocked on Morgan Strickland's door, but this time he waited for his boss to reply before he stepped into his office.

Strickland was sitting behind his desk, fumbling with his phone. He looked up and said, 'Give me one second, Steve. I'm trying to send a text.'

McClaren watched Strickland struggling. He could see that his thumb was spending a lot of time on the Delete key. It was like Strickland had read his mind. He said, 'God, I hate doing this. It would be bad enough with two hands . . .'

McClaren said, 'You don't have to type it yourself anymore, you know. You can dictate it. Make Siri do the work for you.'

Strickland shook his head. 'I don't trust that stuff – these virtual assistants. I don't get why anyone uses them. It's like voluntarily putting a bug in your pocket. They say the system isn't listening all the time, but if that's true, how come they keep subpoenaing the recordings in murder trials?'

'You just don't like other people – or things – helping you.'

Strickland shrugged. 'What can I say? I carry my own water. I don't even like that predictive text thing. And don't get me started on spellcheck . . .'

'You can turn that off, you know.'

'I do know. And I have turned it off.'

'Good. Now, listen, Morgan, I came to apologize. I let my temper get away from me earlier, after the assessments. I'm sorry.'

Strickland put his phone down. 'There's no need to feel sorry, Steve. Your heart was in the right place. I know that. And to be honest, you made some good points. Those recruits weren't great. We should be looking for better. But they're not necessarily completely useless. So how about this. We set up a new unit for people who are stuck at that kind of level, and we use it to target a different market segment. I don't know what, yet. Something less demanding. Private security, maybe. Something where we can build a whole new revenue stream and keep from having all our eggs in one basket.'

'Interesting. I hadn't thought of that. We should explore the idea, at least.'

'Good. Let's get our heads together. Brainstorm it. See what we can come up with. It's getting late today, so how about tomorrow morning? 09:00?'

'I thought Violeta Vardanyan was coming in at ten. Will that give us enough time?'

Strickland shook his head. 'Vardanyan's got caught up somewhere. She's delayed a little bit.'

'What about the meeting with Hewson on Thursday?'

'That shouldn't be a problem. She should be here by then, give or take half an hour. I'll maybe bump the meeting an hour or two, just to be safe. I don't want to postpone any further than that, though. Hewson's flaky enough as it is.'

'There are other people at the Pentagon, you know. Ambitious people. I get that you and Hewson have history together, but if he starts holding us back . . .'

'I hear you. And—'

Strickland's phone hopped around on the desk and 'Enter Sandman' started to play. He checked the screen and said, 'Speak of the devil. It's Hewson. I better take it. See you at 09:00.'

Strickland waited for McClaren to step out and close the door, then he hit Answer.

Hewson said, 'I thought we agreed – no changes.'

Strickland said, 'What are you talking about?'

'The contract. We said no changes.'

'Then don't think of them as changes. Think of them as corrections. If you had gotten it right—'

'Don't be a smart-ass, Morgan. You have no idea how difficult this is at my end. I can't just give it to any random legal guy to deal with. I have to be discreet. There are only maybe two who—'

'Fine. I apologize. So how about this. Find someone who can safely make the corrections. Then on Thursday, right after you sign, you can yell at me all you like. Think of it as a free therapy session.'

'Morgan, I'm being serious.'

'So am I. We need our working relationship to be in top shape. So let's do this. Come here at ten, as planned. I'll push Vardanyan back to noon. That'll give us time to ourselves.' *And time for me to come up with a distraction if she's not ready to play ball*, Strickland thought.

The line was silent for a moment, then Hewson said, 'Sounds good. See you Thursday.'

Reacher stepped back into Weaver's office fifteen minutes later. He wished there was somewhere he could get clean. Not because he'd touched anything gross – he hadn't touched anything at all. Not with his hands. But he felt dirty when he searched someone's home. He always had, even when he was an MP and it was his job to do it. Even when he knew the person was up to his ass in bad deeds. It was annoying, but there was nothing he could do about it. That was just the way he was wired.

Gilmour was still sitting at the desk. Weaver's laptop was open in front of him. Two of the phones were to its left, and one was to the right. He said, 'You find anything?'

Reacher shook his head. 'You?'

'I can tell you what kind of porn the guy was into. Who his sports teams were. The last thousand items he ordered from Amazon, and where his favorite vacation spots were. But there was no mention of Kasselwood, and nothing about me or Patten or Arlon James. Actually, there was nothing about any of his blackmail victims past, present, or future. I think he kept that operation completely analogue. Which makes sense in a way. Paper's impossible to hack. And it's easy to burn. Unless you get shot in the head before you have the chance. In which case I guess the format doesn't really matter.'

'So the computer was a bust?'

'Not entirely. I found one interesting thing. A password-protected document.'

'That's interesting?'

'Usually. Back in Wiesbaden, anytime we had to search a bad guy's laptop, we always started with those. They're like safes in hotel rooms. A place where people stash all their valuables, thinking they're secure, but in reality every housekeeper knows how to open them.'

'You being one of the housekeepers?'

'Right. So I broke into the document, and guess what I found? PIN numbers for a list of phones. Not just these. All the ones he's used, and presumably ditched, for all the past schemes as well. But here's the strange thing. Only three current ones were listed. One PIN unlocked the Maryland Fashion phone.' He pointed to the burner on the far left. 'One unlocked the Safe Harbor phone.' He pointed to the next phone in line. 'But when I tried the PIN for the shipment heist phone, it didn't work.' He pointed to the phone that was sitting on its own. 'So I got in the old-fashioned way. And I realized it was a different phone altogether. He was using it to communicate with his wife, Dr Martin, whenever they needed to discuss an ongoing operation or one of their blackmail victims. He asked her about me when the guy he sent to the coffee shop croaked on the way to our meeting.'

'Okay, so what about a PIN for a fourth phone? For the file Kasselwood must be named in.'

'There's no sign of it. They must communicate some other way.'

'Where's the shipment heist phone?'

'It's not here. We have the PIN, so we know it exists, but we don't have the phone.'

'What about the phone I found in Weaver's pocket?'

Gilmour shook his head. 'I checked. He used that one for regular stuff. It's completely innocuous.'

'Kasselwood must have taken the missing phone. Along with the files.'

'She must have. But listen, I found one other thing. I don't know if it'll help us, but I'll run it by you, anyway. In this document, as well as the PIN numbers, there were details for some online messaging accounts. It seems like Weaver started using them along with the burner phones about six months ago.' He pointed to the phones again. 'See, these are smartphones. You can set them up so that your messages – your texts, if you like – work hand in hand with your computer.'

'Is that a good thing?'

'For most people, yes. It's convenient. But for Weaver it was a great thing. It meant that if he left the house and wanted to stay on top of all his active jobs, he wouldn't have to carry all the separate phones. Which is huge, because if the police stop you with a sack full of burners, they're taking you downtown. There's no question about that.'

'Okay.'

Gilmour caught the expression on Reacher's face. He hit the space bar to wake up Weaver's laptop and said, 'Come around here. I'll show you.'

Reacher made his way around. Slowly.

Gilmour opened a document, copied a bunch of details, switched to a browser, and clicked and pasted his way through what Reacher took to be a complicated log-in process. Eventually a series of speech bubbles filled the screen. Gray ones on the left, blue ones on the right. Gilmour pointed to a blue bubble almost at the bottom of the screen and said, 'See that one? That was sent this morning. Right after I sent Weaver that confirmation about the shipment details not having changed. He was updating his contact based on what I told him.'

Reacher said, 'Then where's your message?'

'It doesn't show up here because I use a dumb phone. Not a smartphone. They work differently. Anyway, the next message down is Weaver's contact – Wait. What the hell?' Gilmour sat up straighter in the chair.

'What's wrong?'

'Look at the very bottom of the screen. The last two messages – they're new. They weren't there five minutes ago when I first found the account.'

Reacher looked. He saw a blue message followed by a gray one. The blue message said: *URGENT. Docking schedule impacted by medical emergency on vessel inbound from China. Package of interest delayed 24 hours. Window now opens 10:00 Thursday.* The gray one was an acknowledgment of sorts. *Understood. Advise if further developments.* The blue one had gone out four minutes ago. The gray one had arrived a minute later. Reacher said, 'You didn't send that update?'

Gilmour shook his head. 'Of course I didn't. It's not true.'

Reacher said, 'It looks like Weaver's contact was in a hurry. His typing is as bad as mine.'

The computer made a sound like a wineglass being tapped with a fork. Gilmour stretched over. He did something with the touchpad and another string of messages appeared. These looked to be between Weaver and Arlon James. A message had been sent from Weaver's account six minutes ago. It said: *CRITICAL. Arrival delayed 24 hrs. Ensure you are on duty Thursday am.* James's reply, which had caused the computer to sound its alert, said: *Will do. Prob 2 late 2 change officially so will trade with buddy.*

Reacher perched on a clean corner of the desk. He said, 'If a message is sent from a phone that's on the same account, will it show up here, on the computer?'

Gilmour nodded.

'Then it must be Kasselwood who sent the updates. That's why she took the phone. And the file with you and Patten in it. Because she's in it, too.'

'How can she be in our file and her own? Could Weaver have been blackmailing her into two things at the same time?'

'No. There is no other file. Only yours is missing.'

Gilmour was silent for a moment. His eyes flicked from side to side like he was reading an invisible book. Then he said, 'Holy hell. It all fits. She took her personal file from Dr Martin's office to shield herself from the police. She took Weaver's file to hide her involvement in the shipment robbery, or the conspiracy, anyway. And she took the phone to send false intel to Weaver's contact and Arlon James so the robbery will fail. She's cleaned house. All the loose ends are tied up. The CIA, or the contractor, can retrieve their – whatever – unmolested. The thieves will show up a day late and there'll be nothing there to steal. Kasselwood's kind of a genius, if you think about it. I kind of want to meet her.'

Back in the car, Patten listened while Gilmour explained what had happened inside the house. When he was done, she said, 'So that's it? We're in the clear? Are you sure?'

Gilmour said, 'Absolutely. Can you believe it? The nightmare's over.'

Patten shook her head. 'It's weird. I've prayed for this moment. I thought, when it came, I'd be overjoyed. I thought I'd be dancing and opening champagne. But I'm not. I feel . . . flat. Maybe it's because two people had to die to buy our way out. I don't know.'

'Two assholes had to die.'

'They were still humans. We shouldn't lose sight of that.'

'They were still assholes,' Gilmour said under his breath.

Patten reached for the ignition, then pulled her hand back. 'There's one thing I don't understand. How did Kasselwood wind up as part of the same conspiracy as us?'

Gilmour said, 'The same way we did, I guess. Dr Martin uncovered some kind of vulnerability during therapy. Weaver used it to make her play along.'

'Sure. I can see how that could happen. But what part did they make her play? Why did they need her? You, me, Arlon James, our roles are obvious. What was she supposed to do?'

'Does it matter?'

Patten shrugged. 'Maybe. Maybe not. I'd just like to know.'

So would I, Reacher thought. He could feel the scratching at the back of his brain again. It was starting back up. Nagging at him.

Patten said, 'Anyway, do you guys have anywhere you need to be tonight?'

Gilmour said, 'I was thinking of leaving town, but I guess that can wait till tomorrow.'

Reacher said, 'I am leaving town.' He took hold of the door handle and started to pull.

Patten said, 'No, wait.' She started the engine. 'Come back to my place. For a while, anyway. I'll make dinner. Or order takeout. It's a big deal, what we've been through together. Even if we thought we were going through it alone. But we survived. We should at least try to celebrate.'

Reacher didn't object. Nor did Gilmour. Patten pulled away from the curb and found her way home from memory. She drove slowly. She seemed distracted. Two other cars had to brake to avoid hitting her. No one spoke the whole way to Patten's street. It was busier than before. More cars were driving on it. More were parked. Ahead of them, a guy in a Mercedes signaled left. It looked like he was going to swing around and pull into a parking spot. It was the last one in sight. But before he could complete his turn, a Maserati coming the other way sped up and nipped into the space ahead of him. The Mercedes guy honked. He rolled down his window and yelled that he had seen the space first. The other driver just laughed and flipped him off.

Patten shook her head. 'This street's going to shit,' she said. 'It started a month ago. A new guy moved in. He's single, but he bought the biggest house in the neighborhood. He throws parties all the time. Invites dozens of friends. They show up in their fancy sports cars and take all the parking spots until there are none left for the homeowners.'

Gilmour said, 'Can't the homeowners park in their driveways? Or in their garages?'

Reacher had no interest in where the homeowners parked or how other people's party guests behaved. Just thinking about things like that made him want to leave town and get back on the move. It didn't matter where to. He had been about to say he'd walk to the Greyhound station instead of staying for dinner, but all of a sudden he felt the scratching at the back of his brain grow a little stronger. He still had no idea what was causing it but knew it would most likely be something connected to Baltimore. The place itself, or something that had happened there, or something that would happen there soon. He felt like the location was key, so he figured he'd better hang around until whatever it was came into focus. He just hoped that would happen soon.

TWENTY-NINE

Patten squeezed her Lexus around the nose of a Ferrari that was overhanging the entrance to her driveway, parked, and led the way inside. Gilmour made a couple of half-hearted attempts at small talk. Reacher didn't say much at all. Patten did everything she could think of to lighten the mood. She played music. She ordered Thai food. She opened a bottle of wine. Then a second. And a third. They sat in a line at the breakfast bar in her kitchen, Patten in the middle, and she started to tell her life story. Parts of it, anyway. How she had grown up in Cleveland, Ohio, wanting to be a dancer. About her string of failed auditions in New York and San Francisco and finally in Baltimore. About a summer spent in Paris. Another in Milan. A short-lived flirtation with stand-up comedy. And an eventual, grudging acceptance that a corporate job was needed, at least temporarily, to repair the hole in her bank account and cover life's other essentials, like health insurance and a 401(k). She'd lost Reacher by the end, but he was aware of one thing: Throughout the whole tale she had been careful to steer clear of whatever it was that had landed her on Dr Martin's couch.

Reacher's interest picked back up when Gilmour started talking about his time in the army. They had four years at West Point in common, but aside from that, their experience was very different. Gilmour had been born in the United States. Reacher in Germany. Gilmour had grown up in one place, Pittsburgh, because of his mother's job. As a kid, Reacher had never spent more than a few months in one place because of his father's. Stan Reacher had been a captain in the Marines, and he was constantly shifted from one overseas posting to another. Gilmour had spent his whole career, aside from training detachments, at one base. Reacher had served all over the world.

Eventually the focus shifted away from Gilmour. Patten took up the slack again, but this time she was mainly asking questions. Of Reacher. She didn't care about his service life too much. It was the choices he'd made afterward that fascinated her. She kept circling back to the things that she felt he lacked. A house. A car. Possessions. Clothes. He tried to explain that he hadn't lost anything. He had gained everything. But he didn't try too hard. People either got his lifestyle or they didn't. He knew that from experience. People wanted roots or they wanted freedom. They wanted to have a boss or to be their own boss. To have structure or to have flexibility.

There was no point in trying to change anyone's mind. And even if it had been possible, Reacher wouldn't have wanted to. Deciding on a path for yourself was pretty much the whole point.

Patten was the first to run out of steam. She tossed the leftovers in the trash, put her empty wineglass in the sink, and stumbled up the stairs, muttering something about spare bedrooms and clean bath towels. Gilmour was the next to go. Reacher waited until he could no longer hear either of them moving around, then checked the time. The clock on Patten's microwave said it was 2:11 a.m. The clock in Reacher's head said 2:08. Either way, there would still be buses running. Reacher wasn't sure exactly how far away the Greyhound station was, but he didn't really care. A walk would be welcome, and he had no interest in sticking around the house for a bunch of hungover goodbyes later that morning. He left the phone Gilmour had loaned him on the kitchen table, picked up his coat, and made for the front door. He took hold of the handle. Then he turned back. The scratching in his head was still there. Maybe worse than before. Certainly more insistent. Leaving town wouldn't help to quiet it. Reacher was sure about that, so he found Patten's living room. He folded his coat to make a pillow and set it down on the longer of her two couches. He unlaced his shoes and took them off. Positioned them so they'd be easy to slip back on quickly if the need arose. Then he lay down, closed his eyes, and prepared to get some sleep.

But sleep didn't come easily to Reacher that night. At least not in the satisfying way it usually did. Something kept him awake, and when he did occasionally drift off, he was bothered by dreams. One in particular. Although when he looked back, he realized it was more of a memory than a dream. A recent memory, of the Mercedes and the Maserati on the street outside the house. The two drivers competing for one parking space.

After an hour of the same loop grinding relentlessly around in his head, Reacher sat upright. He was annoyed with himself. He had no interest in cars. No interest in parking spaces, or neighborhood disputes over party guests. Those thoughts had no place in his head. They needed to leave. He needed to purge his mind so he went to the kitchen, took a drink of water, then returned to the lounge. He lay back down and closed his eyes. He started to slip away. He fell half asleep. Then he was gone all the way, and he stayed under until a minute before six a.m. Then he surfaced and found that the two cars were back in his mind's eye. Two cars, one space. Only this time he knew why they were there.

Reacher sat up. He heard light footsteps padding down the stairs, and a moment later Patten appeared in the doorway. She was wearing a bottle-green nightgown. It was lightweight, made of silk or some other shiny material, and she pulled it tight around herself. Her hair was piled loosely on top of her head. Her face was pale except for the dark circles under her eyes. She looked at Reacher for a moment, like she was surprised to find him there, then said, 'Are you hungry? I could make breakfast.'

Gilmour staggered into sight before Reacher could answer. He was fully dressed, but his hair was damp and drops of water had soaked into his shirt collar. He grunted a kind of primal greeting, brushed past Patten, staggered across to the shorter couch, and flung himself down, glowering at the others through bloodshot eyes.

Reacher said, 'Just coffee. But first I need to know something. Does Kathryn Kasselwood work at the port? Is there some way you can find that out?'

Gilmour grunted incoherently and rolled over.

Patten said, 'Coffee's no problem. But why do you need to know about Kasselwood?'

Reacher shifted to the edge of the couch and said, 'There's something about this whole thing with her and the shipment robbery that doesn't make sense.'

'Life has to make sense?' Patten threw up her hands. 'Shoot me now.'

Gilmour rolled back and opened his eyes just a crack. 'What doesn't make sense?'

Reacher said, 'We figured she's connected with the shipment robbery, like you both are.'

Gilmour hauled himself up a little straighter. 'She has to be connected. There's no other explanation for the things she did.'

'Connected, yes. But in the same way as you? That's where the lines get blurred.'

'How?'

'Think about the file she took from Weaver's desk. Why did she do that?'

'So the police wouldn't connect her with the crime.'

'Then why not just take the one sheet that mentioned her name? She didn't need the whole file.'

'Maybe she was worried that if the police investigated, someone would give her up.'

'Who would? The only people who knew about her were Martin and Weaver. They're both dead. And she knew that for a fact because she killed them.'

'Two murders,' Patten said. 'You know, actually that's been bothering me as well. Doesn't it seem ... disproportionate, if all she was trying to do was extricate herself from a scheme she'd been blackmailed into in the first place? If the robbery happened and she got arrested, she could claim extenuating circumstances. That's what I was planning to do if the shit hit the fan.'

Gilmour said, 'Kasselwood is more proactive than you, I guess. Or maybe she's a sociopath. She was in therapy, after all.'

'So were you. So was I. We're not sociopaths. At least, I'm not.' Patten breathed out slowly, then she said, 'Here's another thing. You figured she took the phone to send the bogus messages and stop the robbery from happening. If there was no robbery, there was no crime to connect her with. No harm, no foul.'

Gilmour slumped back down. 'Maybe she was extra cautious. Maybe she wasn't thinking straight. It's easy for us to be wise here, now. Yesterday she was in the thick of it. Or maybe her plan evolved. She went to Weaver's to get the file. She wouldn't have known she was only mentioned on one page. She took it because that's what she'd programmed herself to do. Then the opportunity to take the phone came up after that, like an afterthought. A bonus. She didn't like the idea of a gang of thieves and blackmailers getting away with a bunch of loot, so she stopped them.'

Reacher said, 'Taking the whole file still bothers me. So

do the bogus messages. If she really wanted to stop the robbery, wouldn't it be better if the robbers got caught, too? Wouldn't she take the one page to keep herself out of trouble, because with Martin and Weaver out of the picture, nothing else could connect her, then leave the rest of the file? No. Draw attention to it. Leave it out on the desk. Stick it on the wall. Staple it to Weaver's cold, dead forehead. Anything to make sure the police found it and acted on it.'

Gilmour rubbed his eyes. 'So why do you think she took it?'

'To make sure the police didn't find out about the robbery. So they couldn't stop it.'

'You think she wants the robbery to go ahead?'

'I do.'

'Why?'

'There's only one shipment coming in, but who says there's only one thief trying to steal it? Maybe it's one shipment, two thieves?'

Patten said, 'Kasselwood was working *against* Weaver's people? Not *with* them?'

Reacher nodded. 'That's what I'm thinking.'

Gilmour said, 'Two thieves. Sounds like a big coincidence.'

'Not at all. If word got out that you had a million dollars in cash under your mattress, burglars would be lined up around the block.'

'If word got out. This is a CIA shipment we're talking about.'

'Other people are involved. You told me that. The agent who filed the special forms. CBP personnel.

Dockworkers. There's plenty of scope for cash to loosen someone's tongue.'

Gilmour sat up. 'So Weaver bought some information about the shipment and sold it to whoever he was texting my updates to. And he sold the same information to Kasselwood as well? I guess Dr Martin could have picked Kasselwood as a mark, based on stuff that came out in therapy. But how was Weaver communicating with Kasselwood? He'd need to send her updates, like he did with the other guy. There'd need to be another phone, and there wasn't one. And there was no record of any messages from him to her, even in the online accounts.'

Reacher shook his head. 'Not if it worked the other way around. If Kasselwood came up with the original plan. If she let it slip to Martin. If she fed it to Weaver. And if Weaver sold it to someone else.'

'If you were planning a crime, would you really tell a shrink?'

'You told her about your situation. Names. Numbers. Enough to get you dragged in over your head. And you only saw her twice.'

No one spoke for a moment, then Patten cleared her throat. 'Personally, from my experience, I would say there's nothing a person could keep secret from Dr Martin once she got a hint of it, however hard they tried. You wouldn't believe what I confided in her. And what did you find in the files yesterday? Judges admitting they were pedophiles. Businessmen admitting they were perverts. Clearly people aren't tight-lipped around her. And another thing. It could all depend on why she was seeing the doctor in the first place. What if the planned crime was tangential? Like if she was in therapy because she went off the rails as a kid after she got abused or something. Then she'd have less reason to keep any future plans out of the discussion. Actually, scratch *tangential*. The plan could be central to whatever was going on with her. It could be her road to redemption.'

Gilmour stifled a yawn. 'I guess.'

Reacher said, 'Okay. Kasselwood could have let information slip to Dr Martin, or she could have bought it from Dr Martin. But either way, how can we find out if she had a job at the port?'

Patten said, 'Wait here.' She hopped out of the chair, left the room, and came back a minute later carrying a laptop. 'I have remote access. Some of us still work from home occasionally, post Covid.' She opened the computer and waited for it to connect. She typed and clicked and scrolled, then checked the screen. She shook her head. 'Nope. No Kasselwoods on the payroll. Never have been.'

Reacher said, 'Can you search by her address?'

'I guess.'

Gilmour said, 'How? I can't remember it. And neither of you saw it on Dr Martin's computer.'

Patten managed a tiny smile. 'No problem. It's still in my Maps from when we nearly went to her house.' She opened her phone, transferred the details to her laptop, and checked the employee database again. This time she nodded. 'Well, look at that. We have a Kathryn Kennedy on the books at the same address. Kennedy/Kasselwood. Same person, do you think? How do we find out for sure?'

Reacher said, 'When did she get hired?'

'She started with us a month before Gilmour.'

'Would her job give her access to shipment information?'

'Most definitely.'

'Is there a photograph of her in your records?'

Patten nodded. 'Same one that'll be on her ID card.'

'Can you make prints of it?'

'Maybe. Why?'

'We need to show it to her neighbors before they leave for work. See what name they knew her as.'

'I can copy it onto my phone. That'll be just as good.' Patten clicked and scrolled, then held up her phone for the others to see. The picture reminded Reacher of a mugshot. It showed a woman looking forward, neutral expression, dark hair tied back, minimal makeup. She looked to be in her late forties, though her face showed signs of a hard life. There was a deep lattice of creases around her eyes. Her hair was shot through with streaks of gray. And there was an angry red scar, two inches long, on her left cheek.

Gilmour's mouth sagged open, then he said, 'Holy hell. There's no need to ask her neighbors. I know who that is.'

THIRTY

Sabrina Patten carried her laptop to the kitchen more out of habit than need. She placed it on the countertop and got busy measuring water and shoveling grounds into the coffee machine. Reacher went with her and watched her work. Gilmour followed a couple of minutes later. He slumped down in the spot at the breakfast bar he'd used the night before, then took a remote from a wicker basket and turned on the TV. It was set to a news channel. The show was basically a rehash of the material Reacher had read in the papers at the coffee shop. It was all about the looming crisis in Armenia. The talk was still centered on the potential invasion. But now it was being presented as a question of *when*, not *if.* The only remaining issue seemed to be whether the operation would be handled exclusively by private contractors, or if there would still be a role for the army. Reacher shook his head and looked away. The segment closed with a clip of the woman who had defected from the Nagorno-Karabakh separatists. She went into all kinds of detail about the help her group was giving Iran with their uranium processing. She looked like she was in her thirties. She was clearly well-educated and familiar with the kind of technologies that are involved with nuclear weapons. A made-for-TV eyewitness, Reacher thought. A far cry from many of the scumbags he'd had to interrogate back in the day.

Patten waited for the coffee to finish, then took three mugs from the dishwasher and poured. She looked at Gilmour and said, 'Cream?'

Gilmour managed a croaky 'Please.'

Patten opened the fridge, then closed it again right away. She said, 'How does black sound?'

Gilmour just grunted this time.

Patten handed a mug to Reacher and set the last one down at her place at the breakfast bar. She switched off the TV, smoothed her robe across her stomach, slid onto her stool, and said, 'Another war. Depressing.'

Reacher said, 'True. But that's not our immediate problem. We need a plan. The shipment's due at the dock at ten. That doesn't give us much time. We need to make every second count. Here's what I suggest: Sabrina, you take Kathryn Kasselwood's neighbors. Show them her picture. Get a positive ID if you can.'

Patten said, 'Will do.'

Gilmour said, 'There's no need. I told you, it's Kasselwood. I saw her up close and personal. She's the woman who was looking for my coworker the first time I snooped on the shipment details. Look.' Gilmour took out his phone and selected an image. He held it up. 'It's the same woman. Check the scar on her cheek. It's identical.'

Patten said, 'Nathan, is there anyone on the planet you haven't illicitly photographed?'

Gilmour looked away.

She said, 'I know Dr Martin's dead, but there are other shrinks . . .'

Reacher said, 'And I still want that positive ID.'

Patten said, 'No problem. I'll ask around her neighborhood.'

'Good. But be careful who you talk to. We don't know where Kasselwood is. She could be home. You don't want to run into her.'

'Don't worry. I'll be careful. And if the shit hits the fan, you haven't seen how fast I can run.'

Reacher turned to Gilmour and said, 'Nathan, get on to your buddy in Wiesbaden. Update him. Stress the additional threat the shipment is under. See if he thinks there's enough to call the cavalry yet.'

Gilmour checked his watch for the time difference with Germany, then said, 'Sure. I'll ask him.'

'Sabrina, is there any way to confirm whether Arlon James is still working today?'

'Of course.' Patten grabbed her laptop from the counter and opened it. She clicked and scrolled and after a minute said, 'He's supposed to be. Seagirt Terminal. Early shift. James and one other.'

Gilmour looked up. He said, 'What about tomorrow?'

Patten checked and said, 'Tomorrow – Seagirt. Late shift.'

'Did he not act on Kasselwood's message?'

'There's no way to tell. It's short notice. If he swapped with a buddy or something, that wouldn't show up on here. It would be an informal thing. It's discouraged, but it happens.'

Gilmour flopped forward, folded his arms, and cradled his head in them on the bar. He said, 'Too much wine. Too little sleep. I'm too old for this.'

Reacher craned his neck to get a look at Patten's computer. He said, 'Is there a picture of James in there?'

Patten clicked her mouse a couple of times, then swung her laptop around. The screen was filled with a photo of a man with a buzz cut and a round, friendly face. She said, 'Here he is. Need a copy?'

'No. I'll recognize him. Nathan and I will find him. We'll bring him up to speed, then head to the place where the rendezvous with the shipment should be.'

'Why?'

'All we can do at this stage is watch. We have two potential scenarios – one benign, one not. If Kasselwood was using the bogus messages to bail herself out of the mess she was in and send Weaver's thief on a wild-goose chase, no one will try to steal anything. The CIA will collect their cargo unopposed. But if she sent it to clear the way for herself, she'll try to steal whatever the CIA's bringing in. If the CIA can stop her, fine. We'll leave them to it. If they can't, we'll call James. Have him lock down the exit. Delay Kasselwood as long as possible while we summon some kind of reinforcements. Sound good?'

Patten said, 'I guess.'

Gilmour raised his head and said, 'Not really. But it's all we've got.'

If the Patapsco River is a finger pointing inland to the heart of Baltimore, the Seagirt Marine Terminal is a callus on the inside edge, between the knuckles. The Francis Scott Key Bridge crosses the river to the south, like a ring, and the Harbor Tunnel feeds under it to the north, like a vein. Gilmour was familiar with both, but that morning he took Reacher through the Fort McHenry Tunnel and approached the terminal from the west, because he had insisted on making a quick stop at his apartment to switch from his own car to the rental. They dropped off I-95, took Keith to Broening, and then Gilmour drove right up to the main vehicle gate. They had agreed on the drive from Patten's house that this was no time for subtlety. Gilmour coasted to a stop, and right away they spotted Arlon James. His shoulders were broader than his HR photo suggested, and he seemed light on his feet for such a solid guy. Reacher and Gilmour scanned the area around the gate, but they couldn't see another guard.

'Come on.' Reacher opened his door. 'The iron's hot.'

Gilmour followed Reacher to the security window. James strolled across on his side of the fence and stepped into the guard booth. He gestured for Gilmour and Reacher to remove their IDs from their lanyards and pass them through. He barely glanced at Gilmour's, but he took his time with Reacher's, checking it front and back and examining it for size and width. He finally handed the cards back and opened the gate. Gilmour drove through and pulled over. They jumped out, and Reacher led the way back to the guard booth. James hopped down from his stool and said, 'What now, fellas?'

Reacher said, 'Can we talk for a minute?'

'About what?' James stiffened, his voice full of caution.

'Relax. We're not offering bribes and we're not from HR.'

'If you say so.'

'You working alone today?'

James nodded. 'The other guy's sick. He called in last minute. It's no biggie. I don't mind.'

Reacher and Gilmour exchanged a glance.

Reacher said, 'Okay, I'm going to tell you something now, and it might come as a surprise. Maybe even a shock. So I need you to think first and act second, all right?'

James said, 'Whatever. Spit it out.'

'Here's the thing. We know why you're here. Not the exact details, but the overall picture.'

James eased back in his booth, but he didn't say anything.

'A guy propositioned you. Not long ago. He said he'd get you out of a fix or keep some kind of a secret for you. All you had to do was get a job here, stay out of trouble, and one day he'd ask you to do something in return. That day is today. Am I right?'

'No.'

Gilmour pressed in closer. He said, 'It's okay. Don't be embarrassed. The same thing happened to me. But the game has changed now.'

James said, 'What do you mean?'

Reacher said, 'The guy who propositioned you was

called Weaver. He's dead. He died yesterday. He was murdered. No one's holding anything over you now. You can walk away if you want. Right now. No one will stop you. But we're here to ask you to stay one more day. One more hour, maybe.'

James's phone made a sound like a bell chiming. He took it out of his pocket and glanced at the screen, and a crease flashed across his forehead.

Reacher said, 'Everything okay?'

James put his phone away. 'Yeah. That was a buddy asking about swapping shifts tomorrow. I guess that won't be an issue now. I won't be here. But why should I stay today if I don't have to?'

'Weaver wanted you here because he was setting up a heist this morning. You probably figured that out already. We think he was killed by a rival group. They took his phone and sent a bogus message saying the shipment they want to steal is delayed until tomorrow. They sent another one to you. We saw it. You replied. You used the number two instead of the word *to*. We think they sent the messages to give themselves a clear run at the shipment today. We're going to watch. See what happens. And if we're right, we're going to need you to hold them here for a while.'

James thought for a moment, then said, 'The shipment's not delayed? It's coming in today, on schedule?'

'Correct.'

'How do you know?'

Gilmour said, 'Tracking it was my part of the puzzle.'

James said, 'Okay, but why do you care if it gets stolen? Or who steals it?'

Reacher said, 'Because of what's in it. We think it's something classified. Maybe something dangerous. We don't want innocent people to get hurt.'

James stared into the distance for a moment, then pulled his focus back. He said, 'All right. I'll stay till you leave. And if you need me to, I'll lock the whole damn terminal down.'

THIRTY-ONE

Morgan Strickland wrestled with the cot until he had forced it into a position that was supposed to resemble a couch. He thought that made it more like a torture device, and he never sat on it. But it did have one advantage. It kept meetings in his office relatively short.

Strickland moved around behind his desk and sat down. He had a few minutes before Steve McClaren was expected, and he wanted to jot down some talking points about his idea to set up a new subsidiary. He had come up with the suggestion on the fly the evening before but didn't want McClaren to see that. And he didn't just want to save face. He figured the idea could actually have legs. Another revenue stream could be good. Diversification could be good. And finding a justification for keeping the hopeless recruits would definitely be good. It would be extremely good indeed, from his point of view.

McClaren knocked on the door at 8:55. Strickland called him in and gestured for him to sit. McClaren did and was still fidgeting around, trying to find the least uncomfortable position, when Strickland's phone buzzed on his desk, just once.

Strickland picked it up and checked the screen. His face tightened.

McClaren said, 'Another text? Want me to type out your reply?'

Strickland shook his head. 'No,' he said, 'but I do need to take a rain check on this discussion.'

'Is there a problem?'

'Not yet. But there will be if I don't get some ducks back in a row, and fast.'

The Seagirt Marine Terminal was shaped like a giant rectangle with one corner lopped off. One long side and the short side faced the water. The other long side was lined with low, wide warehouses and covered storage sheds. The diagonal side ran alongside a narrow service road. The border with the road was secured by a fence. It was eight feet high. The top was angled outward and laced with razor wire. The panels were steel mesh, which was dark with rust after years of exposure to the salty sea air. The posts were square concrete, and rust from the rebar was leaching through and staining the rough surface.

Two ships were in dock that morning. They were moored nose to stern below a line of giant white cranes.

The cranes' booms stretched out across the cargo holds, and some trick of the light made it look like they were leaning down as they lifted out the containers, like prehistoric predators picking the meat off the bones of their prey. The ground beyond the cranes was scarred and pitted from decades of contact with containers as they'd been moved and stacked and loaded onto trucks for onward transport.

Reacher and Gilmour climbed back into the rental car and threaded their way across the terminal parallel with the ships and through the stacks of containers that filled the area. Some stacks were only three containers high. The tallest were seven. The narrowest were two containers wide. The deepest were six. The containers themselves came in all different colors and shades. Some were new and shiny. Some were dull and dented. Reacher remembered Gilmour's intel buddy talking about thieves living out of containers in ports like this one and using them as bases to launch their assaults. Looking at the clusters that had been built up all around the place, Reacher could believe it. They were like little citadels. You could stay concealed in one for weeks. People could be hiding in them now, he thought. Kasselwood could be.

Gilmour continued patiently until the car was almost at the diagonal end of the terminal. Here the containers were formed up differently. A line of them jutted out from the fence at around sixty degrees. It was three containers long, three high, and one deep. Another stack, also three high, cut back at a ninety-degree angle. That left a small gap at the far end between the stack and the fence, like a breakwater at a harbor. Only this wall had been built to protect from prying eyes, not waves or tides. That was clear.

Gilmour dumped the car behind the penultimate stack of freestanding containers. He took out his gun and swung his pack onto his back. Reacher led the rest of the way on foot. He approached the gap between the angled containers and the fence. He stepped into it, moved forward, and saw that the enclosure wasn't empty. A container was already there. It was sitting toward one side, on its own. It was painted a deep red color and the security tags on its door seals were missing.

Gilmour stepped up to Reacher. He said, 'Is that it? Are we too late?'

Reacher said, 'One way to find out. I'll look inside. You keep watch in case this isn't it.'

Gilmour turned and started to move away, but Reacher grabbed his arm and pointed to a ladder set into the side of the nearest container. He said, 'Up there.'

Gilmour said, 'Seriously?'

'Seriously. No one ever looks up. It's a thing. Trust me.'

Gilmour looked at Reacher like he'd told him he had a bridge for sale, but he tucked his gun into his waistband and started to climb, anyway. Reacher waited until he had disappeared onto the top of the stack, then crept toward the red container. He closed to within ten feet. Five. He felt in his pocket. He still had the flashlight he'd used at the warehouse two nights ago. He pulled it out. Took another step. He stretched for the handle that operated the locking mechanism. Then he heard Gilmour's voice from above and behind him.

Gilmour whispered, 'Stop. Incoming. Thirty seconds.'

Reacher dropped the flashlight back in his pocket and ran across to the long stack of containers. He went to the far end with the ladders, which was by the fence. He started to climb. The stack was three high. That gave him ten seconds per level. Say nine, to be safe, allowing for crossing the open ground. Gilmour had gotten up in less time than that. But Reacher was slower than Gilmour. He was heavier. The rungs were small and fiddly for his hands to grip and the gap to the container wall was almost too shallow for his feet. His right foot slipped once. It slipped again. He had to consciously slow himself down. Move steadily. Deliberately. He made it to the top of the first container. The clock in his head told him he was three seconds off the pace. He climbed a little faster and realized he could hear something. A vehicle engine. It was rough and heavy, and it was coming closer.

Reacher ignored the sound and focused on the ladder. He got to the top of the second level one second behind schedule. Then his left foot slipped. That cost him another second. He kept going. Pushed harder. Moved faster. His hands found the top of the final container. He pulled himself up and over and rolled onto his front. Gilmour was at the opposite end of the row, also on his stomach. He'd taken off his backpack and set it down at his side. Ahead of him two things were moving. Slowly. Two pieces of metal. They were held parallel, like vertical rails or girders, and their tips were as high again as the stack of containers Reacher was lying on. They were traveling in unison, like they were floating in the air, but obviously they had to be connected to something on the ground. A vehicle. Presumably the one Reacher could hear approaching. But he couldn't see what kind it was. He was too far back. The containers were blocking his view. Which meant the driver wouldn't be able to see him, either.

Reacher pulled himself into a crouch and ran along the top of the containers, staying to the center, then dropped back down next to Gilmour. He wriggled a few inches farther and the vehicle came into view. It was a giant forklift. Its body was painted bright orange. It was the size of a semi cab. It had four wheels with huge fat tires. Each one was the height of a regular family car. A pair of thick forks jutted out from the tall rails he had first seen and attached to them, broad side on, six feet clear of the ground, was another container. This one was blue.

The forklift slowed then pulled a tight left turn to line itself up with the gap at the end of the stack of containers that Reacher and Gilmour were lying on. It crept forward. There were only inches to spare on either side. It kept going, all the way through to the enclosed space. It twisted left again and stopped. It was still for a moment, then its engine note changed. The blue container it was carrying began to move. It crept down until it hit the ground. A hollow *boom* reached their ears a moment later and the container was left resting on the ground, roughly parallel with the existing red one.

The red container's right-hand door swung open and a woman stepped out. She was dressed all in black. Boots, jeans, hoodie, and gloves. Her hood was hanging down around her shoulders. Her hair was pulled back in a ponytail. It was dark. And it was streaked with gray. Gilmour pulled a small pair of binoculars out of his backpack and focused them on her.

'It's her,' he whispered. 'Kasselwood.' He handed the binoculars to Reacher. 'Check her scar.'

Reacher took a look. He nodded. 'Confirmed.'

'She's beaten the CIA to the punch. Where the hell are those guys? Does she have backup? Should we stop her?'

'No. Maybe this is part of the plan. Maybe the CIA guys want to catch her in the act. We just watch. For now.'

Kasselwood opened the second door, then hurried across to the blue container. She was limping slightly, and seemed to be favoring her left leg. She pulled a knife from her jeans pocket, sliced through the security tags, worked the locking mechanism, and pulled open both doors. She ran back to the red container and disappeared inside it. Another engine fired up. A forklift's. It backed out. It looked more compact than a regular-sized one and its masts were lower. Kasselwood was driving it. She spun it around, lined it up, and drove it inside the blue container. Reacher and Gilmour heard a whirring sound, then a couple of bangs, then the forklift backed out again. It was carrying a wooden crate now, maybe four feet wide by five feet long and five feet high. Kasselwood looped around and drove the forklift into the red container. A moment later she ran across, closed the blue container's doors, and handed an envelope to the other driver. He mimed a salute, cranked the blue container up a few feet, maneuvered the rig around, and squeezed out of the enclosed space.

Kasselwood ran to the red container, darted inside, and a couple of minutes later backed out again in the forklift.

It was no longer holding the crate. She spun it around to the side of the container, killed the engine, ran back, and disappeared inside the container, pulling up her hood as she went. Another engine fired up. A pickup truck backed out. It was a Toyota, some kind of bronze color, sprayed with mud around the wheel arches, and the crate was strapped down in its load bed. The driver hopped out. Her hood was still up. She slammed the container doors, jumped into the truck, drove through the gap, and accelerated toward the terminal's exit.

Reacher said, 'Call James. Tell him to lock it down.'

Reacher crawled to the top of the ladder, swung his leg over the side, found a rung with his toe, and began to lower himself down. He forced himself to take it easy. Hold tight. Move steadily. His left foot slipped once, but he made it to the ground without any major problems. Gilmour caught up a moment later and started for the gap. Reacher grabbed his arm and pointed to the red container. He said, 'I want to look in there first. Kasselwood may have thought she was playing to an audience.'

Reacher took out his flashlight, opened the container's right-hand door, and stepped inside. A lingering smell of exhaust fumes was hanging in the air. There was a small pool of oil on the floor, presumably dropped by the forklift. A crowbar was lying near the left-hand wall. A pair of bolt cutters was tucked behind a reinforcing bar at the far end. A candy wrapper had been dropped in the corner nearest to it. But other than those things, the container was empty. Reacher strode across the floor, grabbed the crowbar, then hurried back outside.

*

Gilmour had been cautious on the way into the terminal, but returning to the gate, he didn't hold back. A couple of dockworkers had to jump out of his way, and they were not shy about sharing their opinion of his driving. They didn't meet any other vehicles, but Reacher did glimpse a black panel van going in the opposite direction, through the channel between the next parallel rows of containers to the north.

James had done his job. The Toyota was sitting just in front of the gate. Gilmour pulled up behind it and Reacher jumped out. The crate was still in the truck's bed. Its engine wasn't running. Reacher moved around to the side and saw the driver hunched over the wheel, hood still pulled up. James was standing by her door with his sidearm in hand.

He said, 'She gave me a name. Kasselwood. But aside from that she won't talk.'

Reacher crossed to the rear of the truck. He released the tailgate, jumped into the truck's bed, loosened the straps that were holding the crate in place, removed them, then went to work with the crowbar. The lid came loose in a couple of seconds. He pushed it aside, looked in, then jumped down.

Gilmour climbed out and said, 'Well?'

James moved closer. 'What did she steal?'

Reacher said, 'Nothing. The crate's empty.'

Gilmour said, 'How can it be? There wasn't time for them to stop and unload it.'

James said, 'Could they have switched it?'

'No.' Reacher got back into the passenger seat. 'It's a decoy. Arlon, keep the woman here. Nathan, come on. We need to get back to the container.'

THIRTY-TWO

Gilmour pulled a J-turn and hit the gas even harder than before. The workers were ready for him on this run. They got clear in good time then pelted the car with soda cans and pieces of trash as it sped by. Gilmour ignored them. He didn't slow down until he was close to the gap at the end of the containers they'd climbed on earlier.

'Stop here,' Reacher said. 'Right in the center. No one gets in or out.'

Gilmour hit the brakes, and as they entered the gap they saw that another vehicle had already gotten in. The black panel van Reacher had just seen. It was stopped nearer the red container than the fence. Fumes were streaming out of its exhaust. Its passenger door was open and a guy was on the other side, between it and the container. He was wearing a generic olive-green military-style uniform, and he was dragging a woman along the ground by her foot. She was dressed all in black. Her hood was up, hiding her face, but strands of graying hair were escaping at one side.

The guy heard the car. He dropped the woman's foot and went for his gun. Reacher was a beat ahead of him. He had already grabbed the pistol from Gilmour's waistband and opened his door. The guy turned, lining up on the windshield. Then he hesitated for a second. He was confused. His first thought had been to shoot the driver, Gilmour, but Reacher's movement threw him.

Reacher did not hesitate. He aimed and pulled the trigger. He'd been going for the guy's center mass but the car hit a rut in the concrete and sent the shot high. It caught him in the throat rather than the chest. The force knocked him back a pace, then his knees gave way. Gravity took over and dragged him down. He hit the ground legs apart, arms by his sides, blood pulsing and spraying from the tear in his neck like an ornamental fountain.

Gilmour hit the brakes. Reacher jumped out. He took a step toward the van and raised the gun. The van's rear wheels started to spin. Smoke rose from the concrete. The van was stationary for half a second, then it lurched forward. It was heading straight for the fence. It adjusted slightly to avoid a concrete post, then accelerated and plowed into the rusty mesh. It slowed a little, just for a moment. Then it burst right through. Reacher ran after it. He got to the boundary in time to see the van race away down the narrow street.

Gilmour was standing in front of the car, looking down at the two bodies, when Reacher turned back. He said, 'What the hell? You just shot a CIA agent. With my gun.'

Reacher shook his head. 'He wasn't CIA.' The arterial spray had dried up. The guy was clearly dead, but Reacher checked for a pulse in the intact part of his neck, anyway. He didn't find one, so he turned to the woman and pulled back her hood. The left side of her face was pointing upward. There was a fresh cut by her temple and an older scar on her cheek.

Gilmour stepped up alongside Reacher. He said, 'Kasselwood's here? Not in the truck. Decoy cargo, decoy driver. So she was just a thief after all. I've got to say, I'm a little disappointed.'

Reacher felt Kasselwood's neck, then he grabbed her zipper and opened the front of her hoodie. She was wearing a Kevlar vest. He said, 'She's still breathing. I guess she took a round, it knocked her down, the vest saved her life, but she hit her head when she fell.'

'Okay, and the guy? If he isn't CIA, who is he?'

'One of the original thieves. We screwed things up for Kasselwood, that's for sure, and the other guys walked away with the prize.'

Gilmour started toward the car. 'Then let's not be here when the CIA does show up.'

'Relax. The CIA's not coming. It's not involved. It never was.'

'How—'

'I broke my second rule of army life. *Never trust the intel*. The shipment wasn't being smuggled *by* the CIA. It was being smuggled by someone who was *ex*-CIA. Someone who'd left recently enough to know the up-to-date shipping codes.'

'Kasselwood was a Company woman?'

'We knew she was some kind of veteran. It was the VA that referred her to Dr Martin.'

'Right. It was. Okay, so what now?'

'I say we walk away. I was worried about something classified getting into the wrong hands, but what actually happened was some thieves ripped off a smuggler. I don't care about one set of assholes over the other. Do you?'

'I guess not.'

'All right, then. I'll call 911 once we're clear. The police can tidy up the mess.'

'What about the guy you shot? We don't want the police coming after us on his account.'

'Is the gun registered?'

Gilmour looked away. 'No.'

'Does it have sentimental value?'

'No. It's a gun.'

'Then we wipe it down and stick it in Kasselwood's hand.'

'She didn't do it.'

'She killed two other guys. Three, if you're right about your coworker.'

'That's not the same thing. Although, I guess she's no angel.' Gilmour turned and looked down at Kasselwood for a moment. 'Here's another thing I don't understand. It seemed like the original guys had bought her bogus message. Why else weren't they here at the start?'

Reacher said, 'I think they did buy it.'

'Then why show up when they did? What changed their minds?'

'It's not what changed their minds. It's who.'

'I don't follow.'

'You had a file at Dr Martin's office. Patten had a file. Who didn't?'

Gilmour thought for a moment. Then he said, 'Arlon James.'

'Remember Patten said she didn't understand the shenanigans to get James the job, because he was actually qualified for it? I think the guy Weaver sold the information to didn't have a computer person. He didn't have an HR person. He needed Weaver to recruit you and Patten to fill those gaps. But he did have someone who could work security. So he only used Patten to put James in place. Not to find him. Then, when we showed up this morning and told James that the message about the delay was bogus . . .'

'. . . He called his boss. His boss sent the guys in the van. Damn. And James has seen us. He can describe us to the police. Come on. Let's go.' Gilmour hurried toward the car.

Reacher said, 'Don't worry. James will be long gone by now.'

Gilmour slowed down. He said, 'I wonder if James knew what was taken. Aren't you curious about that? What could be worth all this effort?'

'It's not *what* was taken.' It was a woman's voice, wheezy and hoarse, low down behind them.

They turned and saw that Kasselwood had opened her eyes. She said, 'It's *who*.'

Kasselwood struggled to sit up. Reacher offered his hand but she batted it away, then noticed the body lying behind her. She said, 'You did that?'

Reacher didn't answer.

Kasselwood pointed at the hole in the fence. 'That's how they got away? Nice job, fellas.' She took a deep breath, winced, but managed to haul herself to her feet, keeping her weight on her left leg. She clutched her ribs and looked at Gilmour. 'You work at the scheduling office. You told them where to be. And when.' Then she turned to Reacher. 'I don't know who you are, but I don't need your help. Stay away from me. Both of you.'

Kasselwood gave them each one more scowl, then set off walking, threading past Gilmour's rental car and toward the terminal's main gate.

Reacher handed the gun to Gilmour then stepped across to the body. He said, 'Turn the car around. We need to stop Kasselwood. I'll be there in a second.'

Gilmour opened the driver's door. He said, 'How are you going to shut her up?'

Reacher started going through the dead guy's pockets. 'We need to talk to her first. She said *who* was taken. You saw the size of that crate. It could have been a child in there. Or a small woman. If human trafficking is going on here, we're not just walking away.'

THIRTY-THREE

Part of Morgan Strickland's rehab after he'd gotten blown up in Iraq was counseling. At their first session his therapist told him that the psychological recovery would be a harder row to hoe than the physical. He told him it would take longer. And he said it would be more important, too. Strickland was going to have to transition into a new role. He would no longer be on active duty. He would no longer be a soldier at all. The therapist told him that a key strategy for survival would be to redefine his identity. At the time, Strickland thought that was the biggest bunch of BS he had ever heard. Now, twenty years later, he had to accept that there was some truth to it. And if he was honest, he would have to admit that despite everything he had achieved with his company in the intervening decades, he still hadn't adapted all the way. That morning was a case in point. Instead of being at the port making things happen, he was left behind, stuck at the base, waiting for secondhand information. He couldn't focus. He couldn't plan. There would be no after-action report for him. There couldn't be if there'd been no action.

Strickland pulled and kicked at his couch until it flopped back down to form a cot, then he flung himself onto it. He couldn't lie still. Every cell was vibrating. The tension was destroying him. Not knowing what was happening was the worst part. If the operation were happening overseas, his tech guys could have extended their radio net to cover the port, but that wasn't possible at home. There were too many regulations. Too many rules standing in his way. He pulled out his phone, stared at it, and willed it to ring. After another ten minutes, which felt like ten hours, it finally did. The man on the line didn't identify himself. He just said, 'We have the woman. One KIA. Out.'

Strickland felt himself relax. He wasn't sure how his guys had managed to take a casualty carrying out such a straightforward mission, but strategically the loss was acceptable. To assess how it ranked financially, he would need more information. All he could do for the moment was hope that the guy on the phone hadn't been stupid enough to leave the body behind.

Kasselwood was in sight a hundred yards ahead. Gilmour resisted the urge to lean on the gas. There was plenty of time to catch up to her before she got close to the gate, and he didn't want to attract attention. He didn't want her ducking into any of the clusters of containers where she would be hard to ferret out. And he really didn't want any of the workers he'd already pissed off intervening on her behalf. That wouldn't work out well for anyone.

Reacher had scooped up the dead guy's gun and had brought everything else he found in his pockets. There was a spare magazine, which he kept. A phone, which he set aside for Gilmour to look at later. A bunch of keys. And a dog-eared leather wallet. The wallet contained $120 in cash, which Reacher took. It was a time-honored tradition, in his mind. Spoils of war. Then there were three credit cards. One ATM card. And a work ID. Reacher pulled it out and showed Gilmour. It was issued by an outfit called Strickland Security Solutions, Inc.

Reacher said, 'Ever heard of these guys?'

Gilmour shook his head. 'Probably assholes.'

'You think?'

They had closed to within ten feet of Kasselwood. Gilmour cruised past her, then coasted to a stop in the center of the channel between the stacks of containers. Reacher leaned back and opened the rear door. Kasselwood dodged around it and kept on walking, still clutching her ribs.

Reacher lowered his window and called after her. 'Let us give you a ride to the exit, at least. It'll be quicker. You're in pain. That's clear. Then you can hook up with your buddy, collect your pickup, and go from there.'

Kasselwood stopped. She stood still for a second, then turned and stalked back to the car. She climbed into the back seat, brushed her fingertips across the scar on her cheek, shut the door, and said, 'Fine. Let's go.'

Gilmour hit the switch that locked all the doors, then cut the engine. He took the gun from his waistband, turned to look at Kasselwood, and said, 'I have a question first. Don't lie, because I'll know. And what you should know is that this is a rental. It's under a false name. I could blow your head off right now and not even have to clean it up.'

Kasselwood looked straight back at him. She said, 'You have a question? Let's have it.'

'All right. Did you kill my coworker?'

Kasselwood held his gaze. Her voice was low and steady. She said, 'No. I did not.'

'You came to our office. You were looking for him. You were mad. Next thing, he's dead. Explain that.'

'I was frustrated, not mad. Someone had been snooping for information about the shipment I was bringing in. Obviously that was part of an attempt to steal it. I assumed he was the spy. But really it was you, using his ID?'

Gilmour nodded. 'You killed him because you thought he was spying on you.'

'No. I wanted to talk to him. I knew I had a leak. I assumed it was Dr Martin. I figured she'd gotten Zack Weaver to recruit the guy and they'd somehow planted him in the scheduling office. I wanted confirmation. So think about it. Killing him before I spoke to him would make no sense.'

'You already knew about Dr Martin and Weaver?'

'Only Dr Martin. I figured she must have been hooked up with some muscle, though. I didn't see her doing the dirty work herself.'

'You were a patient of hers?'

Kasselwood took a moment to reply. 'I was. Were you?'

Gilmour said, 'Briefly.'

'For long enough, evidently.' Kasselwood looked at Reacher. 'And you?'

Reacher said, 'What do you think?'

Kasselwood said, 'I'm guessing not. I'm not sensing much openness for personal growth. So, who are you? How are you involved?'

Reacher said, 'Stick to the topic. You killed Dr Martin. Why?'

Kasselwood was silent for a moment. 'That was an accident. Don't get me wrong. I'm not sorry she's dead. In other circumstances I would have been happy to put a bullet in her head. But yesterday was all about information gathering. I figured she had pieced together what I was planning and passed the details to a partner. I was pressing for that partner's name, but she wouldn't give him up. Not even when I threatened her. And believe me, after what I told her in our sessions, she knew what I was capable of. I worked for the Agency in Iraq, remember. I've done things I'm not proud of. If she could keep quiet in light of all that, I figured some kind of emotional connection must have been in play. A husband or a live-in lover or a kid. Someone she shared a home with, maybe. So I asked for her address. She freaked out, so I was obviously on the money. She tried to strangle me. And when that didn't work, she tried to run.'

'You couldn't allow that.'

'It would only have taken a second for her to warn him, if she'd gotten out of that office. He could have disappeared. I couldn't risk that. So I shot her. I didn't mean to kill her. I was trying to wing her, but hey. This isn't Hollywood.'

'So you went to her house.'

Kasselwood nodded.

'You found her partner. Weaver. And you shot him, too.'

'He shot himself, actually. I made him believe his wife was alive, to make him cooperate. I got what I needed. Then he figured out that I'd been lying to him. He had a hidden weapon that I'd missed. That was stupid of me. He got to it and used it.'

'*What you needed* being the name of the guy they sold you out to?'

'What? No. I already knew that.'

'Who is it?'

'An asshole called Morgan Strickland. You've probably heard of him. His outfit's been all over the news. He's gagging to invade Armenia with his gang of toy soldiers.'

'So what was the point of leaning on Weaver?'

'I needed to know how he was communicating with Strickland.'

'To send Strickland false information. To trick the guy.'

'You make it sound like I'm cheating on my homework. You have to understand the scale of operations here. Strickland literally has a private army. I'm up against him with one other person, plus a crew member we bribed on the ship. I can't go toe-to-toe, as much as I'd love to. I have to box clever. And I would have won if it hadn't been for you idiots sticking your noses in.'

'You had a hiding place in the container. The red one.'

'Obviously. I knew Strickland might not buy my story about the delay. Not all the way, anyway. But I hoped it would plant a doubt in his mind, at least. Cause him to second-guess himself. Then, if he was watching at the original time and he thought the crate was a diversion, he would check the container. If it looked empty, he might be convinced a little more easily than normal. He might go after the crate a little quicker. Then we'd have time to get out and slip away.'

'It must have been a small space.'

'Tiny. At the end opposite the open doors. I couldn't make it too big or the proportions would have given us away.'

'You were going to cut the fence. I saw the bolt cutters.'

'It was the obvious way out. But it all went to shit because I saw you come in. I figured you were one of Strickland's goons. I saw you pick up the crowbar, so I assumed you were going after the crate. We came out. You were gone. And *bang*, Strickland's guys showed up. Tipped off by you, I now understand. Thanks for that. So how about we wrap this little chat up and get moving. A woman's been taken. She's in danger and I need to get her back.'

'She'd be safer with you?'

'Obviously.'

'Why is that? Softer bedsheets? Better clientele?'

'What? Wait. Are you suggesting . . . You are. All right. Get out of the car. Say that again. See what happens.'

'She must be pretty valuable for you to smuggle her in all alone. I thought you guys usually brought dozens of women over at a time. Economies of scale or whatever. There must be a lot of money at stake.'

Kasselwood sighed and acted like she was looking to the heavens even though the roof of the car was in the way. She said, 'I'm trying to stop a war and this is the bullshit I have to put up with?'

'Which war are you trying to stop?'

'The invasion of Armenia, obviously. The special military operation Strickland's pushing so hard for.'

Gilmour leaned in closer. He said, 'Look, maybe this Strickland guy is an asshole. Maybe war for profit is morally dubious. But do you really want Iran to get its hands on weapons-grade uranium? Is that going to make the world a safer place?'

Kasselwood rolled her eyes. 'Listen. There is no uranium. Iran has nothing to do with this. They're just a convenient bogeyman. The Nagorno-Karabakh separatists aren't even involved. They know nothing about it. You have to understand, the entire basis for the invasion is a scam. Strickland fabricated the whole thing, from soup to nuts. He made up the press reports. The eyewitness testimony. The social media posts. Everything. It's all a pretext so his company can make more money.'

'How do you know?'

'Because I know Strickland. I've been watching how he operates for more than twenty years.'

Reacher said, 'Who's the woman he's taken? Why is she so important?'

'Her name is Violeta Vardanyan. She's his star witness in the court of public opinion. And every word she's said on camera so far has been a lie.'

THIRTY-FOUR

Gilmour fired up the engine and continued to the exit, driving a little faster now. The Toyota was in the same place as before, still blocking the gate. The empty crate was still in its load bed. Four semis were lined up on the other side. And there was no sign of Arlon James.

Kasselwood climbed out of the car. The lead semi started to honk. She ignored it, crossed to the Toyota, and opened the driver's door. The woman who was dressed like her was still there. Her hood covered her face. Her right arm had been pushed through a gap in the steering wheel and her wrists had been cable-tied together.

Kasselwood said, 'You okay?'

The woman said, 'Get me the hell out of here.'

Kasselwood took out her knife and cut the ties. The other woman rubbed her wrists, pulled back her hood, tucked a loose strand of hair behind her left ear, and climbed down. Now that Reacher had a clear view he could see that she was a passable double for Kasselwood. Not perfect, but close. She was an inch shorter. A little narrower across her shoulders. Her hair was the same length, but a lighter color – chestnut brown – and it had no traces of gray.

The woman said, 'Is Violeta okay?'

Kasselwood shook her head.

'Damn it. Did Strickland get her?'

'It looks that way.'

'What are we going to do?'

'Get her back. Before it's too late.'

'How?'

'Good question. Where are the keys?'

'That security guy took them right after he trussed me up.'

'He left?'

'The minute after the bozos in the car figured out they'd been duped by the crate. Who are they, anyway?'

'I don't know their names. But it looks like we might have to play nice for a little while. At least till we get out of this place.'

Reacher, Gilmour, Kasselwood, and her lookalike – who was called Ellie Taylor – exchanged rapid introductions and agreed on a division of labor. Kasselwood and Taylor would wipe down the Toyota since they couldn't move it and their prints would be all over it. Reacher and Gilmour would keep watch for replacement security guards, law enforcement, or angry mobs of dockworkers.

The women moved fast. They buzzed around the pickup, rubbing every surface they might have previously touched with alcohol wipes that they kept in the glovebox. Behind them, dockworkers swarmed around the stacks of containers. Cranes and forklifts hoisted and lowered and loaded. Engines roared. Transmissions rumbled. Metal crashed against metal. Rubber squealed on asphalt. But no one paid any attention to the activity at the gate. The two small vehicles and the people working on them were lost in a sea of noise and motion.

When they were satisfied that the Toyota was safe to leave, Kasselwood and Taylor piled into the back of Gilmour's rental. Taylor said, 'How do we get out? We could maybe open the gate, but those trucks are in the way, and they can't get in. It'll take all afternoon to sort out that mess.'

Gilmour said, 'No problem.' He turned the car around, more sedately than the last time, and set off toward the far corner of the terminal. He kept his speed low, and the dockworkers hardly noticed. By now most of them had turned their wrath against a forklift driver who was rumored to be having an affair with the wife of one of the late-shift supervisors. Gilmour cruised past and looped around the end of the row of containers and into the enclosed space. Taylor caught sight of the body lying near the red container. She gasped and said to Kasselwood, 'Did you—'

Kasselwood said, 'Don't ask. He got what he deserved. That's all that counts.'

Gilmour steered a little to the right and bumped the car

through the gap that the panel van had torn in the fence. He paused at the street and said, 'Which way?'

Reacher said, 'Left.'

'Why?'

'It's a rule. When in doubt, turn left.'

Gilmour turned left. No one spoke until the car had covered another hundred yards, as if someone at the port might hear them. Then Reacher said, 'There's an easy way out of this, you know.'

Kasselwood said, 'We're not abandoning Violeta. She's done wrong, yes. But she was tricked into it, to some extent. She's come here to put things right. I promised to protect her, and I intend to do that. We need to help her, and not just for her sake. For the sake of the soldiers – the contractors – and the Armenians who will be killed if this invasion goes ahead. It's completely unjustified.'

Reacher said, 'I'm not suggesting we abandon anyone. I'm just pointing out, kidnapping is a federal offense. You should call the FBI. Let them deal with it. They have the resources and the expertise. It's dumb to ignore them.'

Kasselwood shook her head. 'We can't do that.'

'Why not?'

'Because Strickland has connections. Friends in high places. Taylor and I were at the Agency when I found out what Strickland was up to. I flagged it up the chain. Two nights later, a bunch of thugs were waiting in the parking lot for my building.' Kasselwood pointed to the scar on her cheek. 'See this? They didn't steal my purse. They didn't touch my car. They didn't take my keys and rob my apartment. They just cut me. It was a warning. So I quit. We both did. And now we need to take care of this our own way.'

'What makes you think Violeta's still alive to help? If I were Strickland, she'd be face down in the Patapsco with her throat cut.'

'That's possible, obviously. But I'd be surprised. The public face of the campaign Strickland has built is centered around Violeta. Journalists and politicians are starting to question it. If he has a chance to wheel her out in front of them and have her repeat her story – maybe even double down on the weakest parts of it – he won't want to miss that. If she cooperates, she'll be safe. If she doesn't, she probably has a day or two while he tries to persuade her.'

'How do you know her original story was fake? Maybe she was telling the truth then and is lying now.'

'No. I'm certain. When I saw the first video Violeta made I knew it was bullshit. I tracked her down in Turkey, where she was living at the time. I talked to her. Made her see who Strickland really was. How he was using her. It wasn't easy but I got her to trust me. She agreed to come to the United States and set the record straight. So now we need to figure out where Strickland's taken her. If she refuses to cooperate with him, I don't want to think about what he'll do to her. In case I haven't mentioned it, the guy's a twenty-four-karat asshole.'

'You don't know where his operation is based?'

'I know about the public-facing stuff. Where his corporation is registered. Where he pays taxes. Things like that. But he keeps the operational part under wraps. I guess he thinks it adds to his mystique.'

'All right, then let's figure it out. The guys who showed up this morning must have come from somewhere within a radius of maybe thirty miles.'

'How do you know?'

'Because of the time it took from us talking to Arlon James, the security guard, and them arriving.'

'Okay, but a circle with a thirty-mile radius? That's, what, about twenty-eight hundred square miles. Needle, meet haystack.'

'Not quite that large. Some of it'll be sea. But we can narrow it down. He's going to hold her somewhere private. Probably isolated. Probably somewhere that he owns or leases, to avoid the public walking in on them or hearing her scream if he gets physical or she cries for help. And it'll be a place where there's a lot of limestone. A quarry, maybe. Or a mine. Or even a supply depot for contractors.'

'How do you figure limestone?'

'The guy I shot had little white fragments in the cleats of his boots. It looked like limestone to me. There was the same color powder around the cuffs of James's pants. And around the wheel arches of their van.'

'You're sure it was limestone? What are you, a geologist?'

'No. But I've seen limestone before and this looked the same. Have you got anything better?'

Kasselwood didn't answer.

'It doesn't hurt to look.' Taylor tucked a strand of hair behind her ear, pulled out her phone, and started to google. A moment later she said, 'I've got something.' She showed Reacher and Kasselwood. It was a news report, three years old, about a military contractor that had taken a lease on a decommissioned quarry. The idea was to use it for vehicle storage between deployments, according to the reporter. A photograph showed the first batch of Humvees that had arrived, looking shabby in faded Desert Tan and parked in a ragged line at the base of a cliff.

Kasselwood enlarged the image. She squinted at it for a moment, then said, 'No. Sorry, Ellie. Look at the vehicles. There are logos on the doors. They're like some dumbass medieval coat of arms. The text is too small to read, but I've seen the design before. It belongs to United Allied, which is run out of Florida by a pretentious prick named de Zerbi. It's not connected to Strickland's outfit.'

Gilmour said, 'Could Strickland have taken the site over from these other guys?'

Taylor took her phone back. She said, 'I'll find out,' and started tapping away at the screen again.

Kasselwood brushed the scar on her cheek with her fingertips then turned to Reacher and said, 'You thought I was a pimp or something. What gave you that impression?'

Reacher said, 'You smuggled a woman into the country in a box, then talked about her being taken from you like she was a piece of property.'

'She wasn't in the box the whole way from Turkey. Just the last couple of hours so that we could run the decoy.'

'You're a true humanitarian.'

'What did you think I was doing before you knew about Violeta?'

'We thought you were trying to rip off the CIA.'

'*Rip off* the CIA? What had you been smoking?'

'Gilmour recognized the code you used on the custom forms. We assumed it was a covert shipment.'

Kasselwood looked at Gilmour and said, 'You recognized the code?'

Gilmour nodded.

Kasselwood said, 'How?'

'I'm Military Intelligence. Retired.'

'Oh. Well, that'll do it, I guess.' She turned back to Reacher. 'And you?'

'Military Police. Also retired.'

'Well then. You're not bozos after all. Maybe we have a chance of making this work.'

THIRTY-FIVE

Morgan Strickland lay on his back and focused on his breathing. He visualized calming scenes, the way he had been taught in the hospital years before. He kept it up for twenty-five minutes – which felt like it was going to kill him – until finally there was a knock at his office door. He stood up. He straightened his shirt, moved to the other side of his desk, and called, 'Come in.'

The door opened and a woman stumbled into the room. She was stiff and apprehensive and had clearly been pushed forward by someone who was still in the corridor.

Strickland came out from behind his desk. He glanced at the woman, said, 'Excuse me for one minute,' and stepped past her and out the door.

A man was standing in the corridor. He was the one who'd driven the van to and from the port and had called

Strickland with his report. Strickland said, 'The man we lost. You brought his body home?'

The guy swallowed hard. His Adam's apple bobbed high in his throat. He took a breath, then said, 'That wasn't possible, sir. I had to leave him at the scene.'

Strickland clenched his fist and said, 'Wasn't possible?'

'There was no alternative, sir. I was under fire. Sustained fire. If I had stayed, even for another minute, I would have been unable to guarantee my mission objective, which was the safe extraction of Violeta Vardanyan.'

A goofy expression spread across the guy's face. Strickland wondered if it was his idea of confidence. Or determination. Strickland thought it made him look like a clown. He certainly spoke like one. *Guarantee his objective?* There was no guarantee the guy could find his own ass with a flashlight and a mirror, Strickland thought. He wanted to slap the stupid look off his face. He wanted to see him in a body bag. He wanted . . . He forced himself to calm down. It wasn't the guy's fault he was second-rate and all the competent operators were already deployed. It wasn't his fault that he didn't know the bigger picture, or how much money he had wasted that morning. Strickland made a mental note to prepare a story for the police when they found the body. He'd have to throw the dead guy under the bus, of course. Claim he was part of some unrelated conspiracy. That would be tough on the guy's reputation. Hard for his family to swallow. But that was too bad. It was the cost of failure.

Strickland turned back to the guy and said, 'Let me see if I have this straight. Kathryn Kasselwood had you pinned down under sustained fire. Both of you. One woman.'

The guy shook his head. He said, 'No, sir. Kasselwood was already down. Two other guys were firing. She must have brought hired help.'

'Kasselwood was down? Are you sure?'

'I saw her go down.'

'Down, as in dead?'

'There's no doubt about it, sir. Tim put a round – a couple of rounds – into her and was recovering her body when these other two guys appeared.'

Strickland allowed himself a tiny smile. If Kasselwood was dead, that meant a major thorn was gone from his side. He reached out and slapped the guy on the shoulder, and said, 'All right, then. Good job. You're dismissed.'

Violeta Vardanyan was standing in the center of his office when Strickland walked back in. She was staring straight ahead at the blank wall. Her face was expressionless, like a mannequin's. Strickland was relieved she was there. He was glad the original schedule had held after all. The extra day before the meeting with Mark Hewson could be invaluable if there were any issues to iron out, and so far, Vardanyan didn't seem very cooperative. Not at all like she'd been the last time they'd met, near the border between Turkey and Armenia. He wondered what kind of poison Kathryn Kasselwood had been pouring in her ear. He studied Vardanyan's face, searching for a clue as to what she was thinking, but came up dry.

Strickland forced a smile onto his face, walked around to his side of the desk, and sat down. He said, 'Violeta, I'm sorry for the unconventional mode of transport and the drama at the port. I'm glad you made it through safe and sound. And now that you're here, I'll make sure you have everything you need for as long as you're my guest.'

Vardanyan didn't reply. Her gaze didn't shift from the wall.

'I'll make sure you're well looked after, but I do need something in return. Two things, in fact. First, I want you to sit down with another important visitor. Mr Hewson, who works at the Pentagon. He has the power to sign off on our operation but he'll only do that if he believes your story. I need you to tell him the same things you already told me about the separatists helping Iran. Exactly the same things. And after that, I need you to make another video. We don't have to do that right away, though. You'll have a day or two to learn the script, like last time.'

Vardanyan remained silent. She didn't move a hair.

Strickland said, 'Do we have a problem, Violeta?'

Vardanyan looked at him and said, 'I don't have a problem. You do. Because I'm not your puppet any longer. I won't do either of those things.'

Strickland took a breath. 'Think about what you're saying. Words like *won't*? They're not very helpful. The answer I'm looking for is, *Yes. Of course I'll do those two simple things for you in return for all the money you've paid me.*'

'If you want a ventriloquist's dummy, get someone else.'

'No one else will do, Violeta. The world has seen your face. Everyone has heard your voice. It has to be you. You have to keep going.'

Vardanyan looked away. She said, 'I won't do it.'

Strickland stood up. He lowered his voice and said,

'Violeta, you are going to. You can agree here, now, where it's warm and pleasant. Or you can agree somewhere else, later, where it's neither of those things. So take a moment. Consider your options. Then make the smart choice.'

'It makes no difference where you take me or when you ask me. The answer will be the same. No.'

'Are you sure? Because I'd hate to see you ... discomforted in any way.'

'Save your threats for someone you can intimidate. I won't lie for you anymore.'

'So be it.' Strickland took out his phone and hit a number on his favorites list. When the call was answered he said, 'Is the next bed ready? Good. I'll bring her there in a couple of minutes.'

THIRTY-SIX

Gilmour hit the brakes, pulled into the parking lot of a Target superstore, and coasted to a stop in a space that was well away from any other motorists. He said, 'This is crazy. We can't just drive around the city all day. We need a plan.'

Reacher said, 'Call the FBI.'

Kasselwood said, 'No.'

Reacher said, 'Then we need to keep working on finding where Strickland took Vardanyan.'

Taylor brushed a strand of hair behind her ear and held up her phone. She said, 'I've found another possible place.'

Reacher and Kasselwood turned to look at her screen. It showed another news article. This one was older. It was from four years ago. And it was much lighter on detail. It talked about the sale of a run-down limestone mine to a veteran turned entrepreneur from Kansas. It didn't give the buyer's name. It didn't say what he planned to do with the place. It hinted at the possibility of providing storage for vehicles and other equipment due to the amount of underground space left by the exhausted mine workings. The reporter didn't seem confident that the place had much of a future, though. He wrapped up with a rumor that the previous owner had been forced to sell due to the cost of bringing the facilities up to code. He hinted at multiple violations. The worst was said to be that there was only one way in or out, which could be disastrous if there was ever a fire. The piece was accompanied by a single photograph, which showed the entrance. It was set into a flat, semicircular section of cliff face and it actually had two doors, but they were right next to each other. There was probably a single, joined-up space behind them. One was for people, which looked like a regular house door. And one was for vehicles, like the kind you see at auto shops, only large enough for giant trucks.

Kasselwood said, 'That write-up's not very conclusive.'

Taylor said, 'I kind of hope it's not the place, actually. Look at that approach. Imagine assaulting it. It's a massacre waiting to happen.'

Kasselwood took the phone and pinched the screen. She peered and squinted, then her head tipped back and she closed her eyes for a moment.

Taylor took the phone back to see what Kasselwood had found. She said, 'Damn it,' and passed the phone to Reacher.

Reacher said, 'I see two guys shaking hands. Some kind of a staged pose. The buyer and seller, presumably.

One guy has a missing arm. And an eye patch. He must be the vet. So what's the big deal?'

Kasselwood said, 'Strickland's Humvee was hit by an IED in Iraq. He lost his left arm and left eye.'

Taylor said, 'And guess where he was born. Topeka, Kansas.'

Kasselwood said, 'Sorry, Ellie. It has to be the place. I wonder what he uses it for now. I can't see Strickland settling for a glorified storage unit. Unless he keeps nuclear weapons down there. Or a bunch of Abrams tanks.'

'I wonder if he's changed it much since he bought it.' Taylor took her phone back and called up a mapping app. She entered the address for the old mine and her screen filled with a three-dimensional version of the view from the old news report. There was still essentially only one entrance, but the doors had been painted olive green. A straggly tree that had somehow taken root on a flat spot above the cliff face had grown a little taller. A few new antennae had sprouted. And the hard-standing area outside the mine's vehicle door had been extended so that more vehicles could park on it at the same time. 'Nothing radical's been done on the outside. I wonder about the inside.'

Kasselwood said, 'It's impossible to say from the picture.'

Taylor said, 'It's impossible to say, period. Because it's impossible to get inside. The four of us couldn't fight our way in. And we can't bluff our way in. Strickland knows you and me. And one of his guys saw Reacher and Gilmour this morning.'

Reacher said, 'There's no such thing as impossible.

Only inadequate planning. How long would it take to get to that place from the center of the city?'

Taylor checked her map. 'Twenty-five minutes, give or take.'

Reacher turned to Gilmour. 'The coffee shop where we met. Do you know its address?'

Gilmour nodded.

Reacher said, 'Good. Now give me your phone. I need to call Patten.'

Patten picked up on the first ring. She said, 'Nathan? What's going on?'

'It's Reacher.'

'Oh.' A hint of worry crept into her voice. 'Is Nathan okay?'

'He's fine. He's right here with me. Where are you?'

'In a deli not far from work. I'm not really hungry but I figured it would be best to stay away from the port for a while. The whole Seagirt Terminal was swarming with blue lights a little while ago.'

'I'm not surprised. Now, I need you to do something for me. I'm going to have Nathan text you the address of a coffee shop. Go there and look for a young kid called Kevin. He's a barista. Tell him the guy his boss is looking for is at the old Kinsella limestone mine. Say he has four buddies with him, all the same kind of size. They're only going to be there for another half hour, then they're heading to town. They're looking to cause trouble. Expensive trouble. And everywhere they do, they're going to leave a flier with the boss's face on it and a note saying he tried to stop them but couldn't.'

*

Gilmour pulled out of the parking lot and followed his phone's directions to the old mine. The physical terrain confirmed what the photographs had suggested. The approach to the place was a defender's dream. That made it a nightmare for Reacher and the others. The only entrance was at the end of an arrow-straight, single-track dirt road originally designed for trucks. There was no cover anywhere along it for the last half mile, but even if there had been, the thick white clouds of limestone dust thrown up by any vehicle that drove on it would be a dead giveaway. Gilmour stopped the car three-quarters of a mile shy of the entrance and turned it around. He kept the engine running, ready for a fast getaway if the need arose. He rested his gun on the edge of his seat, next to his thigh. He surveyed their target with his binoculars, then handed them to Reacher.

Gilmour said, 'It looks worse in person. Like a bunker, or a U-boat pen. And it would be no better at night. There are LED floodlights all over the place. It probably has infrared sensors coming out the wazoo.'

Reacher handed the binoculars to Kasselwood. She studied the scene for a minute then rubbed her knee and said, 'I can see three different ways we could get in. The trouble is, they all call for equipment and resources we don't have and can't get.'

Taylor tucked a strand of hair behind her ear and said, 'Is it worth even trying? Maybe we should withdraw. Come up with a new plan. *Discretion is the better part of valor.*'

Kasselwood said, 'There's no time. If Violeta is in there . . .'

Reacher said, 'We'll get in.'

'Are you sure your diversion will work?'

'I'm sure.'

'Who is this *boss* you sent a message to?'

'His name's Kelleher. He's a local asshole.'

'How's he connected to Strickland?'

'He isn't. I just happened to bump into some of his flunkies a couple of days ago. I guess I rained on their parade, a little bit. Kelleher's been bugging me ever since. I figured this was a chance to make up for the aggravation.'

'If you're sure, why is no one here?'

'They'll come.'

'When?'

'Soon enough.'

Five minutes ticked by. Ten. No one left the cave. No one approached it.

Reacher turned to Kasselwood and said, 'Tell me about Vardanyan. How did she get hooked up with Strickland?'

'You can't just turn to the end of that story. You have to start at the beginning. With Strickland.'

'Okay.'

'That'll take a while.'

'You got anything better to do right now?'

Kasselwood gazed out the window for a moment, then turned back and said, 'I've known Morgan Strickland for more than twenty-six years. We went through Basic together. Deployed together a bunch of times. I was in our barracks in Iraq when word came through that he'd been hit.'

'He was on patrol?'

'That was the official story. It's not true.'

'So what happened?'

'First of all you've got to understand a bit about Strickland. He's smart. He's creative. He's determined. But most of all, he's a man in a hurry. You've served. You know the army. You know what a bad combination that can be. Strickland was always butting heads. He had ideas. Good ideas, usually. Sometimes they got implemented. But even when they did, it was never fast enough for him. He was always pestering our CO to push things through. He got to be a real pain in the ass. People started calling him BBFM. Bigger, Better, Faster, More.'

'How did he take that?'

'He didn't care. He just did his thing, right up until '03, when we wound up at a base linked to Camp Ashraf, near the Iranian border. It was early in the war and the rules of engagement were still pretty much gold-plated. First and foremost was that we could not engage the enemy unless he or she presented a clear and present danger. That was taken to mean they had to be armed, which no doubt sounded great on paper in someone's office at the Pentagon or during an ass-covering session in whatever committee in Congress was meddling at the time. But on the ground it was a disaster. It was a gift to the insurgents. Take their mortar crews. We got hit every night, without fail. And there was nothing we could do about it. The mortar operator stayed under cover where we couldn't get to him, but his spotter could stand around in plain sight, calling in the targets on his cellphone. He was the one doing the real damage and everyone knew it, but if he wasn't holding a gun, we couldn't touch him.

We had to watch him, taunting us, as his buddy blew the shit out of our barracks.'

'I remember reading about that at the time. Caused a lot of bad feeling.'

'And a lot of unnecessary casualties. So, as you might have guessed by now, being forced to abide by such a dumb rule didn't sit well with Strickland. He came up with an idea. He wanted to track the cellphone use of the spotters in real time, which we had the ability to do. If we could show they were talking to the mortar operators during an attack, it would be reasonable to assume they were providing updates on range, bearing, etc. Then it would also be reasonable to class their phones as weapons.'

'Then you could take them out.'

'Exactly. Strickland's idea was sent up the line and then, as usual, it got bogged down in the weeds. The brass spent every day weighing the optics and debating the politics, and our guys spent every night getting their asses blown off. So Strickland put pressure on our CO. He said if the method was good enough for General McChrystal and the Special Forces guys to pinpoint targets for their nightly snatch squads, it was good enough for us. Hewson agreed – Hewson was our CO back then – and the rule went into effect. It was unofficial, but everyone figured the brass would catch up one day.'

'I'm guessing this story doesn't have a happy ending.'

'You're right. A few things went off the rails. First, a soldier filed a complaint. The new rule made sense and it saved lives, but technically it was illegal. There was no getting away from that. Nothing happened at that point.

I don't have any proof, but I'm pretty sure Hewson torpedoed the complaint. Then a week later a spotter was out in the open, calling in targets on his cell. The connection to the mortar operator was confirmed and a sniper was given the green light. He took the shot. Visibility was good. There was no wind. No rain. Range was minimal. He would miss that shot one time out of a million. And that day was the one time. He had dirty ammo, he was tired, distracted, I don't know. But he did hit something. A passing car. A civilian vehicle with eight members of the same family on board. It flipped, slid into a residential building, caught fire, then exploded. There were thirty-two dead in total.'

'Then the shit hit the fan.'

'Not immediately. Hewson fought like crazy to keep a lid on it. It was ultimately his ass in the sling, after all. But the deaths and the cover-up didn't sit well with the soldier whose previous complaint had gotten quashed. She decided to break the chain of command. Blow the whistle. Strickland found out about that. He heard she'd taken a Humvee and was heading to Camp Victory. Word was she had reached out to General Jacoby himself. So Strickland jumped in another Humvee and set off after her. What happened in the end, no one really knows. It looked like Strickland caught up to her. Then, whether his breathing down her neck was a factor, or whether it was just bad luck, she triggered a roadside IED. She was closer, so she took the brunt of the explosion. She didn't make it. Strickland did. His injuries you know about.'

'The brass should have acted faster. They should have approved Strickland's idea.'

'They should have. But they didn't. So Hewson should have stood firm. Not jumped the gun. And the rest of us? We knew the law was getting broken. I knew. I could have tried to stop it, but I didn't. Were lives saved? Yes. I'm sure. But how many? There's no way to know. Enough to balance out the thirty-two civilians and the whistleblower who lost theirs? Is there even an equation for something like that?'

THIRTY-SEVEN

Gilmour held up his hand for silence.

'Can you hear that?' he said.

There was a sound in the distance. Car engines. More than one. They were growing louder. Heading their way. Gilmour took his binoculars and scanned the horizon. He said, 'There they are. Four pickups. Two SUVs. Incoming, less than a minute.'

Kasselwood scooted over to the center of the back seat. Reacher tipped the passenger seat down so that it was almost flat. He watched the growing dust cloud drift closer and when he could see the chrome on the lead truck's grill glinting in the sunshine, he ducked down out of view. The dust cloud caught up to the car. The light through the windows grew dimmer and Reacher heard the convoy of vehicles rumble past. Gilmour waited thirty seconds then dropped the car into drive.

He pulled away slowly, made a U-turn, and started up the road toward the mine. Reacher pulled himself a little more upright and risked a glimpse out the windshield. He could see the trucks – three Fords and a Chevy – and the SUVs – both Grand Cherokees – up ahead. They had reached the mine entrance and had fanned out in a rough semicircle facing the vehicle entrance. People were getting out. All of them were men. They were all different ages. Reacher could see guys who looked to be in their twenties, all the way up to some who must have been in their sixties. There was no unifying theme in terms of height or weight or hairstyle or clothing, but they were all carrying weapons. Reacher could see ball bats, pickax handles, nightsticks, telescopic batons. One guy had a length of two-by-four with a bunch of nails sticking out of the business end.

Gilmour was driving smoothly, trying not to attract attention. When they were fifty yards from the mine he coasted to a stop. He opened his door and slipped out. Behind him, Taylor did the same. They swapped places – Taylor behind the wheel, Gilmour in the back. Then Taylor rolled the car forward again. She tacked it onto the left-hand end of the semicircle of vehicles, just a little ahead of a battered blue F150. It had a huge dent in the rear quarter panel and instead of fixing it, the owner had a stuck a Road Runner decal at the deepest part of the cavity.

The mob was getting loud now. Not in the organized, chanting way that you get at political rallies. This sound was more primal. Sinister. Threatening. The men were milling around, circling, approaching the mine's doors, then ebbing back, re-forming, and flowing forward again like an angry sea. Even from inside the car Reacher could feel the tension in the air, like it was full of gasoline vapor. The tiniest spark would ignite the whole thing.

One of the younger guys moved up to the vehicle door and prodded it with the end of his bat. He yelled, 'Come out. All five of you. We know you're in there.'

Another voice picked up on it. 'Out. Out.'

An older guy ran forward and smashed his ax handle against the door. 'Out. Out.'

Two more people stepped forward and started whaling on the door. Three more.

Then Reacher saw what he'd been waiting for. The mine's personnel door was opening. 'Now,' he said. He slipped out of the car and darted forward. Ahead, the mine door was halfway open. Gilmour was running to his left. Kasselwood was behind him. The door kept moving. It was three-quarters open. Fully open. A man burst out. He was wearing a black uniform with a helmet and face visor. He was holding a riot shield in one hand and a baton in the other. He turned away from Reacher, toward the crowd, and started swinging the baton. He was trying to crack heads. That was clear. Another uniformed guy ran out. Then another. And another. Reacher was still heading for the door. It was still wide open. A guy in the crowd recognized Reacher. He yelled something Reacher couldn't understand and aimed a punch at his head. Reacher brushed the guy's fist aside and kept moving. The door was swinging closed now. It was halfway there. Three-quarters. Reacher stretched out. The gap was narrowing. It was almost gone. He wasn't going to get to it in time. He started to slow, so as not to slam into the wall. Then the door swung open again, harder than before. It almost hit Reacher in the face. He caught it by the leading edge and held it steady. Another guy in uniform rushed out. He was breathing hard behind his visor and his stab vest wasn't buckled properly. He looked at Reacher, confused, then turned and dived into the mob, using his baton to clear a path toward his buddies.

Reacher went through the door first. Gilmour and Kasselwood were right behind him. After the mob scene outside they felt like they'd stepped into a monastery. The space was broad and tall and cool and quiet. It had a whitish-gray ceiling and walls, and a smooth, dusty floor. It was the mouth of the central road that had been built to carry giant trucks down to the lower level. That made it the oldest part of the mine. Marks left by pickax blades were visible on some of the surfaces from the days when the digging was done by hand. Some of the old miners had carved their initials into cracks and crevices. Redundant cable conduit still spanned parts of the ceiling from when Strickland had added better lighting after he bought the place. He had built a security barrier and converted the original reception booth on the left into a guard post. And he had added another guard post on the right-hand side of the vehicle door.

There was a guard on duty in the booth. He pulled his sidearm and rushed out. He said, 'Stop. Step back. You are not auth—'

Kasselwood hit him in the face. It was a ferocious punch. A roundhouse, perfectly timed, with all her weight behind it. The impact knocked the guy backward. He stayed upright for a second, teetering against the wall, then he sank down and flopped forward onto his face. Kasselwood took the guy's gun, then checked that he was still breathing.

The guard from the opposite post had also drawn his weapon. He took a step into the road, then raised it and moved into a two-handed marksman's stance. Reacher started moving toward him.

The guard said, 'Stop. No closer.'

Reacher raised his arms and took another step. He said, 'Hold on. We just want to talk.'

The guard lined the gun up on Reacher's chest. 'No closer.'

Reacher slowed a little, but kept moving. He said, 'You don't understand. There's a riot outside, and—' Reacher sprang forward. He covered the last six feet with one step and grabbed the guard's right wrist. He shook it, hard, breaking the guy's double grip, then he pushed up so that the gun was pointed at the ceiling. He spun the guy around, clamped his right forearm across the guy's throat, and began to apply pressure. The guy's windpipe started to collapse. He couldn't breathe. He started to panic. He dropped the gun and clawed at Reacher's forearm with both his hands. He tried to stamp on Reacher's feet. Kick backwards into his knees. He wriggled and twisted and writhed. Reacher pushed his left arm out then bent it up at the elbow. He trapped his own right wrist and pulled back, adding to the pressure on the guy's throat. The guy thrashed harder for a moment, like a fish on a line as it neared the shore, then his body went limp. His head nodded forward and his lips began to turn blue.

Reacher relaxed the pressure and after a second the guy's breathing came back, rough and ragged. His body stiffened and right away he started to struggle again. Reacher pulled his forearm back, hard, but just for a second. Then he said, 'Listen carefully. You have a decision to make. Do you want to live or die? Nod your head once if you want to live.'

The guy nodded one time.

Reacher said, 'I need some information. A woman arrived today. Violeta Vardanyan. Is she still here?'

Reacher eased the pressure on the guy's throat a little more to allow him to talk.

The guy's voice was harsh and raspy. He said, 'Don't know.'

'You saw her arrive?'

'Yes.'

'Did you see her leave?'

'No.'

'Where are special visitors usually taken?'

'Conference room.' The guy gestured vaguely toward the other side of the road. 'Then they get the tour.'

Reacher said, 'Where are they taken if they're here for a meeting? Not a tour.'

'Don't know. That's above my pay grade.'

'Guess.'

'Mr Strickland's office, probably.'

The guy turned his head to the side and dropped like a dead weight, trying to slide out from under Reacher's forearm. But he was too slow. Reacher saw it coming. He clamped down, trapping the guy, then increased the pressure on his throat. He kept his grip firm and steady. The guy struggled for a moment, weakly now, then his head pitched forward again and his lips turned a darker shade of blue.

Reacher carried the guy he'd incapacitated across the road and bundled him into the guard post. It was a cramped, rectangular space with a solid door and a chest-high sliding window. Inside, there was a shallow counter made of unfinished plywood, a fabric-covered office chair with no arms, and a file cabinet with two drawers. There was a clock on the wall, which Reacher noticed was a minute slow, and next to that was an old-school whereabouts board. It was divided vertically into two halves. The left side had a list of names embossed in gold on a black background. A token in a horizontal slot next to each name could slide back and forth. It was moved to the left to show that the person was in, and to the right to show they were out. The other half was just a regular whiteboard. Seven names were scrawled on it in fading blue marker, along with one pair of initials in the top right-hand corner.

   Reacher leaned his head out of the guard post door and said, 'Guys. Come see this.'

   Of the permanent names on the left of the board only one was marked *In*. Morgan Strickland.

   'The senior staff are thin on the ground,' Gilmour said.

   'They'll all be deployed,' Kasselwood said. 'Waiting to slip the leash and rake in more cash for Strickland Security.'

'Seven handwritten guys,' Gilmour said. 'These two sleeping beauties, and the five mixing it with the mob outside?'

Reacher said, 'Makes sense. Then there are the initials. VV.'

Kasselwood said, 'Violeta. It has to be. Too much of a coincidence otherwise. I guess whoever wrote it was being discreet. Or mysterious.'

'Or maybe he's bad at spelling,' Gilmour said.

Reacher said, 'So until the guys with the hats and bats come back in – if they come back, and don't wind up in the hospital – we have the numerical advantage. Strickland has the territorial advantage. He knows the ground but he doesn't know we're here, so he has no reason to hide. Yet. The guard said guests get taken to his office, so let's try that first. If we can find it. Sound good?'

Gilmour and Kasselwood both nodded.

Reacher said, 'Okay. Let's get these two cuffed and gagged, then move out.'

THIRTY-EIGHT

The main level of the old mine was seventy feet below the surface. The gradient of the access road had been capped at five degrees to give the old-time trucks that used to carry the limestone a fighting chance of climbing in and out. That made the walk from the entrance to the first open cavern a hair over eight hundred feet. The walls and ceiling of the shaft that carried the road had been hewn by hand. That had left the whitish-gray surface with a rough pitted complexion that reminded Reacher of pictures he'd seen of the Apollo landing sites on the moon.

The space around the first pair of pillars they came to when the road flattened out was a parking area. It would normally be used for Humvees, Reacher guessed, based on the track width of the tire marks in the layer of gray dust. There were no Humvees there that day. They were presumably overseas, waiting to be used in the invasion of Armenia, if that ever happened. Instead there was a cluster of older domestic pickups on one side – some immaculately cared for, some on the verge of rusting to pieces – and a dark-blue Tesla on the other, with the license plate MS1. Morgan Strickland's personal vehicle, Reacher guessed.

Beyond the Tesla was a door set into a limestone wall labeled Conference Room One. Reacher opened it, found a light switch, and took a look inside. Right away he called for the others to join him. The center of the room was taken up with a rectangular table that was surrounded by steel-and-chrome chairs, but Reacher wasn't interested in the furniture. Two of the walls were covered with giant posters showing scenes from the company's training zones. Each one featured a smiling young man or woman in uniform, swinging on a rope or climbing through a window or scrambling up a sand dune, but Reacher wasn't interested in advertisements, either. It was the display on the third wall that had grabbed his attention. It was divided into three sections. There was a map of the complex in the center. A list of the complex's specifications and facilities on the left. And a table on the right comparing Strickland Security's strengths with the US Army's. Reacher was tempted to rip that one down and throw it in the trash, but he resisted. He focused on the map instead. Gilmour came up alongside him and took a picture of it with his phone. It showed that half the total area was taken up by the training zones. The rest was shared between locker rooms, a mess hall, offices, and machine rooms.

Kasselwood stepped between Reacher and the map. She said, 'I think we're looking at two likely scenarios. Violeta's cooperating with Strickland – or at least pretending to. Or she's not. If she's cooperating, she'll be somewhere nice. Which would be what? The guard thought the offices. Strickland has a fancy ride back there. Maybe he splashed out on his workplace, too.'

Reacher said, 'And if she's not cooperating?'

Kasselwood said, 'Somewhere uncomfortable, I guess. What do you think? A machine room, maybe? Somewhere hot, or noisy? Or cramped, where she can't stand or sit?'

Gilmour said, 'Or a latrine? That's always a favorite.'

Reacher said, 'Let's assume she's playing it smart. We'll stick to the plan. Try the offices first.'

There were three offices in the complex, lined up one next to the other. Strickland's, then McClaren's, then Moyes's. If the whereabouts board in the guard post was accurate, the second two would be empty, but Reacher listened at each of their doors, anyway. He heard nothing, so he knocked. He got no reply, so he moved on to Strickland's. There was no sound from inside there, either, and no answer to his knock, so he barged the door with his shoulder. It barely moved, so he changed tack. He turned around, raised his right leg, then drove it back, slamming his heel into the door just to the side of the lock. The frame gave way, showering the inside of Strickland's office with fragments of wood, and the door swung all the way open. Reacher looked inside. He saw a desk with an iPad lying on it, a giant monitor, and an old-school In/Out tray. There was a chair and a cot. But no sign of

Vardanyan. He busted open the other two offices, just in case. McClaren's was sparse and tidy. Moyes's was cluttered and chaotic. Vardanyan wasn't in either of them.

Reacher said, 'I guess she's not cooperating.'

Kasselwood said, 'Oh God, I hope she's all right.'

Gilmour called up the picture he'd taken of the map and they worked their way around, checking every area they thought a person could be confined in. They moved fast but they were thorough. They looked in, on, and under anything that could be used as a hiding place. They called on all their years of experience. Reacher, at finding people. Gilmour, at hiding people. Kasselwood, at hiding the remains of people. But after an hour they were back outside Strickland's office with nothing to show for their efforts.

Kasselwood said, 'We've seen no sign of Strickland, either, which is weird. Do you think they're still here? Maybe he's taken her somewhere.'

Gilmour said, 'His car's still here.'

Reacher said, 'It's more likely they're here together, someplace we haven't looked yet.'

Kasselwood said, 'Like where?'

Reacher said, 'The training zones.'

'Why would he take her there?'

'Plenty of reasons. Desert zone – bury her up to her neck in sand. Jungle zone – drop her in a pit or dangle her in a cage. Urban zone – shove her in a leaking sewer pipe. Mountain—'

'Okay, I get it. Let's get over there. But I'm telling you now, if Strickland's doing something gross with her, twenty-six years of . . . *acquaintance* aren't going to count for shit.'

Reacher led the way from the offices toward the training zones, but when he got to a spot where they needed to make a sharp left, he stopped. Gilmour stepped up alongside him and pointed. He said, 'It's that way.'

Reacher said, 'I know. But what's that doing there?' He gestured straight ahead. The bottom inch of a metal chair leg was peeking out from behind a limestone pillar fifty yards away.

'No idea.'

'Is there supposed to be anything down there?'

Gilmour took out his phone and pulled up the picture he'd taken of the map. He said, 'No. There should be empty space all the way to the boundary wall.'

Kasselwood said, 'Maybe someone's hiding out down there. Dodging kitchen duty or something?'

Reacher said, 'Let's find out.'

There wasn't one chair at the end of the corridor. There were two. And they were set outside a structure that looked like an odd kind of cage. It was rectangular, sixty feet long by twenty feet wide by eight feet tall, and its walls were made of steel mesh over shiny insulated panels. It had a metal door with no handle. Next to it there was a keypad.

Kasselwood said, 'What the hell is this place?'

Gilmour said, 'Looks like a storage facility.'

Reacher said, 'It's no ordinary store.' He pointed to a pair of heavy-duty electrical conduits that dropped down from the roof and snaked into the room through a hatch in the ceiling. 'There's some major equipment in there.' Then he pointed to the chairs. 'And it's guarded most of the time. Look at the floor. The chair legs are wearing channels in it.'

Kasselwood said, 'Where are the guards now? Is the place abandoned?'

Reacher shook his head. 'It looks new. My guess is the guards are outside. They got called away when the mob attacked.'

Gilmour said, 'Maybe Vardanyan's in there.'

Reacher said, 'One way to find out.'

Gilmour pointed at the keypad. 'What about the code? It could take all afternoon to crack it.'

'Maybe.' Reacher crossed to the metal door, took hold of the keypad, and wrenched it off its mounting. Four wires were sticking out. Reacher selected two and touched their exposed ends together. The door gave an audible *click*. 'Or maybe not.'

The gun Reacher had taken from the guard at the entrance was tucked into his waistband. He took it out, held it ready, and shoved the door. It swung open a quarter of the way, then immediately slammed back. Reacher jammed it with his foot, then shoved again, harder. The door hit something. Reacher heard a groan. He pushed again then stepped into the room.

Chill air hit Reacher in the face. He ignored the sensation and focused on a man who was backing away from him. He was wearing a heavy coat. One sleeve hung empty, and a patch covered a missing eye.

Reacher said, 'Strickland.'

Strickland didn't answer.

Gilmour stepped through the door, followed by Kasselwood.

Gilmour said, 'What is this place? An infirmary?'

Both of the room's long walls were lined with metal cots. There were fifteen on each side. Each had a crisp white pillow and a red blanket pulled tight. Four of the cots were empty. One was occupied by a woman. Twenty-five were occupied by men.

Kasselwood said, 'Morgan?' She took a step forward, then pivoted toward the woman in the bed. 'Oh my God – Violeta? Are you all right?'

Reacher said, 'It's not an infirmary. Look again. All the men in here are dead.'

THIRTY-NINE

Gilmour looked at each bed in turn. All the men's eyes were closed. Their chests were not moving. Their skin was waxy and pale. Some had bullet wounds to the head. Some had shrapnel wounds. The outline beneath the blankets showed that some had lost arms, or legs, or both. And from the small amount of fabric that was visible between the top of the blankets and the men's chins, it was clear they were all wearing uniforms. Twenty-four looked to be a similar shade of washed-out green but the one at the end on the far side seemed to be darker, like it had never seen the sun.

The woman in the bed stared at Kasselwood and said, 'Are you all right? They shot you. I saw you fall.'

Strickland frowned. He said, 'I guess the reports of your death have been exaggerated. That's too bad.'

Kasselwood patted her chest and said, 'I was wearing a vest. I'm fine.' She glanced uneasily at the rows of bodies, then turned to Reacher and Gilmour and said, 'Guys, this is Violeta Vardanyan. Together we're going to stop a war.'

Strickland said, 'The hell you are.'

Kasselwood turned to Vardanyan and said, 'Come on. Let's get you out of here.'

Vardanyan said. 'I can't move. The asshole tied me down.'

Kasselwood moved closer and took out her knife. She pulled back the blanket and cut the ropes that were securing Vardanyan's left wrist and ankle to the bed frame. Then she moved to the other side and freed Vardanyan's right wrist and ankle.

Reacher looked at Strickland. He said, 'Why are you keeping these bodies here?'

Strickland didn't answer.

'Where did they come from?'

Strickland sneered, but he didn't speak.

Reacher took a step toward him. 'Who are they?'

Strickland said, 'Who are you?'

'I'm the one who's asking you a question. What's with these bodies?'

'Yeah? Well, I'm the one who's not answering.'

Kasselwood said, 'It's freezing in here. And these bodies are creeping me out. Can you ask him your questions outside?'

Reacher looked at Strickland and said, 'Take your coat off.'

Strickland said, 'What?'

'The lady's cold. Take your coat off. Give it to her.'

'No.'

Kasselwood said, 'It's all right. I don't need it.'

Reacher kept his eyes on Strickland. He tucked the gun into his waistband and said, 'You can give it up. Or I can take it from you. Your choice.'

Strickland was silent for a moment, then said, 'Fine.' He unzipped the coat, slipped it off his shoulders, and let it fall to the floor.

Reacher kept looking at Strickland and said, 'Kathryn – how much rope is left on the bed?'

Kasselwood checked the bed frame and said, 'A couple of feet at each corner, if you adjust the knot.'

Reacher quickly glanced at the bed Vardanyan had been in. The blanket was missing. He saw that she had it wrapped around her shoulders like a cape. He looked back at Strickland and said, 'Go lie on her bed.'

Strickland didn't move. He didn't speak.

Reacher said, 'If I have to put you on the bed, I'm going to break both your legs.' He stepped back to give Strickland a clear path.

Strickland was still for a moment, then he slowly walked forward. He paused at the foot of the bed Vardanyan had been in, then moved down its far side. He made as if he was going to sit on it, then twisted the other way and flopped onto the next empty bed in line.

Gilmour was the closest to Strickland. He moved forward and reached out, ready to grab him and move him across to the bed with the ropes attached. Strickland sat up. He slipped his hand behind his back, then pulled it around to his front. He was holding something now. It was bright orange, with two spikes sticking out. He lunged at Gilmour's chest. Gilmour spun away but the spikes caught him in the side. They ripped through his clothes and stuck into his skin. His back arched. His whole body shook for a second. His eyes rolled back in his head. Strickland dropped the device and grabbed Gilmour's shirt, just below the collar. He jumped off the bed and dived toward the door, towing Gilmour after him. He took two more steps then let go of Gilmour's shirt. Strickland kept moving. Gilmour fell, sprawling, arms and legs out wide. Strickland was at the doorway. Reacher was moving, too. His right arm was stretched out, aiming for Strickland's back, closing in. His fingertips were an inch away. Then his foot tangled with Gilmour's leg. He stumbled. Almost lost his balance. Corrected. But by then Strickland was through the doorway. He pulled the door behind him. Reacher snatched it open. He dived through and caught sight of Strickland. He was running toward his office, full pelt. Reacher snatched the gun from his waistband and lined it up on Strickland's back. Then he lowered it and tucked it away.

Kasselwood was standing in the doorway. She said, 'You didn't shoot. Why not?'

Reacher said, 'I was thinking of you and Dr Martin. *This isn't Hollywood.*'

'Thank you.'

'For what?'

'Not killing him.'

'After what he did to Vardanyan? And what his guys did to you?'

Kasselwood shrugged. 'It's complicated.'

'I'm listening.'

Kasselwood brushed her scar with her fingertips. 'The soldier who made the complaint in Iraq? It wasn't just the rules of engagement she was upset about. There was a personal thing going on, too. She liked Mark Hewson. But she thought Hewson liked me.'

'Did he?'

'Maybe. Nothing ever happened between us but the woman was still jealous. *Hell hath no fury*, right? I think that's a big part of why she broke the chain of command. To get back at Hewson because of me. So I always felt like it was partly my fault that Strickland got injured. That's one reason I always kept track of him when he left the army.'

As soon as Gilmour was ready to walk, they set off toward the main road running through the mine. Kasselwood checked her phone and said, 'Message from Ellie. All clear out front. A bunch of guys, including the security guards, had to go to the hospital, so there'll be no problem getting out.'

Gilmour said, 'What about the guards we left tied up, at the entrance? We can't leave them there. They've seen our faces.'

Reacher said, 'I'll bring them down here. Show them the bodies. Ask if they want to be around when the police show up.'

Gilmour shivered. 'Should work. No one's going to tie themselves to that horror show.'

Reacher turned to Kasselwood and said, 'Tell Taylor you're on your way.'

Kasselwood said, 'Aren't you?'

'Not yet.'

'Why? You like it down here?'

'I want to know what Strickland's doing with the bodies. That whole situation is completely messed up.'

Kasselwood said, 'Violeta – did Strickland say anything about what he was doing in there?'

Vardanyan said, 'Nothing specific. Just that it was an unpleasant place. He thought being locked in it would make me cooperate.'

'With what?'

'He wants me to talk to some guy tomorrow morning. Repeat my *eyewitness account.* Then make another video.'

'Who's the guy?'

'Someone from the Pentagon. Mark Hewson?'

Kasselwood stopped walking.

Vardanyan said, 'What? Did I do something wrong?'

Kasselwood said, 'No. That's just not a name I was expecting. He's coming here?'

Vardanyan nodded.

Kasselwood said, 'Well, shit.'

No one spoke for a minute, then Gilmour said, 'Reacher, you're right about those bodies. Something's totally screwed up. Why is Strickland keeping them? Where did he get them from? He must have built that room specially. And why are they all in uniform?'

Reacher said, 'I don't know. But I'm going to find out.'

Gilmour said, 'I'll help.'

'You don't have to.'

'I know. But you helped me, and there's safety in numbers.'

Kasselwood looked at Vardanyan and raised her eyebrows. Vardanyan nodded. Kasselwood said, 'We'll stay, too.'

Reacher said, 'Really, guys—'

Kasselwood said, 'I turned a blind eye in '03. I learned my lesson. We're staying.'

Reacher decided to start with Strickland's office. He was hoping Strickland would be there to answer in person but when they arrived, the door was open, the lights were off, and the room was deserted. Reacher hit the light switch and they congregated around the desk, since that seemed to have more potential than the cot.

Kasselwood picked up the iPad. She said, 'I'll see what's in here.'

Gilmour looped around to the far side of the desk and sat down at the keyboard.

Reacher made a start on the In/Out tray. The upper tray was empty but there was a sheaf of stapled papers in the lower one. Reacher flicked through it. The pages were printed, and some had handwritten notes added to them. It was the draft of a contract between the Department of Defense and Strickland Security. Reacher started to skim through the sections and clauses. The whole thing seemed bizarre to him. A dry, arcane document in an underground room in Maryland, meaningless because it wasn't signed – but with the addition of a couple of squiggles of ink, it would translate into boots on the ground on the other side of the world. And inevitably dead bodies on the other side of the world. Reacher was more interested in a link to the dead bodies that were already here but he couldn't see one. He got to the last page. The one with the most scribbled notes. And suddenly everything came into focus.

Reacher said, 'That son of a bitch.'

Kasselwood looked up from the iPad and said, 'Found something?'

Reacher held the document with its last page facing out. He said, 'See that last paragraph? The title is "Special Compensatory Consideration." What do you think that means?'

Kasselwood shook her head.

Gilmour said, 'Damned if I know.'

Vardanyan was sitting on the cot. She didn't respond at all.

Reacher said, 'It means that if any of Strickland Security's contractors get killed in an action carried out on behalf of the US government, the president of the company – Morgan Strickland – gets a compensation payment. Not the family of the dead guy. Not the company. Strickland, personally.'

Kasselwood said, 'That's so wrong.'

Gilmour said, 'How much does he get per body?'

Reacher said, 'One million dollars.'

FORTY

Kasselwood said, 'This compensation clause. Is it a new thing?'

Reacher said, 'It must be. The contract isn't signed yet.'

Kasselwood said, 'That explains the refrigerated room. And why the bodies are in uniform. They must be KIAs from the last operation Strickland's company was involved in. Some minor fracas in Haiti, I think. The bodies weren't worth any money then. Now the contents of that room are worth twenty-five million dollars. That's why Strickland's faking the case for invading Armenia. He's going to pretend those guys got killed over there.'

Gilmour said, 'Will that work? Even refrigerated, those bodies aren't going to look like fresh ones. Surely any decent medic will see through that.'

'Define *decent medic*. I'm sure any doctor *could* tell the difference. And would over here, anyway. In peacetime. With their medical license at stake. But overseas? In the fog of war? With some of that million-dollar love to spread around? I can see it working. Once the shooting starts he'll take them over there. And I can see Strickland trying it, at least. I told you. He's a creative guy.'

'What about when the bodies come home? If even one family gets suspicious and calls for an autopsy . . .'

'The bodies won't come home. These are contractors. Not the US Army. There's no obligation to repatriate. It'll be in the operators' contracts. The company will have the right to dispose of the bodies as it sees fit.'

'That's grim.'

Reacher said, 'Strickland's not going to try this time. I'll see to that. I don't care how creative he is.'

Gilmour said, 'I can't believe anyone at the Pentagon would sign off on this.'

Reacher said, 'I bet Kathryn will believe it.'

Kasselwood said, 'Why?'

'The signature page is set up for Mark Hewson. I bet he's going to sign it tomorrow when he's here to see Vardanyan. I bet that's the plan, anyway.'

Gilmour said, 'How are you going to stop it?'

Reacher said, 'I'll find Strickland and tell him not to sign.'

'What if he won't listen?'

'I can be very persuasive.'

'How will you find him? Do you really want to search this whole place again? And what if he's snuck out of here?'

'I don't need to find him. I know where he'll be at

ten tomorrow. Right here, ready for his meeting with Hewson. I can wait for him to come to me.'

Kasselwood said, 'I have something to entertain you while you wait. Look at this.' She set the iPad at an angle on the desk so that Reacher and Gilmour could see it, then hit Play. 'They take videos of the recruits doing their assessments. And they are *terrible*.'

The screen showed a recruit tiptoeing into an empty garage. There was clutter strewn all around. The guy was looking left and right as he moved, but his pistol was pointing at the floor the whole time. He crept forward, looked the wrong way, and stumbled into a stack of paint cans. The stack collapsed. The cans crashed down and rolled away. The guy jumped and pulled the trigger. And shot his own foot. His whole boot turned scarlet. Fortunately for him, he had only been issued a paint gun.

Gilmour said, "Poor guy. He really put the *ass* into assessment."

Kasselwood said, 'I wonder what he's doing now. Flipping burgers somewhere, maybe.' She leaned over to stop the recording, but it ran on longer than when she'd watched it on her own. A grade box appeared, with a green 70 and the word *PASS*. 'No way. He passed? That's not possible. I mean, what kind of operation are they running here?' She picked the iPad up and started running through its menus. Then she leaned forward. A frown covered her face and she set the iPad back on the desk. 'This is bad. This is really bad. Look. This is the grading history screen. The system originally passed the guy automatically. Then someone called S. McClaren overwrote that score and failed him. Then Strickland reinstated the passing score.'

Gilmour said, 'That's weird. Strickland's the boss. You wouldn't think he'd want screwups in his company.'

'He would.' Reacher frowned. The tendons in his neck stood out like steel hawsers. 'A KIA is worth a million bucks to him now, screwup or not. And a screwup is more likely to wind up KIA.'

'Oh God.' Gilmour looked like he'd taken a gulp of rancid milk. 'He's deliberately picking guys who'll get killed so that he'll get paid more. That's disgusting.'

Kasselwood said, 'The guy we saw isn't even the worst one. Look at this.' She selected another video and set it playing. It showed a guy sidle up to a door inside a house. He went to open it but instead of pulling, he pushed. He struggled with it for a few seconds before he realized his mistake. Then he overcompensated. He pulled so hard that the door hit him in the face. He fell down, dropped his gun, then scrambled up and ran away without stopping to retrieve it.

Gilmour shook his head. 'Are these all from the same class?'

Kasselwood said, 'Looks like it.'

'Where do they find these guys? It's like a clown show. And how do they get accepted into their program? These last two – they must have written unbelievable application letters.'

'Let's see. Their whole history is on here.' Kasselwood swiped through a few screens, then she looked away and shook her head. She said, 'I can't even . . .'

Gilmour took the iPad, read what Kasselwood had

seen, then put it down on the desk. 'Holy hell.' He turned to Reacher. 'These guys didn't apply to join the program. They were invited. Strickland wrote to them. Guess what his pitch was?'

Reacher didn't wait for him to continue. He took the iPad and read for himself. 'Strickland was offering them a second chance. All these kids had tried to join the army and all of them had been kicked out of Basic.' Reacher slammed the side of his fist into the desk, denting its metal surface.

Kasselwood said, 'I've had it with him. Strickland. No more guilt. He's disgusting.'

Reacher was working hard to control his breathing. 'He is. But there's another problem here. How did Strickland know who had failed Basic?'

Gilmour said, 'Someone must have given him a list.'

Kasselwood said, 'Sold him a list. And I bet I know who.'

Reacher said, 'Hewson. I'll confirm it when I catch up with Strickland. If we're right, they're both going to have a very bad day.'

Kasselwood said, 'Hewson's going to have a very bad day indeed. If they're in bed together to that degree, you can bet it was Hewson who squashed the warning I sent from the Agency. Who sent the thugs to cut me.'

Vardanyan jumped up off the cot. 'Guys! I think there's a problem.'

Kasselwood said, 'What is it?'

Vardanyan said, 'I was alone in here for a while this afternoon. Strickland left me when he went outside to talk to the guy who ambushed us at the port. I stood and stared at the wall. That one.' She pointed to the wall behind the desk. 'It just hit me. Before it was blank. Look at it now.'

There was a poster on the wall. A four-by-three representation of Strickland Security's emblem, which was a circle with an eagle and some arrows and a globe, which looked to Reacher like a crude mash-up of the Army's and the Marine Corps's. It was held up by strips of masking tape at each corner. The shiny paper was fighting them, trying to curl, like it had recently been rolled up. Reacher took hold of one edge and tore it down. Behind it there was a hole in the wall. It was square with relatively neat edges. The cavity behind it was empty.

Gilmour said, 'You cut a hole. Stash something. Replace the piece of drywall. Tape the edges. Plaster. Paint. No one would ever know it's there. And if you need back whatever you stashed, it takes two seconds to get it.'

'It was a go bag,' Reacher said. 'Strickland's running.'

FORTY-ONE

Kasselwood took out her phone, put it on speaker, and hit a key. Taylor answered on the first ring.

Kasselwood said, 'Have you got eyes on the entrance to the mine?'

Taylor said, 'I do.'

'For how long?'

'The last hour and a half.'

'Have you seen Strickland leave?'

'Negative.'

'Have you seen anyone leave?'

'Negative.'

'Okay, listen. Strickland's running. He's dangerous. Stay alert.'

'Understood.'

*

Kasselwood said, 'He's still here. Somewhere. We should leave and stake out the exit. Get him when he comes out. He can't stay down here forever.'

Gilmour said, 'If it was me, I'd be waiting just inside the exit. Like in the guard booth. I'd pick off anyone who tried to get by me.'

Reacher said, 'I would have built another exit when I bought the place. I'd already be gone.'

Kasselwood said, 'So is it safe to leave, or not?'

Gilmour said, 'Wait.' He turned back to Strickland's computer. 'I saw a camera icon on here.' He clicked a couple of times, then nodded. 'All right. Success. Let's see if we can find where he's been.'

Reacher and Kasselwood moved around the desk so that they could watch the screen. It was divided into twelve rectangles. One for each camera. Gilmour said, 'He's not on any of these live feeds. Let's check the history.' Gilmour called up the most recent recordings. The top three showed the four of them walking from the storeroom to Strickland's office. The fourth showed Strickland himself. The camera was in the training area, in the central section between the four zones. Strickland was walking toward it fast, with a black pack on his back. He was using a sternum strap to keep it from slipping off his left shoulder. He walked right under the camera and disappeared from view. Gilmour said, 'We could wait. See when he reappears.'

Reacher shook his head. 'We need momentum. I'll go find him. You deal with the guards at the entrance.'

*

Reacher made his way along the diagonal corridor that led to the heart of the training area. The urban zone was to his right, behind an eight-foot wall. The mountain zone was to his left, behind an artificial snowbank. He was moving slowly, smoothly, trying to make no sound. The gun he had taken from the security guard was in his hand.

The mountain snowbank was continuous, but there was a gap in the urban wall every forty feet. When Reacher was level with the second gap, he heard a sound on the far side. It was a crunch, like a footstep on loose gravel. He stopped and listened. He heard the sound again. He looked through the gap. The shell of a ruined house was on the other side. He thought about stepping through to investigate but decided against it. Instead he doubled back five feet, tucked the gun into his waistband, jumped, and grabbed hold of the top of the wall. He scrambled up, lay flat, and scanned the area. Nothing was moving. There was no sign of Strickland. Then he heard the crunching sound again. It was coming from inside the house now. He looked more closely. Parts of its roof were missing. Two of its windows were smashed. He had no way to tell if it was occupied. He lowered himself down. Pulled out the gun. And crept across to an intact window. He ducked under it and continued to another, which was broken. The ground around it was covered with shards of glass. He picked up the largest one he could find. He held it up like a mirror and used it to see through a gap in the frame. It was like he was looking into a child's bedroom. There was a twin bed. A wicker basket full of soft toys. A shelf full of books. Then the bedroom door opened. A robotic figure swung into the gap. It was made to look like a young man. It was dressed in black cargo pants and a Kevlar vest over a black T-shirt, and it had a Hell's Angels–style motorcycle helmet on its head. It was holding a pistol in both hands. Its right hand swung up and it fired twice. It was shooting live ammunition, not paintballs like in the assessment videos. One bullet smashed the shard of glass Reacher was holding. He dropped the remains, counted to three, stood, raised his own gun, and fired back. He hit the robot between the eyes. It twitched and fizzled. A tongue of flame spewed for a second. Then it fell back out of sight.

Reacher turned and started to retrace his steps toward the wall. He made it halfway, then all the lights in the zone cut out. The whole area was totally dark. Reacher stepped left, fired four times in a broad, low spread, then dived to his right, where he thought the gap in the wall would be. He saw a flash, a brief spout of flame, and he caught sight of another robotic figure. This one was dressed like a grandmother. It was holding a tray full of glasses of lemonade, and there was a smoldering hole in the center of its chest where one of Reacher's shots had caught it.

Reacher landed in the corridor, rolled, then jumped back up onto his feet. He moved forward five yards then pulled out his flashlight. He started moving again, slowly, like before, and continued until he got to the central area. Then he switched the flashlight off and stood in the dark, listening. All he could hear was the distant humming of electrical equipment.

Reacher felt the prickling sensation start to creep up from the base of his neck. It was fully dark, but somehow someone was watching him. It must be Strickland. He must be in some kind of control room to have pulled off the trick with the sounds and the robots. Maybe he had night vision goggles, too. Or infrared cameras. Reacher shifted his finger onto the trigger and listened hard, searching for any sense of where the control room could be. He strained his ears but picked up nothing. Then he latched onto an echo from long ago. *No one ever looks up.* He switched the flashlight back on and held it above his head. He saw nothing at first. Then he realized there was a long dark shape over his head, tucked in tight to the ceiling, like a hovering spaceship or the hull of a boat. He played the light all around it and saw that a metal gantry was attached at its far end. It was matte black, making it virtually invisible. He traced it all the way to the far wall of the cavern and saw that it connected to a metal ladder. The ladder was also black, and it disappeared into the shadows of a narrow alcove. Reacher saw where it emerged and crossed over to it. But he didn't climb. He realized there was a problem. If the shape above him was the control room, and if Strickland was inside it, the only way to get to him would be to cross the gantry. It was fifty feet long, and it was completely exposed. Assuming he had a weapon, Strickland could pick him off at will.

Reacher turned and ran back toward the corridor between the urban zone and the mountains. He kept his flashlight focused on the wall. He counted the gaps. Located the one he had dived out of. He stepped through it this time. Crossed to the broken window. Tucked the gun into his waistband. Slipped off his shirt and wrapped his left hand with it. He cleaned as much of the broken glass out of the frame as he could. Climbed through. Crossed to the doorway. And wrestled the Kevlar vest off the remains of the robotic target he had shot.

Reacher didn't try to wear the vest. He knew it would be too small, and that wasn't what he had in mind, anyway. He took it back to the central area and carried it up the ladder, taking his time with the narrow rungs. He made it to the top, then set out to crawl along the gantry. He used both knees but only his right hand. He held the vest out in front of him with his left, like a shield.

The first bullet hit the vest when Reacher was fifteen yards from the end of the gantry. The thump jarred his wrist. Strickland was crouching in the control room's open doorway. Reacher kept on crawling. Strickland kept on firing. Another bullet hit the vest. And another. Reacher did not stop. He was almost at the end of the gantry. Strickland rolled back into the control room and slammed the door shut. He wriggled forward and stretched up for the lock. On the gantry Reacher swiveled around onto his back, pulled his knees into his chest, then slammed both feet into the door. It flew open, hit Strickland, and knocked him down. The gun rattled away across the room.

For a moment Reacher and Strickland were both on their backs, lying feet to feet, two yards apart. They both started to scramble up. Strickland was shorter. Lighter. He could move faster. He was halfway up. There was no way Reacher could beat him so he changed tack. He took all his weight on his hands and his heels then launched himself forward with his body, parallel to the ground. He extended his feet, stretched his calves, and strained for every last inch until his soles smashed into Strickland's kneecaps.

Human knees are complex joints. The product of millennia of evolution. Effective, but fragile. No match for a two-hundred-and-fifty-pound weight. Certainly not one traveling at speed. Strickland's knees snapped back the wrong way. Bones cracked. Tendons ripped. Ligaments tore. He pitched forward and landed face down on Reacher's chest. Reacher rolled him to the side and stood up.

Strickland was screaming, a succession of shrill, primeval howls. Reacher waited for the sound to die down a little, then he said, 'Who sold you the list of Basic Training dropouts?'

Strickland didn't answer.

Reacher said, 'Who sold you the list?'

Strickland started to moan.

Reacher said, 'I know who it was. I just want to hear you say it.'

Strickland shook his head.

Reacher raised his right foot and held it over Strickland's knee. 'You speak, or I stomp. Your choice.'

Strickland didn't speak.

Reacher started to lower his foot. He said, 'You think you're in pain now . . .'

'No!' Strickland was almost crying, 'It was Hewson. Mark Hewson. He sold me the list.'

Reacher nodded. 'Very good. Now let's get you down.'

'Right.' Strickland sighed with relief. 'I'm going to need morphine. A medic. A stretcher. Some splints. Some ropes. A block and tackle.'

'Really? All that paraphernalia? Sounds like the kind of

setup the army would use. I thought you private contractors were more efficient. Faster-moving. I bet we can find a much quicker way to get you down.'

Reacher took hold of Strickland under the arms and lifted him up. He tried to move slowly and carefully but he wasn't quite gentle enough. Broken bones in Strickland's legs mashed together. Strickland shrieked, then passed out from the pain. Reacher kept going, anyway. He carried Strickland out to the gantry. He lifted him up and over the safety rail and held him steady, dangling in thin air. Reacher didn't care how long he would have to stay that way. He had a good grip. Strickland wasn't heavy. And Reacher was a patient man.

'Wait!' Strickland came around. He looked down into the darkness then started to twist and struggle and his voice rose to a screech. 'Stop. What are you doing?'

Reacher said, 'Welcome back. This is an important moment in your life. Let's take a second to appreciate the significance of what's about to happen.'

'What . . . ?' Strickland's voice cracked. 'What is about to happen?'

Reacher said, 'Karma's going to pay you back for all the poor souls you were ready to trade for a million dollars each.' Then he let Strickland go. There was silence for two long seconds, then a sound like a soaking bath towel landing on a hard stone floor.

FORTY-TWO

Mark Hewson was due to visit the Kinsella mine at ten the next morning. He arrived outside the entrance at 9:45. He was riding in the back of a plain black town car, and his two bodyguards were wearing expensive-looking gray suits with prominent bulges under their left arms.

Reacher was wearing the largest uniform he had found in Strickland's stockroom, which almost fit. He opened the door when the first guard was two paces away. The guy stepped through and gave the entrance to the mine a cursory inspection. He had been there before and knew what to expect. The only unusual thing was that Strickland's Tesla was sitting on the roadway just inside the vehicle gate, facing down the incline, in place of the regular Humvee. The guard wasn't worried about that. He didn't care what kind of vehicle his boss was going to ride in for eight hundred feet. He went back to the door, gave the signal, and Hewson and the second guard followed him inside.

Hewson's suit was navy blue. The pants were a little tighter than they had been when he'd left the army, and his sandy hair was thinning on top. He was wearing wire-framed glasses and he had a black leather briefcase in his left hand.

Gilmour was also wearing one of Strickland's uniforms. He stepped up alongside Reacher and they snapped into simultaneous, crisp salutes.

Hewson said, 'At ease.' Then a moment later, 'Are you guys new?'

Reacher said, 'Yes, sir.'

'Where are the usual guys?'

'Deployed, sir.'

'Already? Strickland's not wasting time, I guess. Is he here? He's expecting me.'

'Yes, sir. He's ready for you now. I can take you to him.'

Hewson nodded then turned and told the guards to wait in the car.

Gilmour had moved across to the Tesla and was holding the rear door open. Hewson climbed in. Gilmour got into the driver's seat and Reacher looped around to the passenger side. The car purred almost silently down to the mine's main level. Its harsh blue-white lights bleached the rough rock surface as they passed. Gilmour took it easy on the incline, continued straight for a moment, then swung ninety degrees to the right.

Hewson said, 'We're not going to Strickland's office?'

Reacher said, 'Not today. We're using a different room.'

'Why?'

'We have a video camera set up in there. That way, if you're satisfied with what Violeta Vardanyan has to say, we can record the new video testimony right away.'

Hewson nodded again. He said, 'That's good. I like efficiency. Your boss knows that.'

The storeroom door was standing ajar. Gilmour stopped the Tesla near it and climbed out. Hewson got out of the back seat. Reacher moved around the rear of the car and waited behind him. Gilmour gestured for Hewson to go first.

Hewson pushed the door, took half a step into the storeroom, and saw Kasselwood. He froze. Reacher shoved him in the back. He staggered inside, dropped his briefcase, and almost fell onto the bed Vardanyan had been in the day before. Strickland's remains were in it now. Blood had soaked into the sheets and dried, tracing a crusty black outline around his ruined corpse.

Gilmour followed Reacher inside and closed the door behind him.

Reacher picked up Hewson's briefcase. He gestured to all the dead bodies lying in the beds. He said, 'What would you say they're worth? Twenty-six million?'

Hewson's eyes were hopping from pillow to pillow, death mask to death mask. His mind was frozen. He had no concept of what he was seeing. He was silent for a moment, then stammered, 'I . . . I don't know what you're talking about. Is that Morgan? What the hell happened to him? Who are all these other guys? Who killed them?'

'Twenty-six million. You agreed to the contract. You know the price.'

'No.' Hewson held out his hands, palms facing out, and shook his head wildly. 'I never signed that. I wasn't going to. It was Morgan's idea. I never agreed.'

Reacher lifted the case. He said, 'So if I look in here I won't find a freshly signed copy?'

Hewson said, 'No. Well, yes. But's that's for show. It's a negotiating position. I was stringing Morgan along. I was never going to give it to him.'

'But you did sell him the list. The Basic Training washouts.'

Hewson didn't answer.

Kasselwood said, 'I have a question. When I flagged up the fact that Strickland was trying to start an unjust war, my report landed on your desk, didn't it? You buried it. And then you sent a bunch of guys to hurt me.'

Hewson's stepped back. His mouth was open but he didn't speak.

Kasselwood said, 'After everything that happened in the sandbox? I never told a soul. You know that? So I think I deserve the courtesy of an answer now. A truthful answer.'

Hewson's voice was quiet. He was starting to shiver. 'I told them to scare you. That's all. Never to hurt you. I'm sorry about what they did to you.'

'So make it up to me. Answer the question. You sold Strickland the list?'

Hewson threw his hands up. He said, 'You're really pissed about those guys? You're looking at it all wrong.

They were losers. Dropouts. Their lives were in the toilet. We were offering them a second chance. *Offering*. They didn't have to take it.'

Reacher said, 'So it was all about the second chance?'

Hewson said, 'Right.' His eyes were flitting from corpse to corpse again, homing in briefly on each visible fatal wound.

Reacher took out his gun. He racked a shell into the chamber then released the magazine. He put that in his pocket and tossed the gun onto one of the empty beds. He said, 'How about I give you a second chance? I'm going to count to three. If you get to the gun first, you can shoot me. If you don't . . . well, you get the picture. One. Two.'

Hewson didn't wait for three. He tore his gaze away from a body that had been shot in the face and threw himself forward, going for the gun.

Reacher threw himself the other way, going for Hewson. His left fist slammed into Hewson's chest. It had all his strength behind it. All his weight. All his momentum. It caved in Hewson's ribs like they'd been hit with an anvil. The force crushed his heart. It lifted his body clear off the ground. It flew back, landed, and slid along the floor until the top of Hewson's head smashed into the wheel at the base of one of the metal bed legs.

One of Hewson's guards was sitting in the town car with the passenger door open, listening to the radio, when Reacher stepped from the entrance to the mine. The other guard was standing, smoking a cigarette, tracing a deep red stain on the driveway with his foot.

Reacher said, 'Guys, I have a question from your boss.

He wants to know how much of your share you're willing to split with Gilmour and me.'

The guard with the cigarette said, 'The hell are you talking about?'

Reacher said, 'Hey. Stay calm. This is just business. There's no room for emotion. There's been a change in structure, is all. Strickland has brought Gilmour and me on board now, the same way Hewson brought you guys on. So the question is, can we cut a deal we're all happy with? Or do we need to find a way to reduce head count?'

The guy took a step toward the door. Reacher moved to block him off. The guy said, 'I want to speak to the boss. He needs to sort this shit out.'

'All he needs is a number. A percentage. So what's it going to be?'

'The number's zero percent. We're not splitting dick with you asshats. If Strickland wants to get you involved, it's coming out of his end. Not ours.'

'So there is something to split.' Reacher took out his gun. 'Thank you. That's all I needed to know.'

FORTY-THREE

Reacher and Gilmour changed into their own clothes while Taylor collected the rental car from the parking area and drove it up to the main entrance.

Reacher used Hewson's phone to call 911 and report an accident at the mine. He didn't care too much about what happened to Strickland's remains, or Hewson's, or the guards', but he figured there were twenty-five other families out there who deserved some kind of closure.

Gilmour used his own phone to call Patten and give her a summary of the things that had happened since she'd visited the coffee shop the day before. When he was done, she said, 'So it's over?'

Gilmour said, 'It is.'

'Really over this time?'

'Really over.'

'I still don't feel relieved.'

'Me neither.'

'Got any plans for tonight?'

'No.'

'Does Reacher?'

'Hold on.' Gilmour looked around, then said, 'I was going to ask, but I can't see him. He was here a minute ago.'

'Want to come to my place? I'll order takeout. Not Thai this time. And not so much wine.'

'Sounds good.'

'Great. Bring Reacher if he's up for it.'

'Will do. See you later.'

Gilmour hung up and saw that Kasselwood and Taylor were already in the car. Vardanyan was sandwiched between them in the back seat. Gilmour strolled over, opened the door, and said, 'Where's Reacher?'

Kasselwood said, 'You missed him.'

'What do you mean?'

'He left.' She gestured to the dirt road. 'While you were on the phone. He said he wanted to walk. But he left this for you.' She lifted Strickland's go bag out of the footwell and handed it to him. 'He said you'd know what to do with it.'

Gilmour moved to a spot where he could get a clear view down the road. There wasn't much to see. Just a plume of dust maybe half a mile in the distance, moving steadily away like it was being blown by a strong wind. He pulled out his binoculars and took a closer look. He picked out a figure in the center of the cloud. It was

Reacher. Even from behind, and at that kind of distance, his size gave him away. He had nothing in his hands. He was covering the ground fast, but not hurrying. It was the kind of pace he could keep up all day, Gilmour guessed. He watched him for another two minutes. Three. And not once did Reacher look back.

The next bus scheduled to leave Baltimore after Reacher walked into the Greyhound station that afternoon was headed to Salt Lake City, fifty-five minutes later. He went inside and bought a ticket and a cup of coffee. Then he took a seat in the waiting area.

The bus showed up dead on time. Reacher tossed his cup in the trash and made his way to the designated stand. A couple got off. No one else was waiting to get on. Reacher was twenty feet from its door when he heard footsteps behind him, moving fast. He glanced over his shoulder and saw Gilmour running toward him. He slowed to let him catch up, then nodded toward the bus. He said, 'Whatever you want, make it quick.'

Gilmour was carrying Strickland's go bag. He hoisted it up and said, 'You left this.'

Reacher said, 'I know. I left it for you.'

'Do you know what's inside?'

'A bunch of cash.'

'Did you count it?'

'I didn't see the point.'

'There's half a million dollars.'

Reacher said nothing.

Gilmour said, 'You can't give that kind of money to a gambler. It's irresponsible.'

'Did I give it to a gambler?'

Gilmour was silent for a moment. 'I don't know. I hope not.'

'You'll find something good to do with it.'

'Like what?'

'If you're asking me for investment advice, you've got bigger problems than gambling. But I hear there's a bar in Harbor East coming on the market. The Butcher's Dog. And maybe a cab company.'

'Me, an entrepreneur?' Gilmour turned and strutted up and down like he was trying a new persona on for size. 'A small business owner? Nah. I don't see it. But you know what? I could reach out to the guy at the card club. Tell him, any vets who get in too deep, don't send the leg breakers. Let me take care of it for them, quietly. And with no strings attached. No shipments to report on. No robberies to get involved in. Just a clean exit strategy for anyone who needs one.'

ABOUT THE AUTHORS

Lee Child is one of the world's leading thriller writers. He was born in Coventry, raised in Birmingham, and now lives in England's Lake District. It is said one of his novels featuring his hero Jack Reacher is sold somewhere in the world every nine seconds. His books consistently achieve the number-one slot on bestseller lists around the world and have sold over one hundred million copies. Lee is the recipient of many awards, including Author of the Year at the 2019 British Book Awards. He was appointed CBE in the 2019 Queen's Birthday Honours.

Andrew Child is the author of nine thrillers written under the name Andrew Grant. He is the younger brother of Lee Child. Born in Birmingham, he lives in Wyoming with his wife, the novelist Tasha Alexander.

On Monday September 5th, 1994, at home, at the dining room table, I sat down to write. An hour later, I gave the first chapter to my wife. I asked, 'Should I continue?' 'Yes,' she said. 'I like it.'

From global bestseller and creator of Jack Reacher comes Lee Child's first-ever autobiographical collection, featuring twenty-four fascinating personal reflections on his life and work.

'Essential reading for all Reacher fans.'
STEVE CAVANAGH

dead good

Looking for more gripping must-reads?

Head over to Dead Good —
the home of killer crime books,
TV and film.

Whether you're on the hunt for an intriguing
mystery, an action-packed thriller
or a creepy psychological drama,
we're here to keep you in the loop.

Get recommendations and reviews from
crime fans, grab discounted books at bargain
prices and enter exclusive giveaways
for the chance to read brand-new releases
before they hit the shelves.

**Sign up for the free newsletter:
www.deadgoodbooks.co.uk/newsletter**

Find out more about the Jack Reacher books at www.JackReacher.com

- Take the book selector quiz
- Enter competitions
- Read and listen to extracts
- Find out more about the authors
- Discover Reacher coffee, music and more . . .

PLUS sign up for the monthly Jack Reacher newsletter to get all the latest news delivered direct to your inbox.

For up-to-the-minute news about Lee & Andrew Child find us on Facebook

f /JackReacherOfficial

f /LeeChildOfficial

and discover Jack Reacher books on

𝕏 /LeeChildReacher

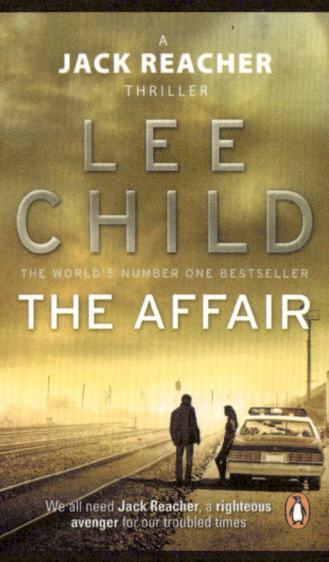
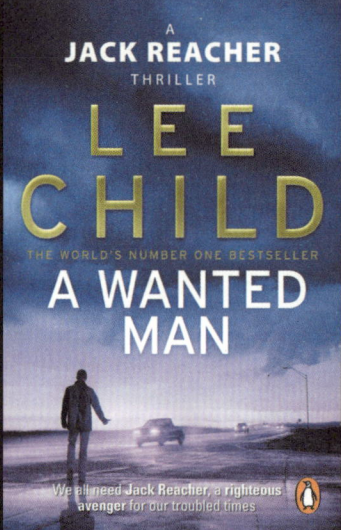

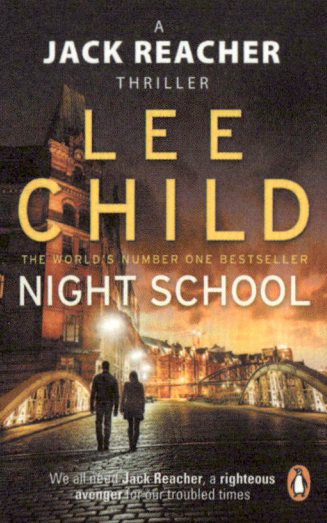
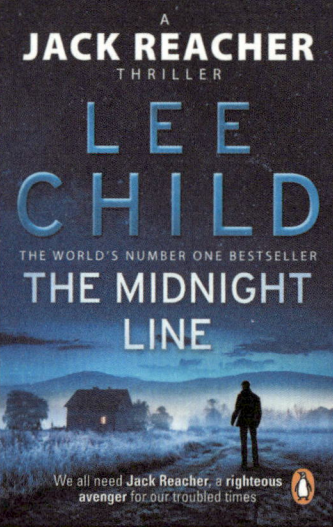
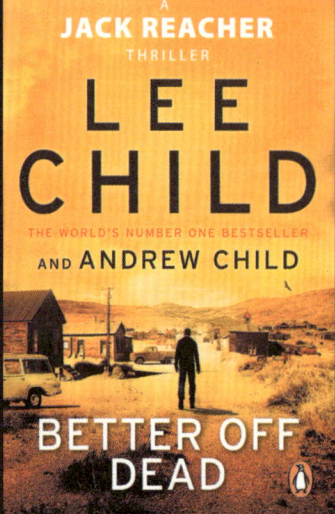
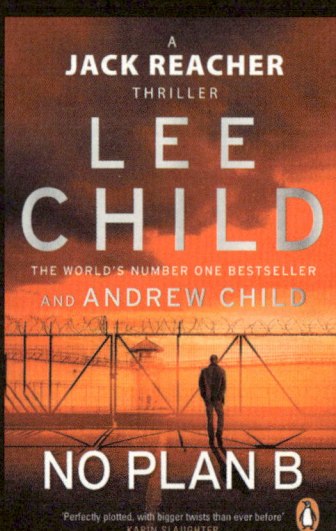